A Matter of Death

Justice #3

Suzan Harden

A MATTER OF DEATH
(Justice #3)
ISBN-13: 978-1-938745-54-6
Copyright 2019 by Suzan Harden
All rights reserved

Published by Angry Sheep Publishing
Findlay, Ohio

Cover Design by For the Muse Designs
Interior Design by QA Productions

More books by Suzan Harden

(Each series is in suggested reading order)

Bloodlines

Blood Magick

Zombie Love

Zombie Confidential

Zombie Wedding

Amish, Vamps & Thieves

Blood Sacrifice

Love, War & a Bulldog

Zombie Goddess

Ravaged

Sacrificed

Reality Bites

Ghouls in the Grocery (Coming Soon)

Resurrected (Coming Soon)

Seasons of Magick

Spring

Summer

Autumn

Winter

Justice

Sword and Sorceress 28 ("Justice")

Sword and Sorceress 30 ("Diplomacy in the Dark")

Justice: The Beginning

A Question of Balance

A Modicum of Truth

A Matter of Death

A Touch of Mother (Coming Soon)

888-555-HERO

Hero De Facto

Hero Ad Hoc

Hero De Novo

Miscellaneous

Sword and Sorceress 31 ("Pig-Headed")

Sword and Sorceress 32 ("Unexpected")

For more information or to be added to her mailing list, visit
Suzan's website at www.suzanharden.com
Or check her out on Twitter or Facebook.

To Dad

Prologue

After Child repaired the World and gave life to Woman and Man, Love defied Balance and snuck back into the World from which She had been banished. Love discovered Woman and Man, Child's imitations of Mother and Father, and She was delighted with these new beings. She taught them pleasure and from that pleasure more humans came into existence just as Child Herself had.

However, Conflict discovered Love had abandoned Him in the Void, and He followed Her back into the World. When He discovered Her new obsession, He flew into a rage. But rather than injure the humans directly, He whispered into their ears and convinced them to hurt each other.

Child, seeing Her people's grievous wounds both physical and spiritual, asked Mother to help Her heal them. Mother enlisted the aid of Vintner and together they aided Child in restoring the humans. Meanwhile, Light caught and banished Conflict once again, and the human race prospered.

But as time went on and new humans and creatures were born, their numbers grew vast. So vast that the human race and all the beasts of the land filled every square league of the world. The fish filled the water, and there were so many birds that they forgot how to fly because there was so little sky left for them to do so.

Once again, the human race cried out for Child to help them, but She did not know what to do. She went to Mother and Father and pleaded for guidance.

Father turned to Mother and said, "Balance must come back to the world." Sadly, She agreed.

So She became Balance once again. She freed Conflict from His prison and unleashed Him, not just upon the human race, but the animals and the fish and the birds as well.

Balance took a new form, Death. Instead of healing those harmed, She took their energy and returned it to Light. When a thousand of each creature was left, She bade Conflict to stop, which He did for fear that Balance and Light would banish Him for a third time.

Balance then decreed that each living thing would be allotted a certain length of time, no more, no less, so that the World and its beings would not suffer as they had. However, no creature, whether it ran or swam or flew, or any plant would know the length of time it was given.

While the other living things understood the necessity and accepted their fate, the human race wailed at the unfairness and cursed Death for Her relentless adherence to Balance's decree.

And Child wept for Her creations.

- The First Book of Death, Verses I thru XI

Chapter 1

Bone-deep weariness dragged on my limbs. So much so, I leaned against the parapet of the Neighbor's Gate watchtower. I wasn't sure if it were night or day anymore. Heat seeped through my sleeves from the stone.

"Anything, Chief Justice?" Reverend Father Nizhé'é' of Diné joined me in staring at the demon army camped outside the city of Tandor. Camped wasn't the right word. They did not sleep or cook as humans did. They crouched in alternating rows surrounding the walls of the city. Not moving. Not even breathing from what I could see.

"From Orrin or from the demons?"

"From Orrin." His tone was far too hopeful, and I hated dashing that hope.

"Not since this morning, sir." The demons' magic pulsed against the warding spells imbedded in Tandor's walls. My warning to Sister Shi Hua of Light had been abruptly cut off when our foes surrounded the city.

"And the demons?" the Reverend Father asked.

"Nothing yet, sir." I shook my head. "But they're plotting out there. I can feel it."

He lowered his voice. "Get some sleep, Anthea. You've been awake for nearly two days straight."

"You don't have anyone who can see them the way I can." Normally, I would have shouted the words at anyone who questioned my abilities, but I couldn't muster the strength.

"And the Twelve Temples have survived a thousand years without a clergy member with red eyes who can see demons through their glamours," he almost sounded amused, but then, he always did when he spoke to me. "You're of no use to me if you kill yourself, young lady."

"Young lady?" I bristled. Maybe I had some energy after all.

"I have you by sixteen winters, so yes." He smirked. "Young lady. Go back to Light and get some sleep."

I gave up the argument and nodded. The little bit of respite from my weariness had died under his logic.

As Luc had pointed out, all the clergy and wardens of the combined Diné, Cliffdweller, and Plains Nations army reported to Nizhé'é' as the seniormost priest of Conflict. Even though, the Reverend Father wasn't Issuran, the surviving Temple seats of Tandor had followed High Brother Aduba's lead in reporting to him as well. Therefore, Luc, our two wardens, and I acceded to the Reverend Father's command, too.

The main purpose of the Temple of Conflict was to prepare for the exact situation we faced—a demon army on the loose. It merely made sense for the senior priest of Conflict to head our . . .

What in Balance's name were we? A delaying action? A last resort?

High Sister Bertrice said our seconds in Orrin had destroyed the demons and eggs planted there, and the queen's army was marching south from the capital in our last contact we had from home. Unfortunately, Bertrice depended on the only distance speaker we had in Orrin. And we hadn't heard from Shi Hua since the demons arrived on our doorstep.

Though I was fairly certain it was the demons' spells that blocked the young Jing priestess from talking to us, I prayed that nothing more had happened at home. Even though Balance didn't deign to answer my pleas directly, the fact that the demon army remained camped outside our walls gave me hope. If the rest of Issura had been lost, they would have left a portion of their number here and marched east for Diné.

No one was on the streets as I trudged back to Light, neither clergy nor civilians. How late was it? Or was it early? With the Temple bells silent and the sky overcast, I had no way to tell.

We had to disable the alarm spells on the bells. Otherwise, they would be constantly clanging due to the demons camped on our doorstep. The din would have driven everyone insane over the last several hours.

I glanced at Balance, but only a trickle of magic came from the remnants of the building compared to the other Temples. Even if its structural integrity weren't questionable, Chief Justice Elizabeth and I were reluctant to step inside it. We'd used all of Balance's magic in a desperate effort to kill a skin-walker and its renegade allies who'd quietly taken over Tandor before anyone noticed there was a problem.

My thighs and calves ached when I climbed the steps of Light. What I wouldn't give for a good soak and a goblet of Pana red right now. But the damn demons had destroyed a large section of the aqueduct into the city, so we needed to conserve water. And the healers needed the wine for the injured since our medical supplies were as finite a resource as our water.

Instead of heading for the room I currently shared with my warden Tyra, I headed for the bedchambers of the former high brother of Tandor. Luc had taken them over, not to mention drafted his own army of the city's children to bring books and scrolls from the Temple of Knowledge for him. If it was as late as I suspected, he should be alone.

I entered without an invitation.

Luc jerked upright from where he'd fallen asleep at the table he used as a desk. "What? Where?" He fumbled for the sword hanging at the side of his chair.

"It's only me."

"Anthea?"

Magic tingled across my skin. Luc squinted and blinked.

I cupped his cheek. "Extinguish the light ball, my love. We've both been ordered to get some sleep."

"I thought we'd been ordered to mate." He pulled me closer for kiss.

"I don't think we'd stay awake long enough to do so," I said with a laugh when we parted. Shi Hua and Jeremy had shared that little tidbit in our next to last communication with them. The clergy of Light from our allies confirmed they received the same directive from their home temples before the demons' spells cut off all contact with the outside world.

In theory, the new order validated mine and Luc's illegal affair. After the messages had been received, he grumbled the Twelve had a warped sense of humor by giving us permission to lay together in the middle of a demon siege.

"Well, technically, I'm the only one who needs to be awake."

"Not necessarily," I teased as I straightened. "I recall a few mornings by our campfire while we were on circuit."

He grabbed his specially designed crutches and crossed to the bed. I quickly stripped off my gear and clothes and joined him. I turned on my side, and he curled around my back.

"It smells much better in here."

"Mmmm." He tightened his arm around my midriff. "Luckily, the master carpenter rallied some other civilians. They managed to clean out the bathing pool and drain before the demons arrived and destroyed the aqueduct."

The renegades hadn't even allowed poor High Brother Dav a chamber pot for his use. Even though he'd been driven mad by a skinwalker's mental torture, he retained enough of his faculties to use one spot for his waste.

"What do you think is happening at home?" I whispered.

"Don't." Luc kissed my shoulder. "You'll only drive yourself insane asking that question."

"But Yanaba—"

"Is alive. Mya, Aaron, and their respective staffs will take excellent care of her mental and physical health."

I knew our high sister of Child and head of the Healers Guild would do everything in their power to help my own junior justice. Luc's words didn't ameliorate my guilt that I left Yanaba alone to face both the Assassins Guild and demons.

"But Shi Hua wasn't telling us everything," I muttered. "Not with Bertrice in the link."

Luc reached down and playfully smacked my left buttock before he resumed his hold of my waist. "What did I say about driving yourself insane?"

I inhaled deeply and released the breath. He was right. All the speculation in the world couldn't change our predicament much less Orrin's.

I'd closed my eyes for barely an instant it seemed when the temple alarm bells clanged. Both Luc and I were out of bed and dressing before we were fully awake. The rasp of demon magic grated against my own power, but it wasn't from the direction of the city walls.

It came from below my bare feet.

Luc muttered a few obscenities in Cantish. "The damn demons are in the tunnels."

Chapter 2

Shi Hua released High Father Jerrod's hands and tried to surreptitiously wipe his sweat from her own palms. "My thanks for your assistance in our efforts, High Father."

The elderly priest merely nodded before he sagged in his own chair. Despite the warm glow from the magically charged alabaster globes, his skin looked terribly pale.

High Sister Bertrice released Shi Hua's shoulders and collapsed onto another chair in the small consultation room within the Temple of Light. She reached for the decanter of wine on the table, poured three goblets, and passed two of them to Jerrod and Shi Hua.

"We must prepare for the worst." She took a sip of her own drink.

Jerrod took a huge gulp of his wine. "The duke has called the outlying estates to arms, and we have all sent couriers to the home Temples. What else can we do?"

Shi Hua didn't touch her goblet. The thought of wine turned her stomach. The last time she'd had any was the night the demons had hatched inside the corpses of Peacekeeper Dante and his family. Once she realized she had survived the battle in Death's morgue, she'd vomited, and wine had been nearly the only thing she had at dinner before the incident.

She took a deep breath to settle her nerves. "We assist The Temple of Conflict in their preparations."

"But—" Jerrod waved his hand, the one holding his goblet. Deep red wine sloshed over the rim and stained his robes.

"We can't assume anything at this point other than there's a demon army at

Tandor's gates as Chief Justice Anthea last reported." Bertrice's voice was stern, solid, even though she was near the same age as Jerrod.

"The good sister cannot even detect the other eleven Temples within the city," he protested.

"I can still feel the demon magic." Shi Hua repressed a shudder. The alien touch of their power repulsed and tempted her at the same time. No wonder human sorcerers fell under the demons' influence. "If Tandor's wards had failed, they wouldn't be expending so much energy in one place."

Bertrice shook her head. "No sense in us expending any more time trying to contact Anthea and Luc. May the Twelve guide everyone trapped within the city." She finished her wine and placed the goblet on the table with a solid *clank*. "I'll go see what High Brother Han needs."

Jerrod reached over and patted Shi Hua's hand. "You made a good effort, my dear." He stood.

I also killed more demons in Orrin than you have.

She quelled the nasty thought at his patronizing tone and schooled her expression to a more appropriate smile. "Thank you, High Father."

Bertrice followed Jerrod to the door, but she turned to face Shi Hua. Wisely, she said nothing, merely rolled her eyes and smirked. But then, she had fought demons in the morgue with Shi Hua, Brother Jeremy and Captain Iakepa. Jerrod would most likely wet his small clothes at the sight of a real demon.

Work would normally distract her from her worries, but the usual tasks of a Temple of Light, especially at the start of the trading season on the Peaceful Sea, had dwindled to nothing. Only the Sea Peoples fleet had arrived in the last month.

To add to the political complications, half of the Sea Peoples fleet still anchored in Orrin's harbor. Prince Alika and several of his captains refused to leave Issura after the discovery of the demons and their eggs in the city. While captains and sailors of the departing ships had been truthspelled, no one could guarantee the ships weren't carrying demons or eggs without Chief Justice Anthea's odd sight to search people, ships, and all property for demon contamination.

However, Prince Alika didn't have a distance speaker with him, and it would be nigh impossible for Shi Hua to contact someone in the islands she didn't know. So he sent half his fleet home on the chance they could success-fully raise the alarm.

What made matters worse was she hadn't been able to contact Reverend Father Biming either. Her mentor from Jing's Temple of Thief had ordered his ship out of Tandor after Luc had warned him of demons. That was the last anyone from Issura or Jing had heard from him. She feared he and the crew of the *Unbridled* had been killed in their attempts to intercept the shipment of demon eggs they had been chasing.

Shi Hua pushed to her feet and extinguished the globe so the rest of the Temple personnel would know the room was free. When she entered the main sanctuary, Warden Mateqai stood near the eternal flame, speaking with one of the new wardens for Love.

From the wardens' attention on her, she'd been the subject of their discussion.

She crossed the polished oak floor. "What's happened now?"

"Warden Jocasta, with a message from the high sister, m'lady." The Love warden bowed to her. "She requests your company for the midday meal."

As if on cue, the Temple bells pealed the time. Shi Hua knew exactly what Dragonfly wished to talk about, but she couldn't think of a single polite reason to refuse the invitation. And from the smirk on Mateqai's face, he was enjoying the situation a bit too much.

"You have no further appointments today, Sister," he added.

Schooling her expression, she inclined her head. "My thanks, Warden Jocasta. I accept the high sister's gracious invitation."

Thankfully, the Love warden gave no indication she thought of anything else but her duty. She led the way out of the Temple of Light and down the front steps.

Two wardens escorting Shi Hua to a friendly meal seemed like overkill. But since the renegades' slaughter of the former wardens of Love, the Assassins Guild's attempts on Chief Justice Anthea, followed by the demon infiltration of Orrin, none of the Temple personnel were taking any chances. Brother Jeremy complained about Warden Tadhg's obsession with someone sabotaging his privy.

The city's main thoroughfare wasn't as busy as it should have been with the Spring Rituals nine days away. Only the Sea Peoples fleet and a few traders from the outlying parts of the duchy had arrived recently. The discovery of demons disguised as humans within the walls of Orrin sobered the normally joyous atmosphere. The news of a demon army camped outside of Tandor had totally destroyed the mood of the citizens.

Some civilians had started evacuating their children to Standora. Shi Hua couldn't blame them for that. The demons would spare no one, not even the tiniest babe.

The Temple of Love was still officially closed for business, though a few young women knelt before the statue of Love Herself and prayed when Shi Hua and the wardens arrived. One of the eunuchs who served the Goddess bowed low and gestured for Shi Hua to follow.

While the high brother of Light's dining room was more of a utilitarian affair, the high sister's in Love was decadent. Low couches covered in scarlet velvet spread like rays of the sun from a circular stone table. Tapestries covered the walls. However, these exhibited a collection of hedonistic views and ideas.

Thank Light, she had been inside the Temple of Love in Chengzhou during her training with her Aunt Yin Li. Otherwise, her face would be burning hot enough to peel her skin.

Love's new high sister Dragonfly gracefully rose from her couch, the bells on her robes tinkling and her bright red veil covering her face, and bowed. "Your presence honors our Temple, Sister."

Shi Hua return Dragonfly's bow. "Your graciousness honors ours, High Sister."

The Love priestess made shooing motions at the two wardens. "Bipbipbip. Outside you two. This is a private meeting."

Shi Hua's heart plunged into her stomach. That was exactly what she feared. It could be worse. Dragonfly could have decided she needed to talk to Shi Hua and Jeremy at the same time.

Mateqai frowned. "With all due respect, High Sister—"

"Acting High Sister," Dragonfly corrected. "And I'm not embarrassing your charge by having this conversation in front of you." She jabbed a forefinger in the direction of the door. "Now, go."

"I'll be tasting everything you try to give her," Mateqai warned.

"As no doubt Warden Jocasta will as well." Dragonfly crossed her arms and tapped a sandaled toe so rapidly the bells on her robes danced and jingled.

Mateqai huffed and looked at Shi Hua for support.

"I'll be fine, Warden," she murmured. Dragonfly was right. Shi Hua really didn't want to have this conversation in front of him.

He finally inclined his head in acceptance. "I'll be right outside if you need anything, Sister."

Once the door closed quietly behind the two wardens, Dragonfly heaved a deep sigh. "Do you mind if I dispense with my veil, Sister? After the last few months, I find it claustrophobic."

"I don't mind at all," Shi Hua said. And she really didn't. Just the few stories she'd heard of what the disgraced priestess Gerd and her renegade allies had down to the sisters here turned her stomach. "But you know your confirmation could come any day now, so please let the wardens get used to addressing you properly."

Dragonfly pulled off the fine red lace, revealing pale blue eyes outlined in coal. Her golden blond hair rippled in waves over her shoulders and down her back. As Chief Justice Anthea would say, Dragonfly's features were somewhere between a very handsome woman and a very beautiful boy.

"Pfft." She flicked the veil toward an empty couch, dismissing Shi Hua's words as easily. "Have a seat, Sister." Dragonfly gestured at the couch next to the one where she'd been sitting.

Shi Hua sat on the edge of the velvet cushion. Somehow, she managed to rest her palms on her knees instead of clenching her fingers.

"First of all, I will not play games with you," Dragonfly started. "My Temple has been ordered to assist those of you from Light and Balance with your recent orders. If you are uncomfortable talking to a *berda*, any of the other sisters would be happy to assist you in your new duties."

Nervous laughter burbled from Shi Hua before she could stop it. "I apologize, High Sister. My discomfort stems from the orders, not you personally."

Dragonfly cocked her head. "If you are sure?"

"Yes, m'lady."

"Tut, tut, my dear." The Love priestess resumed her seat. "If we're going to be discussing matters of such a personal nature, no titles."

"Yes, m'lady, er, Dragonfly." Shi Hua smiled. Or tried to. From the Love priestess's laughter, her expression probably was more of a grimace.

Shi Hua desperately wished she could talk to Aunt Yin Li instead, but she couldn't go to the Jing ambassador's residence without raising a lot of questions. Not when the wardens were keeping a close eye on all the clergy. She'd learned her aunt had arrived in Orrin on Reverend Father Biming's ship, but everyone simply thought Yin Li was Ambassador Quan's new concubine.

But then, everyone had thought Shi Hua herself had been the ambassador's paramour for the last five years. Funny how no one questioned her about her relationship with Quan. Or were the people of Orrin simply that blind?

At a knock on the door, Dragonfly held up a forefinger and called out, "Enter!"

Two maids came into the room with the promised meal. Both women had sour looks on their faces. From both wardens' stances, Shi Hua could guess why. After everything that happened at this Temple, trust needed to be earned.

The maids laid their trays on the table. From the odor, the pot on the tray set before Shi Hua held Jing white tea. The tray intended for Dragonfly carried a wine decanter. Otherwise, both trays were the same—chicken and vegetable pies made from acorn flour with finger holes in the crusts.

When drinks were poured and the door closed once again, Dragonfly shot Shi Hua an amused look. "I hope you've been making your wardens wash their hands frequently."

She giggled again. "Our head of household has been quite paranoid. He's been sniffing the cook and kitchen staff's hands."

"I wish I could say our own staff were overreacting." Dragonfly sighed as she poked at her pie with a spoon.

"If you don't feel up to this . . ."

"No." Dragonfly waved her free hand and smiled once again. "Do you have any questions or concerns before I simply start lecturing like a Temple instructor?"

Shi Hua laid aside her spoon without taking a bite. "How does one . . . find joy in the act of love if you . . . don't find the other person attractive?" she finished in a rush.

Dragonfly released her utensil and took a huge gulp of wine. "If you do not find Jeremy or Luc attractive, you can always head for Standora—"

"No, there's nothing wrong with Jeremy." Shi Hua twined her fingers together. She couldn't meet the Love priestess's gaze. "My problem is he isn't a woman."

"Oh, dear." Dragonfly rose and sat beside Shi Hua. "Do you like Jeremy as a friend?"

"Yes, but when the orders came, he admitted he was attracted to me." Her eyes burned. "I don't want to hurt him."

"I know you don't." Dragonfly took Shi Hua's hands in hers. "But I can help you both so you do not find the experience as . . . difficult as you might under other circumstances."

"Thank you, Dragonfly." And she meant it with all her heart. She'd never dreamed of having children. But now that she was faced with the necessity of having one, she was terrified out of her mind.

Chapter 3

If the demons were in the tunnels, that meant—

"Oh, sweet Balance!" I swore.

Luc's expression was equally shocked before he roared, "Go!"

I jerked on my borrowed boots, grabbed my sword, and ran. Tyra appeared out of the cross hallway.

"Send clergy to the vacant temples!" I ordered as I passed her. "Demons are in the tunnels!"

She whirled and started shouting the Diné words for "demon" and "tunnel". If nothing else over the past few days of battling the skinwalkers and the siege, we'd learned the important terms in order to communicate with each other. With the alarm bells ringing, people raced to their assigned posts, some in a half-dressed state.

One of the Diné Light priests caught up with me at the cracked marble steps into Balance. Elizabeth would have been a better choice to augment my efforts, but my doubts about her loyalty would have leaked through our link.

I realized I had no idea where the Diné justice who'd accompanied their army was staying.

The bones and debris had been cleaned out of the main courtroom and the hallway to the sleeping quarters. Magic tingled behind me as the priest ignited a light ball. In my hurry, I'd forgotten it was dark inside the Temple to normally sighted folk.

ANTHEA! Reverend Father Nizhé'é's silent speech echoed through my head.

Whatever is happening at the gates are a feint. I sent a wordless impression of what Luc and I had felt. *The demons are in the tunnels.*

He issued orders through silent speech, ones that were echoed by a high brother of Conflict from each of the four nations trapped inside Tandor in their native languages. I had to tune out the noise inside my head.

Elizabeth's former quarters were as bare as High Brother Dav's had been when we arrived in Tandor. We'd destroyed anything organic in the Temple with our efforts to take out one of the skinwalkers. I skidded to a stop before the sandstone block that served as the Balance entrance to Tandor's tunnel system. My sword clattered to the floor when I dropped to my knees and held out my palms.

Alien magic scratched on my psyche from the other side of the wall. It seemed . . . hesitant.

"Does the energy seem odd to you, Justice?" the Diné Light priest asked in the Peaceful Sea trade tongue as he knelt beside me.

I frowned. "It's too much to hope they've learned to fear me."

The Light priest chuckled. "I pray to Thief you're wrong. They should fear you."

The magic within the block was nearly as low as it had been after I activated the Balance defenses. The demons must sense the weakness here.

We were fools. We should have recharged this entrance once we'd retaken the city. We should have brought down the tunnels with flashbangs when we had the chance. If only we could prime a light ball like a flashbang—

A memory went off like the Jing device inside my head. I turned to the Light priest.

"There's spell in the Light library that can produce the same effect as a flashbang. Do you know it?"

He looked at me as if I were mad. Maybe I was.

"Yes, but it won't do us any good on this side of the wall, Justice."

"I'm going to put it on the other side of the wall, only a couple of days ago. The last time this passage was opened. Can you delay the spell's activation?"

"I can't." A sly look appeared on his face. "But you could."

Three spells enfolded on each other. Well, it couldn't be any more difficult than the layers of a truthspell, the blocker, and the counter to the blocker. Balance help us if I was wrong.

I frowned and looked around the bare room. "Once I've frozen your flashbang spell, get in the bathing room."

"Why?"

"In case this goes very badly." I grinned at the Light priest. "You can tell High Brother Luc I was an idiot if you survive."

The demon magic scratched more insistently at the weak essence of Balance. We needed to hurry. I motioned for him to start the flashbang spell. On his last two syllables, I concentrated and murmured the time freeze spell.

Very carefully, he set the contained explosion on the floor beside me and scrambled into Elizabeth's bathing room. I tried not to think about the possibility of my freeze spell failing before I finished, but I couldn't freeze the whole room. Nor could I put it in a container since I couldn't guarantee I could pass a three-dimensional object through time.

Balance take me, I wasn't sure I could pass energy through time either, but I was out of options.

I sucked in a deep breath and concentrated on two days ago when Elizabeth and I came in to close the passageway to the tunnels. Time rewound. I shoved the writhing ball of Balance and Light magic through the block that was there and not there.

Footsteps in the hallway sent a trill of alarm through me, and I jerked back. There were voices. I shuddered when I recognized my own and Elizabeth's. We were coming to seal the passage.

I knew how cynical and suspicious I could be. If I saw myself, I could quite literally destroy my own spell. I scrambled to the bathing room, yanked my cowl low over my face, and folded my hands into my sleeves.

The faint outlines of the time ghost versions of Elizabeth and me entered the room. We didn't appear to notice the spells on the floor of the tunnel or my sword I'd carelessly left on the floor. Of course not. The magic was literally a few minutes behind them unless or until I yanked it forward. And the sword was two days ahead of them.

Elizabeth cocked her head as if she heard something. She looked over her shoulder, and her eyes widened.

She was totally blind. She couldn't possibly see me, either as a real person or a time echo. It was the whole reason our order needed someone to recite events when we rewound time. But her mouth opened, and she reached out toward the past me beside her.

I held my index finger to my lips and prayed to Balance Elizabeth would take the hint if she could see me. Finally, she nodded. I relaxed and let the timeline run forward. When time synced again, I yanked on my other spell.

A crack of thunder pounded against the wall. It was followed by screeches of angry and injured demons. However, the scratching of their magic against the Temple entrance stopped.

"That was impressive."

I jumped at the voice. The Diné Light priest. In my panic at Elizabeth being able to perceive me, I'd forgotten he was in here, too.

"I hope the demons were impressed as well." I marched over to the wall, knelt by the block once again, and placed my palms on the sandstone. The alien presence of the demons seemed to be receding. Despite their efforts, the weak seal on the passage was intact.

For now.

"The Reverend Father will need to assign watches on all the Temples." I rose to my feet and picked up my scabbard.

The Light priest nodded. "I'll stay here and keep guard. He will want your report, and he'll need your vision if the demons still assault the city gates."

"Thank you—" I cocked my head. Despite real effort on my part, I still had trouble with people's names, but I was fairly sure the priest and I hadn't been formally introduced.

He smiled. "My public name is Bumblebee."

"Bumblebee?"

He shrugged. "It was a childhood nickname. My grandmother said I was destined for Light because I could not stay away from sunflowers."

"Thank you for your assistance, Brother Bumblebee." I bowed and strode from the room.

The instance of Elizabeth seeming to see me through time bothered me more than I cared to admit. She wasn't a skinwalker. That I was certain of. But if she were a demon dressed in a human skin, why did she try to warn the past me instead of the demons?

I had too many questions and not enough answers. If we held back the current offensive wave against Tandor, I needed to truthspell Elizabeth. I couldn't put it off any longer.

Chapter 4

When Shi Hua and Mateqai returned to the Temple of Light, High Brother Han stood in the main sanctuary. Even without his orange-red hair standing on end, he towered over Istaqa, Light's head of household, who fidgeted nervously beside the priest. One of the Conflict wardens stood a little to the side, a position from where he could watch everyone.

"He wouldn't let me send a messenger to fetch you," Istaqa blurted before Shi Hua could greet Han. "And you didn't inform me you weren't taking your midday meal here."

"I apologize, Istaqa," she replied smoothly. "My presence was requested at another Temple at the last moment." He should not have spoken to her in such a disrespectful manner because she outranked the man, but most of the personnel within Orrin's Temple of Light were discomfited by her presence. The Queendom of Issura did not allow women to serve Light. As Ambassador Quan often said, a little bit of manners could go a long way in paving a diplomatic road.

Shi Hua turned Han. "How may I be of service, High Brother?"

He shot a glare at Istaqa. "May we speak privately, Sister?" The deep rumble of his voice thrummed through the planks beneath her boots. The seat of Conflict was distraught enough his power leaked and affected their surroundings.

She nodded. "This way, High Brother."

He and their respective wardens followed her to the same private consulting room she'd used this morning with High Father Jerrod and High Sister Bertrice. Mateqai closed the door and took a stance on the opposite side of the room as the Conflict warden. Shi Hua lit the alabaster globes, one indicating the room was in use, the other so the participants could see each other now that the sun had passed the south side of the Temple.

"Bertrice said you still haven't made contact with those in Tandor."

A statement, not a question.

"No, m'lord, we did not." Shi Hua wearily sat down. For having so few formal tasks lately, exhaustion plagued her. "I've tried with all of the Temple seats and their seconds supporting my efforts."

"And you truly believe our people are still alive?"

So that was his real concern.

"Yes, m'lord, I do." She leaned her elbows on the table. "If the demons have taken over Cant as we suspect, they have to eliminate Tandor or control it to launch direct attacks into Issura, Diné, and the Cliffdwellers' Territory."

He nodded and smiled. "Not bad for someone from Light."

She shrugged. "I spent some time at the home Temple of Conflict in Chengzhou."

His eyebrows rose. "My compliments to both of your novice masters." His surprise shifted to something more uncomfortable. "Um, Sister, if I'm overstepping, please tell me, but we've heard a rumor that Light and Balance have had their restrictions regarding, uh, . . ." His face turned nearly as red as his hair and beard.

She sagged in her chair. After the afternoon she spent with Dragonfly, this was the last subject she wanted to discuss with anyone.

"It's true," she bit out.

He cleared his throat. "If any of you need volunteers from my Temple . . ."

She squashed her own irritation. Han meant well and was offering help in his own way.

"I appreciate your offer, High Brother. I will relay it to acting High Brother Jeremy." She tried to smile graciously. "However, we've both made our own arrangements, and I fear Justice Yanaba won't be able to participate at this time. High Sister Mya and Chief Healer Aaron are still tending to her."

"Oh, of course the justice's health is of paramount concern!" Han waved his hands and chuckled uncomfortably. "Some of the younger members of our order were merely offering assistance."

"Please tender Light's gratitude for their offer." She sighed. "If we were at full strength, the circumstances would warrant their assistance."

"All right then." Han pushed himself to his feet. "That was all. We'll see ourselves out." He and his warden practically ran out the door.

Mateqai shook his head, a wry smile on his face. "I really hope he wasn't planning on seducing you."

She scrubbed her face. "No, that was him feeling out his chances with the chief justice if she survives the siege in Tandor."

Mateqai's smile faded to a frown. "That won't go over well at all."

"Not when Balance and Light are second most likely to produce a Light child."

"I'd still wager a month's pay on High Brother Luc if it came to blows."

Shi Hua laughed. "What are you talking about? The chief justice would never let him get a lick in."

"At least, they won't have to hide their feelings anymore," Mateqai said softly.

"What feelings, Warden?" she snapped.

He opened his mouth, then though better of what he was about to say. "I misspoke, Sister. I apologize."

Wonderful. If Mateqai knew, then probably everyone else in Light knew as well. Anthea and Luc were never obvious about their private relationship, but it wouldn't do if it became common knowledge that it existed prior to the orders from the home Temples. It wouldn't do at all.

The bells tolled Third Evening. Shi Hua's stride slowed as she approached Jeremy's quarters. She thought she was ready for what they were about to do.

Dinner had been an awkward affair now that it was down to just the two of them. She'd made an excuse of needing to bathe first, and she soaked until her skin shriveled and the water chilled.

"You don't have to follow through with this, Sister." Mateqai, ever her shadow, stood at her side.

"We've been ordered—"

"That's not what I meant." He took her shoulders and turned her to face him. "Love making should be a pleasurable experience for all participants. Right now, you are upset and anxious—"

"And we may all die in a few days." A bitter laugh erupted from her.

"That, too," Mateqai remarked dryly. "What I meant was it might be better to wait until you're in a better frame of mind. Like after you've had a barrel or two of wine."

She shook her head, and her second laugh was much lighter. "If I don't do it now, I'm afraid I never will."

He nodded and an odd expression flashed so fast she thought she imagined it. It almost seemed like regret.

Warden Tadhg stood watch at Jeremy's door as they approached. He inclined his head before he knocked out a specific pattern. The deep *thunk* of the bolt sliding back set Shi Hua's nerves dancing again. The door opened, but instead of his normal sleepwear, Jeremy was still dressed in his uniform.

Maybe the skirt and vest she wore wasn't such a good idea. Maybe she should have kept this experience as any other Temple duty.

"If you need anything before morning, summon me, Sister." While Mateqai's words were directed at her, he aimed a very pointed look at Jeremy.

"I will," she promised before she sucked in a deep breath and stepped across the threshold.

Chapter 5

By the time I reached the Neighbor's Gate, the demons had ceased their assault. They oozed back to their original positions in alternating rows surrounding the walls. It was the only description I could think of for their movements.

I leaned over the parapet of the watch tower. Well, not all of them were back in formation. A dozen lay at the foot of the gate. Dead from the way the blackness spread from the corpses to the surrounding packed earth.

Except the odd contamination only I could see didn't leach from one of the bodies.

"Reverend Father," I called out.

He strode over from a consultation with priests from Conflict and Light. "What do you see?"

"The third demon from the right, lying below the gate, isn't dead."

He signaled for the Comanche Light priest he had been speaking with to join us. "We have a demon playing possum. Could you encourage them not to try this particular trick?"

The priest leaned over the parapet and launched a light ball at the demon. With a loud screech, it raced around as it burned. None of its fellows tried to help it. They remained as silent and as still in their ranks as they had before. The demon fell quiet a moment before it collapsed into a pile of red ash. No contamination spread from the cooling remains.

The Reverend Father frowned before he turned to me. "How does a dead demon look different to you than a live one?"

"They don't look different per se." I shook my head. "Eggs and grimoires tend to contaminate what they touch, so the item takes on the color of demons." I peered down at the corpses. "These are the first demons I've seen that weren't killed by Light magic." I looked at the Reverend Father again and shrugged. "Maybe our brothers of Light are the antidote to the contamination."

The Reverend Father folded his arms over his chest. "Why those things, and not an actual demon?"

I shrugged once more. "That's something we've been trying to figure out ourselves. The single egg smuggled into Orrin last fall turned the cask it was carried in, but the demon already residing with the imperial sorcerer in the Jing embassy didn't leave any traces. In fact, it looked like a sash to everyone else until it realized I was a danger to it."

"And the grimoires?" the Light priest asked.

"The grimoires—" I couldn't help a shudder at the memory of touching the one High Sister Gerd had wanted to sell to the renegades. "The leather of the grimoires appears to be made of demon skin, except the one I confiscated felt . . ." I shook myself to drive away the whispers I still heard in my dreams. "I would have sworn it was still conscious."

"But you still aren't sure if it's a difference between the demons summoned to our plane and those that are hatched here?" The Light priest cocked his head as he regarded me.

I shook my head again. "How did you know?"

He grinned. "Some of us have paid attention to High Brother Luc's reports from Orrin." His attention turned back to the Reverend Father. "May I dispose of the rest of the demon corpses, sir? I wouldn't want anyone trying to make them into books."

"Do it," the Reverend Father ordered.

While the Light priest burned the rest of the demon corpses lying at the base of Neighbor's Gate, the Reverend Father tilted his head. We retreated away from the edge of the parapet.

"Brother Bumblebee relayed your recommendation of keeping a guard at the tunnel entrances inside the Temples," he said quietly. "I'd like to hear your account of the demon's attempt to breach Balance."

I laid out our actions, including the odd behavior of Elizabeth during my rewind of time. "I'm not sure what to think concerning her behavior anymore," I finished lamely.

"Yet you are still suspicious she may be part of the original conspiracy?" He eyed me.

"Or the skinwalkers could have broken her."

"I recall hearing her voicing the same concern when I eavesdropped on your conversation."

That day in the desert when I tried to keep Elizabeth from harming herself once she realized I'd drugged her and dragged her arse out of Balance before I set off the Temple's defensive spells seemed like another lifetime ago.

"I don't know if a truthspell could even work if she isn't aware of her deception." I hugged myself. There were simply too many unknowns in this equation. If any of the clergy from Tandor's Temple of Knowledge were still in the city, surely they would be driven mad trying to calculate the outcome.

"Do the truthspell anyway to relieve both yours and Chief Justice Elizabeth's minds."

"Yes, sir." A little part of me was glad someone else was making the difficult decisions for once. My body literally ached from shouldering so much responsibility. I turned to leave.

"And, Anthea?"

I faced the Reverend Father again. "Yes, sir?"

"Get some real rest before you do the truthspell." He grinned. "I don't need you and Luc accidentally cooking yours and Elizabeth's brains because you've been too busy following a certain other mandate issued by Light."

I should have been embarrassed or furious at the Reverend Father's overly familiar jocularity. Instead, it just reminded me how exhausted I was.

And thanks to my birth mother, I'd never be able to conceive a child even if I had wanted to. But there was no sense in rehashing the pain of my past.

"If we ever have the energy to get around to fulfilling the Light mandate, we'll be sure to use the private facilities inside Love and lock the door," I said wryly.

The Reverend Father chuckled behind me as I climbed down the ladder.

I repeated the Reverend Father's odd conversation to Luc when I returned to Light. We sat in the high brother's quarters and picked over our rations. The innkeepers were cooking for the entire city, and they did the best they could with the ingredients on hand. We'd be looking at this meal differently in another couple of weeks when the water ran out.

Luc blew out a deep breath. "All the ladies of Tandor, civilian and Temple, are taking the mandate seriously. I fear that's why Bumblebee is hiding inside Balance. He begged me not to tell anyone where he was."

I winced as I tore off a bite of flatbread. "He's not interested in men, is he?"

Luc shook his head. "The problem is he's an attractive young man." He waved a hand. "With the destruction and deaths here, the women of child-bearing age could use the stipend for producing a child with a Temple talent. He's had an overabundance of offers, and some weren't exactly subtle."

While I had a bit of sympathy for poor Bumblebee, I had difficulty swallowing the bread in my mouth. Luc was ignoring our obvious problem, but one of us needed to address the issue.

"You should be taking advantage of the women's hospitality in that regard." I stared at my plate. "Especially with the Spring Rituals coming up."

He held out his hand. "I couldn't do that to you, no matter the reason."

I looked up at him. "You don't have a choice, Luc. You need to produce children with your talents. I can't give you those children."

"Since when have you cared about edicts from the home Temples?"

"Since we didn't ride for Cant after the Samael DiRoy affair." Maybe he really had thought I was joking after the Reverend Mother of Balance sentenced me to the Temple seat in Orrin. I wasn't sure how serious I was until this moment.

Luc pulled back his hand. "If we'd done that, we'd be demon fodder by now. And that's assuming we weren't tracked down and executed for defying your sentence."

"It doesn't change the fact you've been given specific orders from the home Temple."

"I am not arguing with you about this." He seized his crutches and headed for the door to his quarters.

"Where are you going?"

"I have to deliver a research report to Reverend Father Nizhé'é."

Before I could reply, he slammed the door behind him.

It was so rare for Luc and me to argue, especially over a personal matter. And yet . . .

Was this my fault? Did I really want a declaration of his undying devotion in the midst of a demon invasion? Or was I simply a jealous lover?

The survival of human race might very well depend on what happened in Tandor. And here we were, fighting over him laying with other women. Which he'd been ordered to do.

My birth mother's attempts to end her pregnancy left me blind and unable to bear children. For the first time in my life, I wasn't angry with her. She had been a selfish fool. My grandmother Thalia had been just as much a selfish fool in her own way for pursuing her illegal affair with Kam and bearing Gerd.

Here I was, acting just as selfishly and foolishly. Maybe it was a good thing I couldn't have children after all. I'd only be cursing them with my family's idiocy.

Chapter 6

"Good morn."

A shriek tore from Shi Hua's throat before she was fully conscious.

"Wh-What's wrong?" Jeremy sat up in his bed so abruptly he dragged the covers from her torso.

Her very naked torso.

She snatched the blanket and pressed it to her chest. "I'm sorry. I forgot where I was."

He frowned at her. "Why are you covering yourself? For Light's sake, we've bathed together."

"Bathing together isn't the same as . . . as . . . this!" She flicked her fingers at their bodies in his bed.

"We were following a directive from the home Temple." He looked confused and a little hurt.

"I-I'm sorry." Shi Hua sat up, keeping hold of the blanket.

"W-was it that bad for you?"

"You were fine." With his quizzical expression, she rushed to reassure him. "You did everything right and took your time and it felt good." She hesitated before she added in a small voice, "Wasn't it all right with you?"

"It was incredible!" At her wince, he amended his statement. "It was better than I expected."

The absurdity of their situation hit her. She broke out in loud laughter.

"What's so funny?" Jeremy frowned at her, which only made her laugh harder.

When she could catch air, she grinned at him. "I've been playing the role of Ambassador Quan's concubine for so long, I forgot neither of us have done this. Now, we're both acting like nobles in an arranged marriage who don't know each other, but they're supposed to . . ." She waved helplessly at the rumpled covers as another fit of giggles overtook her.

Jeremy raked his hands through his long locks and shook his head before a low chuckle came from deep in his chest and burbled from his throat. "You're right. You are being ridiculous."

"Hey!" Shi Hua protested.

"Would you like to bathe before breaking our fast?" he asked, but his eyes glinted mischievously. There was no doubt what would happen if she bathed with him.

She was having enough trouble dealing with her own emotions this morning, but she didn't want to hurt his feelings either. She grinned and climbed out of his bed. "I have other duties to attend to, High Brother."

"Acting High Brother." However, he did grin back at her. "And I haven't assigned you any other duties."

"As the only distance speaker in Orrin, I will attempt to contact our superiors in Tandor. Again." She pulled her skirt over her hips and tied the belt at her waist. "Then I'll need to relay messages to Standora for the other Temples."

The reminder sobered Jeremy. "Istaqa has the preparations for the arrival of the queen's army in hand." He tossed aside the blankets, rose, and stretched. "Have you noticed him being snippy with the staff?"

Shi Hua hesitated for an instant. Even though the head of household had been a major thorn in her side, she wasn't about to argue over personality conflicts. "No more so than usual."

Jeremy grunted as he yanked on his own leggings.

"Do you want me to keep an eye on him?" She shrugged on her vest and fastened it.

"No, it's probably just nerves with the Reverend Father coming to Orrin." He pulled on his silk tunic. "We need to get ready for morning prayers."

His words sounded like a dismissal, so she head for the door.

"Shi Hua?"

His tone clawed at her nerves, but she turned to face him. He wore the same expression of a child unsure of whether he did something wrong.

Jeremy crossed his bedchambers and stood before her. "I'm not sure what the etiquette is in our situation. High Sister Dragonfly's lessons don't seem to apply here."

Shi Hua rose on her toes and kissed him on his left cheek. "We are friends. I had a duty to perform, and I chose you to help me accomplish that mission. After that, I don't think there's anything in the Book of Love or the Book of Light that can truly help us figure out this path."

"Can we leave rank at the doorstep on those nights we spend together?" he asked softly.

That sensitivity, that questioning of their relationship, reminded her too much of her classmate Jian. Part of her wondered what Jian was doing now. And who he was doing it with.

She forced a smile. "We can treat this however you want."

He nodded and bent to kiss her forehead.

Shi Hua unlocked the door. Mateqai stood in the hallway exactly where she'd left him.

"Did you stay awake all night?"

"No, m'lady." He examined her as if looking for any harm.

She turned to Tadhg, who had been assigned to Jeremy for the night. "I don't have the energy this morning to truthspell him. Is he speaking honestly?"

"Yes, m'lady." The corner of his mouth twitched, but he managed to suppress his smile. "Warden Gad relieved Warden Mateqai shortly after you retired for the evening."

"Very well then." She shook her head. "Let's get ready for sunrise prayers, my shadow."

Dear Light, why couldn't she bed another woman to produce a child? It would be so much easier than juggling so many male egos.

Chapter 7

I had trouble sleeping after my argument with Luc, so I dressed again and headed for the rear courtyard of the Temple to practice my forms. Maybe if I wore myself out, I would be able to rest.

But Ambassador Quan sat on the back porch. He reclined on a chair with cushions while he propped his legs on two kegs. Despite the heat, a blanket covered his lower half. He looked up from the book he held.

"Good afternoon, Chief Justice."

"Good afternoon, Ambassador. What are you doing out here by yourself?"

"Attempting to stay out of everyone's way since I can barely stand." There was a faint hint of disgust in his tone.

"I thought the healers with the Diné army took care of your injuries inflicted by the renegades." I frowned.

"If you are referring to the torture, they did." He flipped back the blanket. His left foot was swollen and dark pink.

"An infection?"

"A scorpion sting." A short bark of laughter erupted from him. "Brother Hadar told me to check my boots before I put them on, but I forgot this morning."

"The healers—"

"Bah!" Quan flicked my concern away with his hand. "According to High Sister Reby and Warden Tyra, the type of scorpion seeking shelter in my footwear cannot kill a man. No sense wasting a healer's talent or any medical supplies."

Despite his nonchalance, the last thing I needed in this current madness was the brother of the Jing emperor dying due to a trivial and easily dealt with sting. "But the healers can—"

"Why, Anthea, you almost sound like you care about my welfare?" He gave me a lascivious leer that was more comical than seductive.

I crossed my arms. "Is the lifting of Balance restrictions the real reason you're displaying your dainty foot to me?"

"Oh, I'm sure a certain brother of our acquaintance is keeping you quite busy in his bed." Quan immediately sobered. "What's more interesting is the journal of Tandor's chief warden of Balance."

"What?" My arms dropped to my sides. "You still have it?"

He shrugged. "I had it in my coat pocket when you called for our original evacuation of the Temple. I wanted to compare what happened here in Issura with the recent events in southwestern Jing."

"The attack on Shakya by the renegades who'd taken over the Jing Temple of Light near the border?"

He nodded. Luc and I learned about the incident shortly before we set sail for Tandor.

"And?" I drew a bench closer to him and sat.

Quan flipped through the pages. "The renegades in Issura took their time. The changes to Temple personnel here in Tandor didn't start a year ago. The chief warden's journal only goes back three years, but it appears that Balance Clerk Minerva's role was to intentional seduce him."

"Except she couldn't convert him to their cause. Nor could she keep all of his attention on her instead of Temple business." I smirked though the situation was hardly amusing.

"That's part of it. The other is High Brother Dav."

I leaned my elbows on my knees, wishing I had gotten my spell to give me normal eyesight correct. Otherwise, I wouldn't have to rely on Quan to read the blasted journal to me. "What about Dav?"

"We've been assuming Dav recruited Gerd."

"We have?"

"Are you saying you Issurans haven't?"

I groaned. "Please, quit toying with me, Ambassador. I haven't had enough sleep to guarantee your safety if you continue playing word games."

"Very well, then." He fingered the beads at the left end of his moustache. "If Minerva's task was to get the Balance wardens under her thumb—"

"Gerd initiated the relationship with Dav to convert him? Their affair started years ago." So long ago that at one point, I feared the idiot was my biological father until Dragonfly confirmed the relationship between Gerd and Dav started after my birth.

"Most likely Ural DiSand learned of Dav's abandonment of his vows of chastity." Quan tapped the page he was looking at. "Elizabeth's chief warden noted that Dav was 'indisposed' for a week at a time, always in conjunction with DiSand leaving Tandor."

"And taking him to a Temple of Love in a different city disguised as a merchant allowed Gerd to get her hooks into him." I wiped my hands over my face. "Every little bit of power made her desire more. So much so, she abandoned her own vows."

"I hate to suggest this, but the renegades may have recruited your mother before she even took her vows, Anthea," he said softly.

"She's the woman who bore me. She was never a mother." I leapt to my feet and stalked back into the Temple.

But as I strode toward Luc's quarters, Quan's words sank past my emotions to the logical part of me. Luc and I had discussed the very possibility the demons and their renegade allies had started to infiltrate the Temples after the last major battle a century ago. So why had Quan's statement bothered me so? It felt like it was more than my resentment of how Gerd treated me as a child or my shock to learn she tried to illegally abort me. However, the connection was beyond my reach with my current exhaustion.

When I entered the bedchambers, Luc hadn't returned. I needed to get some sleep, especially if he didn't come back soon and I had to perform the truthspell on Elizabeth. Quan's new information meant it had now become an urgent necessity.

However, frying her mind or killing her accidentally in my current state wouldn't give us the answers we needed.

I stripped off my clothes once again and lay down. Despite the anxiety, doubts, and anger plaguing me, I drifted off before any answers came to me.

Chapter 8

Brother Xander, Bertrice's second from the Temple of Death, arrived as the morning service ended. He and his warden approached Shi Hua since Jeremy was speaking with a shopkeeper about sending her youngest children to the home Temple in Standora. Of course, Mateqai moved to intercept the two.

Shi Hua glared at her warden. He backed off a pace, but he showed no sign of contrition. Was everybody in Orrin as jumpy?

"Sister." Xander bowed. "Might I have a word with you—"

Exasperation filled her exhale. "Let me guess. Your seat wishes you to observe while I try to make contact with Tandor?"

"Actually, there is a private matter I wish to discuss with you and High Brother Jeremy." Dark rose suffused Xander's cheeks.

"Have you broken your fast yet, Brother?"

"No, m'lady."

"Join us, and we'll address your matter." She smiled and leaned closer to the priest. "It'll give us an excuse to kick out the wardens for a little while."

"You did that last night," Mateqai muttered.

Shi Hua slowly pivoted to face him. "Are you in need of correction, Warden?"

He stiffened at her thinly veiled warning. While she didn't know if she could go through with ordering Mateqai lashed, he needed to understand he had crossed a line.

"No, Sister." He stared at the floor. "I beg your forgiveness."

Jeremy blessed the woman he spoke with and crossed the sanctuary. Shi Hua silently informed him of Xander's request and her offer to eat with them.

"As long as you don't need us to deal with pest infestations in your morgue again, you are more than welcome at our table." Jeremy grinned at Xander.

"Nothing of that sort, this time."

"Good, because I'm starving," Jeremy stated.

Istaqa harrumphed at adding another setting to the table in the high brother's dining room, but otherwise, let their extra guest be. Once Jeremy shooed all the wardens out of the room, Light and Death alike, he poured the men's wine and took a seat next to Shi Hua, instead of the chair at the head of the table.

"What issue have you brought before us to solve?" he said cheerily.

Once again, dark rose filled Xander's cheeks, and he gulped some of his wine. "Have you, um, have you made arrangements with Justice Yanaba o-over the recent edicts from the home Temples?"

"Arrangements?"

Shi Hua bit her lower lip to keep from laughing at the flush spreading up Jeremy's neck. She took a sip of her water before she said, "I've already laid claim to his time."

"Ah, th-that's good." Xander gulped more wine. "How is the justice doing? A-after the demon attack, I mean?"

"Physically, much better." She hesitated before she said, "Did Bertrice put you up to courting Yanaba?"

"Yes." The air rushed out of the Death priest, and he sagged in his chair.

Until he realized how his answer sounded.

He straightened and waved his hands. "It's not that I don't find her attractive." He stared at his bowl. "I would have preferred to do it my own way. Nor do I want to harm her with everything she went through with trapping the demons."

"Trust me, being ordered to bed each other doesn't make for the easiest experience," Jeremy said.

Shi Hua faced him. "I beg your pardon?"

"Don't act so offended because you know exactly what we both mean," Jeremy grumbled. He turned back to Xander. "Does Yanaba prefer men or women?"

The poor man had a thoroughly confused expression. "I-I don't know," Xander said.

"Then let's eat and try to contact Tandor." Shi Hua picked up her spoon. "Afterward, I'll perform a scouting mission over at Balance for you."

Xander's relief was a palpable thing. "Thank you, Shi Hua. I owe you a huge favor for doing this."

"Don't get excited just yet." She shook her spoon in his direction. "If the Chief Healer or High Sister Mya say it's not a good idea, that's the end of it. And I'll have words with High Sister Bertrice myself if she dares say a word to you or Yanaba contrary to her best interests."

Another try to reach Tandor through the demon barrier failed. If Shi Hua didn't have her visit with Yanaba to look forward to, she would have pulled out a few chunks of her own hair in frustration.

But as both Jeremy and Xander pointed out, the demon shield was still stationary, which meant Issura remained in control of the city itself.

Shi Hua considered the issue as she and Mateqai crossed the main boulevard to Balance. She couldn't imagine being subject to a demon siege. Her handful of encounters with the creatures had each been terrifying by themselves.

Warden Noko stood guard in front of Balance's main doors. "Sister." She inclined her head. "The justice is expecting you. She's in the main reception room."

"She's out of bed?" Shi Hua's heart leapt at the news.

The junior justice had nearly killed herself defending the city from the demons who'd snuck into Orrin wearing human skins. Shi Hua shuddered. They'd come so close to losing the city, and its defense had been costly.

Noko nodded as she opened one of the Temple doors. "Journeywoman Bly has been assisting with the justice's physical therapy."

The fact the warden didn't mention Yanaba's mental and emotional health in public sent Shi Hua's heart plummeting. She pasted on a smile despite her worry. "Thank you for keeping me informed, Warden."

Shi Hua stepped into the Temple. This time of the year, it should be bustling with preparations for the aftermath of the Spring Rituals. Invariably, a few citizens lost control during the holidays or simply celebrated a little too much. Instead, it was quieter than even Death's morgue.

The statue of Balance Herself loomed ahead in the courtroom. She seemed to be watching Shi Hua from the dark recesses of Her hood. A shiver rippled through Shi Hua. She was being silly. Or maybe the unease had more to do with her vision when Yanaba had set off the Balance defenses the day of the demon attacks.

"Sister Shi Hua. Warden Mateqai."

She turned at the voice of Balance's head of household. Sivan strode down the right hallway toward them.

"What may I bring you for refreshment?"

"I don't suppose I can trouble you for some Jing black tea." Shi Hua smiled.

Sivan leaned closer to her. "I can even bring you some from the chief justice's private stash." She straightened and beckoned them to follow. When they reached the reception room, she gestured for them to enter. "Make yourselves comfortable. I'll be right back."

Shi Hua walked inside to find Yanaba sitting at the table, a book in Balance's raised symbols in front of her. Her hood was pushed back from her black, silky braids, and her delicate fingertips drifted over the lines of code. Warden Gina stood nearby.

"Greetings, Justice."

Yanaba turned in Shi Hua's general direction and smiled. "It's about time you arrived, Sister. You're late for my daily welfare check."

They both laughed, and Shi Hua walked the short distance to hug her friend.

"What are you reading?" With her assignment as Ambassador Quan's bodyguard for the last five years, she'd had little time to practice reading Balance code.

"It's an alleged history of the Assassins Guild," Yanaba said with a sigh. "It's translated from an obscure tongue of a tribe from the Middle Mountains of the Old Continent."

"Then translated from Issuran to Balance code?"

"And was probably sourced from one of the Middle Sea trade languages prior to that." Yanaba laughed. "I think some things were lost in the multiple translations."

Sivan returned with a tray she sat on the table. The sweet scent from the steaming pot triggered a bit of homesickness in Shi Hua. She sat down, and Sivan served the tea to her.

"Do you require anything else, Lady Justice?" Sivan asked.

"No, thank you," Yanaba replied.

"We're about to be told to leave," Mateqai said to Gina.

"You can stand by the door and try to eavesdrop," Shi Hua shot back.

"We both know you're going to ward the room so we can't." But he leavened his words with a smile.

"What's so secret we can't be present?" Gina said.

"It means it's none of our business," Sivan replied at the same time as Mateqai said, "Sex."

"Show some decorum!" Sivan followed her reprimand with a snap of her towel on Mateqai's backside.

"What was that for?" he protested.

"You're lucky it was my towel and not a lash," Sivan hissed.

"Then perhaps you should all leave so Sister Shi Hua can corrupt me while she drinks her tea," Yanaba said primly.

Gina laughed as Sivan herded her and Mateqai out of the reception room and closed the door behind them. As soon as the door latch clicked, Yanaba burst into giggles.

"I wasn't joking," Shi Hua said. "He will be standing by the door, attempting to eavesdrop."

"Stop worrying." Yanaba waved her right hand. Bluish purple energy sprang to life and sank in the walls, ceiling, and floor of the reception room.

"H-how did you raise your wards so fast?" Shi Hua murmured. Balance magic purred against her mind.

"I believe it's a side effect of my efforts to track and trap the demons in Orrin." Yanaba cocked her head. "Despite the Goddess's and Brother Turtle's efforts to stick me back in my body, I think there's a bit of myself left in the walls." She sighed. "The real experiment will be attempting to leave the city once I'm well enough."

"You cannot be serious!"

"Very," Yanaba assured her. "I may have trapped myself in Orrin far more ef-fectively than the Reverend Mother's sentence did Chief Justice Anthea." She carefully took a sip from her goblet. "So, are you here to play matchmaker with me and Xander?"

Shi Hua froze in place.

"I'm sorry. Was I supposed to let you plant the idea in my head?" Yanaba smiled, the first real one she'd shown since the demon attacks.

"Well, yes!" Shi Hua spluttered.

"Then go right ahead. Convince me." Yanaba giggled. "Or are we going to share Jeremy?"

Shi Hua laughed and shook her head. "You are a truly wicked friend."

"I know." Yanaba carefully set her goblet on the table, well away from her book. "In all seriousness, it makes sense for you to conceive with Jeremy. The odds are in your favor to produce a child with Light abilities."

"If this is so damn important, why restrict us from sex in the first place?" Shit Hua grumbled.

"You know why," Yanaba said. "However, I fully plan to take advantage of our permission. Not to mention, I like Xander. Plus, I deduced there was a motive in visiting me daily beyond concern for my injury."

"You could have your pick of any priest from any Temple." Shi Hua sipped her tea.

"Yes, but Xander has made the effort to know me." Yanaba chuckled. "No one else has besides Brother Turtle, and I'm not his choice of a bedmate."

"Maybe it's more fear of what the chief justice may have taught you," Shi Hua teased.

"Her heart belongs to Luc," Yanaba said softly. "It always has even though she'd deny it with her dying breath."

"I know." Shi Hua ran her finger around the rim of her cup. Leave it to Yanaba to see the lie she'd been telling herself for so long. "I'm not her choice any more than you are Turtle's."

"Still no word from Tandor?"

"The demons haven't left, which gives us some hope." Shi Hua took another sip of her tea. "Are you sure you're healthy enough for bedplay? I don't want to give Xander false hope."

"Why do you think I've followed Journeywoman Bly's instructions so closely?" Yanaba laughed. "Seriously though, I must hold court tomorrow. I need to show I'm capable to the people of Orrin. The demon attacks here have terrified them. The knowledge there's an army of them four days south . . ." She shook her head. "Not to mention the chief justice would berate me for getting behind on the caseload."

"What caseload?"

They both chuckled, but deep down, Shi Hua knew it was the black humor of people facing the possibility of their deaths.

When their laughter died, Yanaba said, "Now, how do I invite Xander for dinner without scaring him?"

Chapter 9

The screams woke me out of a sound sleep. It took me a moment to realize they were inside my head. Once again, I rushed to dress. This time, however, I was alone in the high brother's bedchambers.

Luc hadn't come back.

I ran through the Temple. This time, the wardens and priests stared at me with various expressions of surprise. There had been no alarm bells. I was on the street, racing for the business district, when the real screams started.

"Justice!"

I ignored the shout behind me and darted down the side street where the cries were coming from. People lay in front of one of the inns. People who were convulsing and foaming at the mouth.

People who were dying.

Civilians. Wardens. Two or three priests.

Aduba, Tandor's high brother of Conflict, slid to a stop besides me. "By the Twelve!"

"Check fingers and toes!" I ran to the closest person, a female Conflict warden, and knelt beside her. I grabbed her flailing hand. The tips of her fingers were such a bright red the color edged into pink.

Balance help us! I was no healer, but the symptoms seemed to be those Master Healer Devin had described as southern blue poisoning.

"The fingers are the color of red grapes," Aduba called.

"We need honey! Sorghum! Sugarcane! Cider! Anything sweet!" Remembering Devin's comments about alleviating the symptoms when a healer wasn't available, I waved at the inn. "Nothing from their stores!"

One of the Comanche Conflict brothers repeated my orders in his language and Diné. People scattered in all directions.

The warden whose hand I held tried to speak. "Wa-wa-wa…" She pointed toward the inn. Her body gave a shudder, and she went still.

My fingers sought a pulse at her neck. No breath either. Nothing.

I gently folded her arms across her abdomen and pulled her robes around her. More shouts surrounded us.

I didn't know I'd moved from the warden's side until Aduba's huge palm clasped my shoulder. We stood in the doorway of the inn.

Dead. So many dead lay inside. Overturned pitchers and bowls spilled their contents over the tables. Liquid pooled in the grout of the stone floor.

"I was about to come here for a meal," Aduba muttered.

"Thank Thief for whatever delayed you," I murmured.

We drifted through the corpses strewn through the room. Bodies sagged in chairs, flopped onto tables, or collapsed on the floor in the throes of their seizures as they died. We carefully checked, but not a one was breathing. There was no thrum of a heartbeat beneath our fingers.

I silently crossed to the kitchen area and peered inside. A woman with a small boy huddled in a corner, still alive. However, a man and two other women had been stricken, like the guests. At the faint smell of burning meat, I realized one woman's hand landed too close to the hearth when she collapsed. I gently tugged the corpse away from the fire. At least, I could justify I was trying to preserve evidence.

Returning to the living pair, I knelt beside them. "Did either of you drink or eat anything from the evening meal?"

The woman shook her head vigorously.

Her son from the way they clung to each other stared up at me. "Can you help my papa? He got sick."

A hard lump formed in my throat, and I shook my head. "I'm sorry."

Silence ruled as I escorted the pair out the back door. The boy didn't need to see the horror the inn had become. The priestess from Mother who had accompanied the Diné forces met us. With a brief nod to me, she led the pair through the back alleys and away from the disaster.

When I returned to the front courtyard, Aduba crouched near one of the afflicted along with two healers. One of the healers shook her head. Aduba gently folded the corpse's arms and drew its hood over its face.

The Light priest insignia on the corpse's robes caught my attention, and my heart threatened to leap from my chest. I whirled and strode back inside the inn. At least, half of the Diné and Comanche Light priests and a good chunk of their wardens were here to eat their evening meal.

I walked more slowly out of the inn, not liking how the objective part of my mind was twisting this puzzle. High Brother Nantan of Tandor's Temple of Death stood beside Aduba. The Death priest's countenance was a sickly yellow-green.

"You heard them, didn't you?" he murmured. Not an accusation, but as if he needed an affirmation.

I nodded. "The screams woke me."

"You were already running for the inn before the screaming started," Aduba said with a frown.

Nantan tapped his temple. "When that many die in such agony, we hear them. Sometimes, those from Balance do, too."

"The people inside couldn't literally scream, not in the grip of seizures from the poison, but their pain and silent cries invaded my dreams." I glanced around. The wardens who'd come running at the commotion had established a perimeter. Frightened civilians peered at us from behind the line of men and women of the Temples.

"High Brother Aduba," I said. "Could you send for High Brother Luc and Wardens Tyra and Yar? We need to investigate this matter and quickly. Unfortunately, the four of us have too much experience with this type of thing."

"We can't leave this many corpses lying out in this kind of heat," Nantan muttered as Aduba issued instructions to one of the Conflict wardens who had accompanied him.

"We'll work as fast as we can," I promised.

"It's First Evening." Aduba rejoined us. "Darkness brings cold at night here in the desert. You'll have your time, Justice."

The still form of the Conflict warden I tried to aid lay on the dirty street. She'd pointed at the inn. She had tried to tell me. Warn me.

Balance help us! What if she were using one of the few Issuran words she knew?

I laid a hand on Aduba's arm. *Go to each of the tanks and shut down the outflow. We can't risk that the water reservoirs haven't been tempered with.*

A grim look fell over the Conflict priest as he understood my fear. If we didn't have water, we'd die long before the queen's army arrived.

Luc would barely look at me when he arrived at the inn, and from his orange-red skin color, anger still pulsed through his veins.

The priestess from Mother brought the innkeeper's wife and son back to the inn's garden where Luc and I truthspelled the pair. They'd been about to eat their own meals when the rest of the staff collapsed. They hid when they heard the strange noises in the dining room and the screams outside.

And they definitely had not knowingly placed poison in any of the food or drink.

Light magic tingled across my skin from the globes illuminating the scene inside the inn for Luc and our wardens. I prowled through the dining room, sniffing various dishes and cups. Unfortunately, that task was becoming more and more difficult as the bowels of the dead let loose.

"It had to be the water," Tyra murmured. "Everyone was either eating the stew or drinking the water." She sniffed a bowl at another table. "That Cantish hot sauce would hide any scent of almonds."

"It's also the only thing that makes dried fish palatable," Yar said as he entered the main dining room from the kitchen. "The Reverend Father and High Brother Luc request your presence, Chief Justice."

Which meant Reverend Father Nizhé'é' had returned from personally checking the tanks that fed this section of Tandor.

I strode into the kitchen as Luc twisted the lever for the hot water faucet for the inn. An odd burbling came from the pipe before a mass shot out of the opening followed by steaming liquid.

Both men jumped back from the basin. The scent of almonds filled the air.

I snatched a clean roasting fork from where it hung on the wall and turned off the water flow. Poking at the red gelatinous mass in the basin didn't produce any action.

"What is that?" the Reverend Father murmured. "What do you see, Anthea?"

I shook my head. "Something that's scarlet from sitting in hot water too long. "Wardens!"

Tyra and Yar raced into the kitchen, swords drawn.

"You're too late," I said dryly. "It's already dead." I waved at the basin. "What do you two make of this?"

The two wardens peered at the mass.

"It looks like someone didn't drain the carcass properly before making head cheese," Yar muttered.

"Holy Balance!" Tyra sheathed her sword and held out her hand for the roasting fork, which I gave to her. She poked and shifted the dissolving substance. "It's gelatin candy."

"I beg your pardon?" The Reverend Father scowled, but I don't think it was meant as a reprimand of Tyra.

"Powdered bone and hooves are mixed with water, sweetener, and sometimes fruit," Tyra answered. "The texture depends on how long the mix is cooked. It ranges from your basic jelly to spread on bread to a tougher texture that can be stored without the need for a wax seal. A confectioner in Standora made hollow ones they filled with different flavorings." She chuckled. "Vintner has been experimenting with the candies to deliver medicine to children and those with difficulty swallowing."

"Or deliver poison," Luc whispered. He and I stared at each other. His trepidation crawled along my psyche.

"This is, was, much larger than what the confectioner back in Orrin makes," Tyra commented. "Who knows how long it took Tandor's hot water system to soften it?"

"But how did the renegades deliver a giant hollow candy into the system?" the Reverend Father growled. "We had guards on the water tanks."

"We don't have guards inside the pipes," Luc said quietly.

That still didn't answer how the damn things had been introduced into Tandor's plumbing. Unless these hollow balls filled with poison had been placed in the system five hundred years ago when it was built, we had to face the possibility that more renegades resided within our walls than the ones we caught.

Or a demon had infiltrated the city despite our best efforts.

A chill ran through me, and I poked at the gelatinous mass. "Ask the healers if they have anything to test for southern blue. If the tanks themselves are clear, we still have some water. Regardless of how they were delivered, we have to assume these poisonous jelly balls are inside all the pipes."

The true question of Tandor's survival rested on whether there was enough clean water left in the tanks to last until the queen's army arrived.

If they arrived.

Chapter 10

"We have demons on our doorstep, and you two are playing chaperones for a justice and a priest!" Istaqa threw his hands into the air, and his high-pitched shriek bounced off the high ceiling of the main sanctuary.

"That comment was uncalled for," Shi Hua said calmly. She resisted the urge to slap some sense into their head of household. His behavior was getting on her last nerve.

"And you couldn't have told me before the kitchen started preparing the evening meal," he snapped.

She folded her hands behind her back. "Everyone else in this Temple needs to be fed, Master Istaqa."

Instead of answering, he stomped in the direction of the staff offices.

"What was that all about?" Jeremy murmured behind her.

Shi Hua slowly pivoted to face him, mainly to get her ire under control. "I informed him we would be dining at Balance tonight."

"We are?" At least, Jeremy didn't seem put out by her taking the initiative.

"I don't want Yanaba to scare Xander off before he's made his case to her."

"She's interested in him?"

"You find that surprising?"

"No." Jeremy shook his head. "She's never seemed that forward to me, edicts aside."

"Oh, she plans on taking full advantage of the change in Temple policy." Shi Hua grinned.

"Don't blame her one bit on that count." Jeremy grinned back. His smile faded though as he stared in the direction Istaqa. "However, if our head of household doesn't shape up, High Brother Luc will send him packing back to Standora. And Light help me, if something happens to the high brother, I will, too."

"You aren't being overly protective on my account, are you?"

"While Istaqa's behavior toward you has been abominable, it hasn't been his only slip up in the two years I've been assigned here. He harangued Mat . . ." A shadow crossed Jeremy's face at the memory of the renegade who'd infiltrated their Temple. He took a deep breath and released it.

"It's understandable to be angry over a friend's betrayal," she murmured.

"What's done is done." He shook his head as if to dislodge his disturbing thoughts. "Let's find a couple of our wardens and have dinner with our friends."

Shi Hua glanced around the empty sanctuary. "We could walk over by ourselves. It's only across the street."

"If Nicholas were anything like the other eleven chief wardens in this city, I'd do it." Jeremy started walking in the direction of the staff quarters, and Shi Hua trotted to keep up with him. "But he won't yell at me. He gets the same look of extreme disappointment when I do something stupid like my grandfather used to."

"Then I guess we don't want Nicholas to give us such a look," she said.

"Besides, I'm an acting seat, not the youngest priest on whom everyone dumps their boring assignments."

"Actually, that's my job." She grinned up at him.

He chuckled. "I wouldn't call playing matchmaker boring."

Nor was it. Yanaba seemed determined to charm the leggings off Xander, so there wasn't much for Shi Hua or Jeremy to do. They made their excuses and left the Balance dining room at Second Evening.

But Shi Hua made a point to seek Sivan on their way out.

"Has the justice been acting in an unusual manner?" Shi Hua said softly.

"If you're talking about her sudden interest in bedding our brother from Death—" A wry smile crossed Sivan's face. "According to Brother Turtle, it's not uncommon for someone to act out in a peculiar manner after nearly dying." She shrugged. "With the recent edict about breeding, it actually gives her an approved outlet." She leaned closer to Shi Hua. "Don't worry. Little Bear and I will keep an eye on them."

"I know you will." Shi Hua hugged the other woman. "Thank you."

But as Shi Hua, Jeremy, and their wardens crossed the street back to Light, she had to wonder if she were really that concerned over her friend's welfare or scared of her own situation.

Chapter 11

I stood watch at the Neighbor's Gate when Luc joined me later that night. The clergy and wardens on the tower gave us a wide berth. Once again, the demons looked like decorative rocks arranged in a pattern outside the walls if it weren't for their bone-chilling color. Only the heat leaching from the blocks of sandstone gave me any indication darkness had fallen.

"The healers had enough supplies to check half the tanks," Luc murmured.

"How many?"

"Only one." Luc shook his head as he watched the still and silent demons. "The Reverend Father is questioning everyone who guarded that tank."

A tremor ran through me that had nothing to do with the rapidly cooling air. "Please tell me it was the tank serving the inn where the deaths occurred."

He shook his head again. "That one tested clean, but the Reverend Father doesn't trust it."

We now had less than half of our water supplies we could safely drink. I didn't want to speak my thoughts aloud where the wardens could hear. *That's what the demons are waiting for. Everyone to die of thirst.*

The Reverend Father suspects so as well. Luc's expression was grim when he turned to me. *He also believes the Light ranks were specifically targeted.*

Your order has the greatest success in killing demons. Part of me was grateful young Bumblebee wasn't among the dead within the inn or on the street. He reminded me too much of Brother Jeremy back home.

We were quiet for a long time before Luc said, "I don't want to die angry with you."

"I don't want to die angry with you either." I chuckled. "Our situation renders our argument rather moot, doesn't it?"

A wry smile filled Luc's face as he turned to me. "It is one of our more ridiculous ones." He took my hand and brought my palm to his lips. "I beg your forgiveness, Chief Justice."

Smoke tickled my nose. I turned toward the city center. A faint pinkish white glow rose from the Temple District. Nantan and his people performed their duties, but Tandor's Death clergy were working on a scale they never imagined.

I squeezed Luc's hand. *I fear we're going to run out of oil and wood to burn the bodies before we run out of water.*

If it comes to that, the demons won't wait for us to die of hunger or thirst.

A shudder ran through me. The possessed dead was how the Battle of Britannia was lost.

When I climbed down from the Neighbor's Gate tower at First Morning, High Sister Reby of Wildling waited at the bottom of the ladder to collect me. The Reverend Father had called a meeting of the senior clergy.

The funeral pyre embers in front of Government House still glowed white-hot as we passed. Smoke and the stench of burnt flesh tainted the air. Had Death already run out of incense to bless the corpses and disguise the scent?

Most of the original furniture within Conflict had been damaged or destroyed when the renegades tried to assassinate the clergy. A few chairs and benches had been scrounged for the meeting in the main sanctuary, but there wasn't enough for everyone. I dropped to the floor beside the chair reserved for Luc. Reby and her second Sisquoc sat on the other side of me. Everyone from Death looked like they hadn't slept at all last night as they sprawled on the glazed tiles. Aduba and a few others leaned against the rear wall.

Surprisingly, Ambassador Quan and Duchess Nadine had been included. But none of the guild chiefs were present, which was odd.

Unless the Reverend Father suspected one of them to be our renegade who poisoned our water supply.

I peered up at Luc, but he merely shrugged one shoulder. So, he was as confused as I was.

Reverend Father Nizhé'é' stood before the altar to address everyone, nor did he waste words. "Since the demon army came from Cant, we have to assume they are lost. And frankly, we can't assume any more support will be coming from Issura or Diné either since the demons cut off our contact with them.

"The Issuran army was supposedly marching south. However, it's been over two days since our last contact with Orrin, and the army hadn't made it to there yet. No ships have arrived, including Ambassador Quan's personal vessel, despite the spring trading season having started. You all know the situation with our water supply. If we do nothing, we could all die within these walls in two weeks' time."

"You can't be considering an evacuation," Aduba said. "The demons will cut us down before we take a step beyond our wards."

"We fight them?" Pecos, one of the Comanche Conflict high brothers, asked.

The Reverend Father shook his head. "They have greater speed, greater strength, and greater numbers."

"But Chief Justice Anthea and High Brother Luc have killed demons by themselves," Reby protested.

"We were never by ourselves," Luc chided. "And in every case, we barely stayed one trick ahead of the demon or their summoner. I'm not foolish enough to believe we can take on an entire demon army and win."

"I have to agree with Luc," the Reverend Father said. "I fear we may have to activate Death's last resort spells."

An uproar of objections filled the sanctuary.

"One at a time," the Reverend Father shouted. Magic amplified his voice, and everyone grew silent though their anger prickled against my mind.

"Perhaps Anthea should speak first," Nantan murmured. "She's the only one who didn't protest the Reverend Father's plan."

The feel of everyone's attention on me was worse than their anger at the Reverend Father's proposal. I straightened my back. "Triggering the Death spells aren't my first choice, but whatever we decide, we need to find who sabotaged the water supply. The tanks and pipes may not be the only things compromised."

"You think someone of my Temple is a renegade?" Surprisingly, Nantan's voice was contemplative, instead of accusatory.

"Not necessarily," I murmured. "The person most likely to alter the last resort spells outside of your order would be mine."

The anger from the others abruptly turned to worry and concern as everyone looked at my counterpart in Tandor. Chief Justice Elizabeth had been tortured by skinwalkers for months. She may have even been possessed without knowing it.

Her sightless gaze faced my general direction.

"Normally, I'd recommend the suspect be truthspelled," she murmured. "I'm not sure it would do any good in my case."

"Are you refusing?" the Reverend Father asked.

Elizabeth plucked at her robes. "I don't know if it's that simple. The skinwalkers could have broken me as they did Dav, and I may not even know it. He certainly didn't realize they were using him in that manner until they completely destroyed his mind." She shook her head sadly. "I should have listened to my chief enforcer more closely. He noticed oddities in the city long before I did. I—" Her voice caught for a moment. "I chalked up his theories to a man's pride over a relationship parting. But if our own clergy at Child can create a subpersonality so compelling High Brother Aduba could pass among the renegades with magic talent . . ." She shrugged, a helpless, worried gesture.

No one said anything for the longest time until Duchess Nadine added softly, "Even if our chief justice isn't compromised, I may be. One of the skinwalkers possessed me in order to murder my son and my husband." The sadness in her voice made my eyes burn.

"Oh, demonfire," Quan snapped. "Any of us who were the skinwalkers' prisoners could be their agent." It was good to see his spirit returning after what the renegades had done to him. And he wore his boots again, though he still limped from the scorpion sting.

"Including those of us who came down from Orrin." Leave it to Luc to say my internal fears aloud.

"That's what I fear as well," I said. "Reverend Father, it might be best if you locked up all of us from Orrin."

"He'd have to include me and Brother Hadar, too," Quan said. "I have no doubt Reverend Father Biming sent him as my replacement bodyguard, but we have no true accounting for Hadar's time between leaving the *Unbridled* and joining Tandor's surviving Temple loyalists."

"For that matter, we should be suspected of corrupting your man." Exhaustion laced Nantan's words. He gestured to include the Tandor clergy.

"If we start chasing desert hares, we might as well kill ourselves and save the demons the trouble." The Reverend Father's gaze swept through the assembled clergy. "None of you Issurans have any idea whether our forces were compromised when we crossed the desert either. We can't spend our time blaming each other."

He turned back to me. "Anthea, is there a way you and Nantan can confirm no one has tampered with Death's embedded spells without releasing them?"

Nantan and I exchanged glances before we both nodded.

"Very well." The Reverend Father's gaze swept the assembled group. "High Brothers Pecos and Aduba will put together battle plans in case the Temple of Death has been compromised. We have two seaworthy ships in the harbor. High Brother Luc, High Sister Reby, and Brother Hadar will be in charge of plans for making the best use of them. I want multiple ideas. If any of the rest of you are granted inspiration by the Twelve, then take your concept to the team leaders. You are dismissed."

Nantan and I climbed to our feet while the others set off to perform their tasks. Luc and Reby were already murmuring to each other as they left the sanctuary. The Death priest didn't look happy, but I had the sensation it wasn't due to me. He gestured for me to join him in an alcove.

"Have you truthspelled Elizabeth alone?" he asked in a low voice.

I shook my head. "It's been one emergency after another since our arrival."

Nantan glanced over at my fellow justice. Tyra had entered to escort the other justice back to the Temple of Light. Obviously, Nantan wanted to trust Elizabeth as much as I did.

He turned back to me. "Even if she is right about the skinwalkers breaking her, she can't be responsible for the poisoning. How could she possibly get the poison into the plumbing?"

Tyra glanced in my direction, her expression asking if I needed her. I gave her a slight shake of my head.

"Unfortunately, they could have put a subpersonality into her that could cast a spell on a sighted person who could accomplish such a task for her," I murmured.

Nantan's chuckle held no real humor. "I agree with the Reverend Father about chasing desert hares. That's a far more difficult plan than it needs to be."

"At least, she's not hiding a demon on her person." The oddity I noticed earlier flitted through my tired mind. "Is there a reason the Reverend Father excluded the Tandoran guild leaders from this little meeting?"

"You caught that, too." Nantan rubbed his chin before he relaxed and shrugged. "Strategy probably. Perhaps he knows more than he's telling us."

I looked over at Reverend Father Nizhé'é. He spoke with the Conflict priests and the handful of remaining Light clergy. He turned to leave with a Diné brother and must have felt my attention on him. He smiled at me before they left the sanctuary.

His behavior toward me was odd. Discomforting. Almost parental without being patronizing. He reminded me too much of Kam.

The wave of grief caught me off guard. Nantan laid his hand on my left arm. The emotion passed through me and into him. I blinked away the tears that had started to form.

The Death priest merely smiled at me. "Your pain is mine."

I'd always believed the words were mere ritual. But then, I'd never lost any-one close to me until Kam's murder. Never sought succor at a fellow Temple.

"Thank you," I murmured.

"Feel well enough to go to Death?"

My laughter was bitter. "What I really want is a bath and a pot of tea, but I might as well wish for a bag of gold while I'm at it. Let's do this before I fall asleep on my feet."

Balance knew how many candlemarks later, Nantan and I were sure the spells embedded deep in the stones of the Temple of Death hadn't been altered in any way.

"I hate to say this, but I'm sorely disappointed the Temple magic is intact," he said as he sprawled on the flagstones in the main sanctuary.

I laid down beside him. There was simply nowhere to sit, and every mus-cle in my body ached. Unlike the issue of the damaged furniture in Conflict, Death's main sanctuary was always empty, save for the statue of the goddess Herself.

Unlike the basalt used by my Temple, Death carved their representations from obsidian, or dyed onyx in areas where obsidian was unavailable or too expensive. Her face was hidden by her hood as Balance's was. The statue held out her hands in welcome, instead of holding a sword, for we all experience Her embrace eventually.

"As am I," I murmured. "While I can accept the inevitability of death, I do not wish to rush the process, contrary to what many of our peers believe. Despite our short acquaintance, I don't believe the Reverend Father would have suggested this course of action without due consideration."

Nantan rose up on his elbows. "What if we replace Death's defensive spells with Balance's?"

I shook my head. "That would take Elizabeth and me several days, time we may not have. Second of all, how would we lure all the demons into your Temple? In my experience, they have not been that cooperative."

"What if we used the city walls instead? Use Balance to contain Death?"

I sat upright as I rolled his idea around in my head. "We would still need a representative from all twelve orders. My second nearly killed herself trying something similar in Orrin."

Nantan nodded. "We have you, Elizabeth, and Spotted Fawn for Balance. While the majority of the Diné, Cliffdweller, and Plains Nations forces are Conflict, Light, Wildling, and Thief, there's at least one representative from the other six orders with their support staff."

Slowly, I nodded. His idea had a decent possibility of success.

We spent the rest of the afternoon in Nantan's office sketching out our plan. The only problem was how to get the demons inside Tandor and the humans out at the same time. If we couldn't figure out how to pull off that simple task, this entire exercise was for naught.

But the Reverend Father wanted alternative strategies, so by Balance, we were going to give him one.

Chapter 12

When Shi Hua awoke, there was a certain comfort in recognizing her surroundings. At least, she didn't shriek like a child this time. Jeremy still slept, the rise and fall of his chest visible in the faint light seeping under his door.

She eased from under the covers and quickly dressed. The queen's army should arrive sometime tomorrow. With Reverend Father Farrell appropriating rooms within the Temple, this would be her last chance for any privacy in the bathing pool.

While Istaqa was a pain in her backside, Light only knew how the Reverend Father would react.

Tadhg nodded to her as she stepped out of Jeremy's bedchambers. Gad fell in step behind her as she strode down the hallway.

They turned the corner to the entrance to her own quarters. She rested her hand on the latch and faced Gad.

"I'm going to the bathing room by myself. I promise not to leave the Temple until it is time for me to attend court in Balance."

"I can't let you go anywhere without an escort, m'lady." His expression was somewhere between amusement and embarrassment.

She rubbed her forehead. "You don't take orders from the head of household, Gad."

"I know. However, I do take threats from Mateqai quite seriously."

Shi Hua stared at the junior warden. "What did he say to you?"

Gad shrugged. "Merely that if I let you out of my sight for anything more than, uh—" His face darkened in the dim lighting of the corridor. "—your and the High Brother's private times and something happened to you, he would flay me before he salted and burned me alive."

"Can we come to a compromise?"

"It would depend on the nature of such a compromise." But from Gad's expression, he'd be willing to acquiesce as long as she were reasonable.

"I want a quarter candlemark alone with my thoughts. Would you be willing to stand guard at the bathing room doorway since there is no other egress into that room?"

He cocked his head. "You could escape out one of the windows."

"I'd have to break the glass to create an opening large enough. You would hear me and catch me before I made it to the postern gate."

"True." He nodded. "I accept your proposal, m'lady."

The quarter candlemark turned into a half candlemark as Shi Hua tried to sort through her feelings. She could have done worse than Jeremy. He was gentle and went out of his way to please her in bed, but he wasn't . . .

He wasn't a she.

Shi Hua climbed out of the pool and grabbed a towel from the warming rack. She couldn't blame Jeremy for being what he was. He was a good friend and would be a good father to their offspring for the first years of the child's life.

However, it would be odd seeing children racing about Light and Balance the way they did at the other ten Temples. And it would certainly drive Istaqa insane.

She combed out her hair, braided and pinned it. She was pulling on her leggings when the shouting started.

"Sister!" Gad called. "The high brother needs you! A man has taken a hostage in our main sanctuary!"

Chapter 13

Inside the Temple of Knowledge's library, I hung on to my last thread of patience for Reverend Father Nizhé'é' to comment on the plan Nantan and I had developed.

The Reverend Father's gaze shot around the roomful of clergy as he repeated our plan in his language before he added in the trade tongue, "It has potential."

The Diné Knowledge priestess asked a question.

"That will be the trick, won't it?" The Reverend Father tapped an index finger along the side of his nose. Once again, he answered in his own language, but from his gestures, he explained my plan to open up the Balance passage to the tunnel system and lure the demons guarding that egress into the city. That was assuming we could kill them, sneak the civilians out through the tunnels, and lure the rest of the demon army through the gates to destroy them.

"How are we going to keep from losing you and Elizabeth? If it weren't for Jeremy and Shi Hua freeing Yanaba and Turtle reeling her back into her body, we would have lost your second" Luc asked.

"Because I'm not using my soul to trap the demons. We're casting Death's destruction spell, but using Balance's containment to keep the last resort spell from expanding past the city walls," I replied.

"And unlike Orrin, Tandor's walls extend across the waterfront as a tide break." Elizabeth shrugged. "There's no shifting beachfront that must be anchored through time. We have the three dimensions we need to control the fourth to protect the surrounding region and keep from killing the civilians we're trying to save."

"The demons aren't fools." The tomes and scrolls on the shelves surrounding the large table absorbed Aduba's deep rumble. A map of Tandor was spread over the top, its corners weighted by other books so it wouldn't curl.

A map I couldn't truly see.

He traced a line across a section. "The natural rock formations of the harbor extend past the walls. Can we extend your spells to the sea chain? Otherwise, some of our damned foes could escape by running out onto the spits and docks."

"Sea chain?" the Reverend Father asked. "What's a sea chain?"

"When pirate attacks were common along the Peaceful Sea two generations ago, the Temples, guilds and nobles of Tandor created a giant chain to block the harbor since our entrance is much narrower than Orrin's or Standora's." Aduba tapped two other spots on the parchment. "The winches rest in the lighthouses on the harbor points."

"Have you used the chain since then?" the Reverend Father asked.

"Not since Justice Thalia broke their power twenty-five years ago," Nantan said softly.

"Surely, this chain has rusted through?" The Reverend Father appeared puzzled by this feat of engineering.

"Not if there are spells to protect the metal." Luc leaned forward and examined the map. "Not that your idea isn't an excellent one, but using it to extend the reach of Anthea and Nantan's plan is out of the question. We'd have to risk someone going outside of the wards to set the spells. The demon will be inside the walls before you could blink if we drop the wards."

Aduba raised a fist, but gently struck the tabletop. "We can't take the chance of any demons surviving. We're back to the Reverend Father's original plan of destroying the entire duchy to be sure."

"Maybe not." Luc looked up at Aduba. "What if we arm one of the ships with Light and Conflict priests?" Luc turned to the Reverend Father. "The other one with the more experienced crew takes the children and invalids out first. When we bring down the wards, send volunteers out to the lighthouses. Those of us on the remaining ship can keep the demons off them while they raise the sea chain and set the balance spells."

"That would leave anyone on the ship or the prominences in too close proximity to the city when we set off the defensive spells," I protested.

"And where will you and Nantan be when they are set off?" Luc gave me a rather pointed look.

"Before we all start volunteering to be the noble sacrifice in this siege, let's figure out how we're getting the demons into the city in a controlled manner," the Reverend Father said dryly.

"They won't come into the city just because we whistle for them," Aduba added.

"You're right," I said. "They won't unless the demon already within the walls tells them it's safe."

Everyone in the room stared at me once my words were translated.

"You think there's a demon within Tandor's walls?" The Reverend Father's face held the same deep orange shock as everyone else in this meeting.

"Demons can change the density of their bodies. One moment, they are as wispy as fog. The next, they are harder than steel." I waved in the direction of the nearest water tank. "It would explain how the poison was placed in the pipes. If my sword passed right through the first ones I fought, why can't they pass through a pipe?"

"And use their magic to make an object they carry the same density as their bodies." The Reverend Father frowned, obviously not liking my conclusion. "Otherwise, the demons wouldn't be able to do anything in their fog state."

Reby muttered an oath. "That would explain why the guards on the tanks didn't see anything. All the damn demon had to do was reach through the bottom of the tank from inside the building and release the poisoned gelatin ball."

"Or reach into a pipe through a wall," Luc added.

"Twelve take them!" Brother Bumblebee banged his fist on the table. "The bastard could be in here, hiding between the pages of a book and listening to everything we say."

"It's not here," I said.

"How can you be sure?" one of the Comanche Conflict high brothers asked.

"Because I'm here. It's being careful. Staying out of my sight." I gestured at my eyes. "Thanks to the renegades, the demons know I can see them."

"But if it can become so thin to fit between pages . . ." the Diné Knowledge priestess hesitated while the Reverend Father translated her words.

"They can change their forms and their density," I replied. "But they can't change their color to my eyesight. I assure you it's not in this room."

"So how do we find the blasted thing and manipulate it before it poisons our remaining supplies or reports our plan to its brethren?" The Reverend Father frowned at me.

"I don't know," I said softly.

Chapter 14

Shi Hua yanked on her boots and raced after Gad. She skidded to a halt at the sight that greeted her in the sanctuary.

Benches had been scattered across the floor, many knocked over in people's haste to flee. Early worshipers crowded against the walls and muttered fearfully. Wardens ringed the central altar, weapons drawn.

A man crouched before the statue of Light, far too close to the eternal flame for Shi Hua's comfort. He held a knife at a little boy's throat. Nearby a woman huddled on the floor with another boy and an older girl while all three wept silently.

Jeremy stood near the man, unarmed and reaching out. "...let us talk about your grievance."

"That's all you priests do! Talk, talk, talk!" The man appeared more distraught than mad. "You were planning to take my children from me!"

"I didn't authorize—" Jeremy began.

"You conspire with my wife and the blind bitch! First, the Red Justice brings the demons! Now, you all want to take my babies!"

A gasp ran through the crowd, but Shi wasn't sure if it was the insults to Justice Yanaba and Chief Justice Anthea or the accusation of abduction that caused the uproar.

Shi Hua stepped forward. Gad and Mateqai both laid hands on her shoulders. She glared at each man in turn. Realizing their slips, they released her.

She walked slowly and silently toward the man. He twisted toward her, but he was careless. The child's hand waved through the eternal flame, and he let out a wail.

Do you trust me? she asked Jeremy.

Yes.

Shi Hua sat down cross-legged on the section of floor where the oak planks met the flagstone circle beneath the statue and the eternal flame. Her hands rested loosely on her knees.

"Do your children have talents?" she asked softly.

The man stared at her as if she had lost her mind. Good. If she could keep him distracted, Jeremy or Nicholas could get that knife away from the throat of the sobbing boy.

"My name is Shi Hua. What's yours?"

Again, he remained silent. His attention flicked between her, Jeremy, and Tadhg who stood near the weeping woman and the other two children.

"Daddy, tell her!" the little girl cried out.

His attention jerked back to Shi Hua though she hadn't moved. "Liar! Women don't wear Light colors."

"You're right. In Issura, women are not admitted to the order of Light." She took a deep breath and released it. The man matched her inhale and exhale. Good. She was creating a rapport without the use of magic. Her novice master Brother Lin said the less magic used in negotiations, the more likely the parties will stick to their agreement because there was no assumption of coercion.

"However, I am from Jing. Both our leaders recognize working together is best for all of us. What's your son's name?"

Fury filled the man's face. "None of your business! I won't let you spell him."

"It's Cricket," the little girl said before her mother shushed her.

"Cricket is a good name." She gauged the situation. "Cricket, can I look at your hand?"

"Why?" the man snarled. He shifted the boy back toward the eternal flame, and the child shrieked.

"He's been injured," she said gently, not assigning blame. "Look at his skin."

The man released his hold on the child's chest, but that damn knife glittered too close to his throat. He seized his son's arm and stared in horror. The skin on the boy's palm had already blistered, cracked and oozed.

"Cricket needs to see a healer now, or he could lose the use of that hand," Shi Hua said.

"You're just trying to take him from me like my wife is!" He panted and his wild gaze darted in all directions. "You'll put a demon in his place!"

Does Thief know about these crazy ideas? Jeremy whispered in her mind. *If this is a common theory among the populace, we've got bigger problems.*

Shi Hua silently acknowledged Jeremy, but she kept her attention on the man. "If you let Cricket go see a healer now, I'll be your prisoner."

"You could use your magic."

"You have my word I won't, and those of us in Light are not allowed to lie."

Once again, his attention flicked from face to face. She gambled that he still cared about his children's welfare.

"You could fight me," he said uncertainly.

"But I won't," she assured him.

"Why not?" He seemed genuinely curious.

"Because the life of my unborn child would depend on it."

Chapter 15

I couldn't put it off any longer. Now Luc was speaking to me again, he could perform the truthspell on Elizabeth. While I had little guilt concerning the horrible way the fake priest Mat had died under my truthspell, I would feel terribly guilty if I accidentally killed one of the few people who showed me kindness in my childhood.

Luc and I headed back to the Temple of Light after our meeting with the Reverend Father, but his confidence in my ability to find the demon didn't inspire me one little bit.

"Why does everyone expect me to come up with the miracles?" I grumbled to Luc as we crossed the street.

"Because you keep pulling them out of your arse," he teased.

Normally, I would have laughed at his words, but after so many deaths, not even my black humor could cheer me.

There was very little activity on the main thoroughfare as we walked. The funeral pyre in front of Government House still glowed a dull pink that had nothing to do with the growing heat of the day. A few children ran errands, as did a few adults. The steady clangs from the Smiths Guild had quieted for the afternoon. The least amount of activity during the hottest part of the day would require the least amount of water.

"I don't think I can this time," I murmured as we climbed the steps to the Temple of Light.

"Let's deal with Elizabeth before you try to reach up your—"

"Luc!"

Two of the Cliffdweller wardens stood guard at the outer doors. One of them obviously knew enough Issuran he understood Luc from his cheeky smile.

Luc cheerfully greeted them in their own language as they held the doors open for us. When we reached the quarters Elizabeth used, I knocked.

Tyra opened the door. "The Chief Justice has been expecting you."

"Can we dispense with the titles?" I said. "Otherwise, we'll be here all day, and frankly, I need some sleep."

Elizabeth had more guests than just us. Hadar sat on her right, but across the table sat the Diné circuit justice Spotted Fawn and her clerk, a thin man whose manner reminded me too much of Istaqa, Luc's head of household back in Orrin. Spotted Fawn's warden stood between us and her charge.

Neither of the justices wore their hoods. Spotted Fawn's hair was pulled back in a neat bun at the back of her head, which irritated me. I'd been forced to braid my own damn hair the last several mornings since Tyra had been caring for Elizabeth.

Spotted Fawn continued to stare sightlessly in Elizabeth's direction while Elizabeth had turned her head in the general direction of my voice. The odder thing was the Diné clerk's frank appraisal of me.

"By all means, please," the clerk said. "Otherwise, we'd need more water to quench our throats than we can afford."

At his breach of decorum, I stared at him.

"It's actually me, Spotted Fawn, speaking through my clerk Bidzii, Anthea," he said while she smiled at me. "Even though my circuit is on the Issuran border, my proficiency in your language leaves something to be desired. Bidzii, however, is quite fluent."

"You control him?" A shudder ran through me at the thought. The skin-walkers I'd encountered scared the water out of me.

"It may seem that way, but no." The clerk shrugged. "We've worked together long enough his translation is almost instantaneous."

"You don't travel your circuit with someone from Light?" Luc asked.

"Of course, I do. Or I did," she said sadly through her clerk. "My trainee was one of the young men poisoned yesterday."

"I apologize," I murmured while glaring at Luc. "That was insensitive of us."

The objects on the table finally registered in my exhaustion. An ink bottle, quill, and parchment sat before Hadar. Stamps and another piece of parchment rested in front of Bidzii.

"This isn't an official inquiry," I said.

"Yes, it is," Elizabeth said firmly. "It has to be, or I can never hear a case again. There will be too many questions concerning my efficacy and impartiality. As such, two or more justices must hear the testimony."

"How fortunate we have two justices here," I muttered.

"I wouldn't dream of chiding someone of higher rank—" Spotted Fawn started.

"But you will anyway," I shot back.

"If necessary," she immediately responded. "I don't like the situation any more than you do, Anthea. I grew up with stories of the Corrupted. I have a better idea of what they can do to a person, and Balance help me, I wish I were simply boasting on that fact."

"Elizabeth experienced enough trauma at the hands of those renegades!" I threw my hands up though neither of my sister justices could see the gesture.

"Anthea, I need to know for my own peace of mind," Elizabeth said.

"But as we discussed earlier, a subpersonality may exist," I pointed out. "One we can't detect."

"You can find trouble anywhere you go, my dear." Elizabeth smiled. "If there's trouble with my mind, you will find it."

My gaze swept the small room. "All right, if we're going to do this, we're doing it my way. If something goes wrong, the Reverend Father can't afford to lose all three of his justices."

We pushed the bed and the table into diagonal corners for maximum space. The junior priests didn't have private bathing rooms like the senior priest did, so we only had one exit to worry about.

Tyra ran next door to the room we supposedly shared. She brought back the skirt she'd worn when we first entered Tandor, and she had been disguised as my handmaid. With Elizabeth's door closed, she and Hadar ripped the fabric and stuffed it into the gaps around the door.

While I was fairly certain Elizabeth wasn't possessed at the moment, the effort of sealing the room mollified the Diné. We already knew a skinwalker couldn't pass through Temple wards, but we didn't know for certain personal wards could hold them in their smoke state.

Hadar warded the room. His magic stroked my skin, the sensation of warm water trickling over my limbs. However, the rest of us knew from training sessions Thief wards were the most difficult to penetrate because of their ever-changing nature.

Luc and I sat with Elizabeth on her bed. The two wardens stood guard with swords drawn, Tyra closest to us. Everyone else sat at the table to observe and record this session.

I gave the traditional opening statement, identifying myself. Luc laid the counter to the truthspell blocker we'd recently learned that Love had developed before he cast the truthspell itself. Elizabeth answered my initial questions as to her name and personal history.

Before I asked the next question, I sucked in a deep breath. "Have you ever been possessed by a skinwalker?"

"Of course, she has." Elizabeth turned toward me as if she could see me, her grin maniacal. "It's not any fun if you can't make your puppets do acts they'd never dream of performing. That bastard chief warden of hers refused to eat the stew Minerva poisoned. I had to do something. You should have seen the look on his face when poor, helpless Elizabeth stabbed him in the heart."

Chapter 16

Another series of shocked gasps ran through the civilians at Shi Hua's proclamation. The procreation edict probably wasn't widely known outside of the Temples because the changes only affected three people currently in Orrin. On the other hand, considering the speed at which gossip spread in this city, she was a little surprised everyone *didn't* know she'd been bedding Jeremy.

"It's a strong possibility." She shrugged. "With the Assassins Guild killing so many Light priests, our respective Reverend Fathers have ordered Acting High Brother Jeremy and me to breed."

"Th-then the rumors are true?" The man wrapped his arm around the boy's chest once again, but the gesture seemed more protective than threatening.

"What rumors?"

"The Assassins Guild truly exists, and they have allied themselves with the demons." He lowered the knife a fraction.

"The guild exists, and we of the clergy suspect an alliance, but we have no proof," she answered. "However, the guild's actions have directly benefitted the demons' efforts to take over both Tandor and Orrin."

He looked down at his weeping son. "She wants to take them to Standora."

"Your children?"

The man nodded. Tears glittered in his eyes.

"Who wants to take them to Standora?" Shi Hua asked softly. "Your wife?"

Another nod.

"Don't you want your children to be safe?"

Huge drops rolled down his cheeks. "If we're going to die, I want us to be together." The knife hit the flagstone with a clatter. He pulled the boy in a tight embrace.

Nicholas took a step toward him, but Jeremy silently told him to halt.

"Many people are sending their children north to keep them safe and alive," Shi Hua said. "It's difficult to defend the city if we're worried about our children. That's one of the reasons those of us pledged to Light do not normally have romantic relations."

"I'm so sorry, Cricket," the man murmured, rocking his son. "I'm so sorry."

Jeremy summoned one of their pages and sent the youth running for a healer. *Shi Hua, see if you can get him to take Cricket to one of the empty priest's quarters.*

Yes, sir, but we're going to need someone from Child, too, for both the father and the son.

Jeremy silently relayed the request to the squire.

"Can you and I take Cricket to a bedchamber to rest while we wait for the healer?" Shi Hua asked.

The man shot a suspicious look at her over the top of the boy's tousled hair, but the older girl jerked out of her mother's grasp and stalked over to Shi Hua.

"We're coming, too," the girl said fiercely.

Shi Hua looked up at her. "You've been keeping the peace between your parents for a while, haven't you?"

The girl nodded solemnly.

"Then please join us. I will need your guidance." Shi Hua and Cricket's parents stood, the boy still in his father's arms. The knife lay forgotten on the flagstones.

Jeremy silently ordered the wardens to sheath their weapons.

As Shi Hua walked toward the hallway leading to the priests' quarters, she paused next to Mateqai. "Would you please inform Justice Yanaba I will be late for court?"

Chapter 17

"Who are you?" I watched Elizabeth very carefully. Her skin color had changed from its normal golden color to orange-yellow, but she had neither the greenish-yellow cast of possession nor the awful gray-green of a skinwalker wearing dead flesh.

"You know who I am."

I wanted to run screaming from the room, both from Elizabeth's eerie transformation and my own idiotic incompetence. Running my tongue over my dry lips, I collected my thoughts. I had to be smart about this, or we could lose Elizabeth just as we had lost High Brother Dav.

"What is your name?" I tried again.

"Elizabeth."

Luc's knuckles stood out against his skin from his tight grip on his crutches. His concern prickled along my psyche.

"Are you a different personality than the Elizabeth I've been talking to for the last three days?"

She hesitated, then gasped as the truthspell inflicted its punishment for withholding a truth. "Yes."

"How was the second personality inside Elizabeth created?"

She cried out and clutched at her middle.

"I-I planted a copy of myself inside her."

"Who put the copy inside of Elizabeth?"

She glared at me as if she could see me. "I am power incarnate."

A lie. She groaned.

I didn't like speculating, but an awful suspicion formed in my mind. "You're nothing more than the ghost of a skinwalker, aren't you?"

"Yes," she spat.

"But you miscalculated. By binding yourself to Elizabeth, you made yourself vulnerable to the same things she is." I smiled. "How do I purge you out of her?"

"I am more than anything you could possibly conceive, witch!" But her, or rather its, defiance sent Elizabeth writhing on the bed.

"Answer me, then the pain will stop," I said fiercely.

"You can't get rid of me!" Elizabeth's body lay panting on the bed. I wondered if the real Elizabeth knew what was happening to her.

"How would you purge yourself from her?"

Another maniacal grin. "I never bothered to learn because there was no need."

Time for a different track. "Is there a demon inside the walls of Tandor?"

Once again, it writhed. However, its refusal to answer was the confirmation I needed.

"Where has the demon been hiding most of the time of the siege?"

A scream ripped from Elizabeth's throat.

Both Luc and I rose and took a step away from the convulsing body.

"This is why we chain people before we truthspell them," he said dryly over its screeching.

"Anthea," Spotted Deer said. "The fragment of the skinwalker will let the truthspell kill Elizabeth before it will let her go."

"She'd be dead already if I had cast the truthspell." Except my quip wasn't the least bit amusing. Luc's magic would only kill Elizabeth more slowly than mine would if we let this continue. "We need to purify her. Somehow. Saltwater?"

With one more throttled cry, Elizabeth passed out. I laid two fingers along her throat. She still had a pulse, and she breathed. The silence allowed us to think more coherently.

"No." Luc wore the intense expression he had when he was puzzling something out. "Why do they wear human skins or possess people?"

"Because they like to toy with us," I snapped.

"I think there's more than that." He pivoted toward Spotted Deer. "Lady Justice, in the Diné legends, are skinwalkers ever seen in the daylight?"

"Only when they wear skins, but they have no real power during the day. At First Evening . . ." A look of consternation crossed her features.

"Sundown," I murmured. "The demons may not be susceptible to the sun's rays—"

"But they are vulnerable to Light magic, which is energy similar to the sun's but more focused." Luc's eyebrows rose. "However, the skinwalkers are humans using demon magic, so that may make them more vulnerable to the less concentrated power of daylight. Has she been outside in sunlight since we arrived in Tandor?"

"When they dragged us from Light to Balance after I lied about you using the Temple to destroy them." Luc and I met each other's gaze.

"Minerva yanked her hood up before we went outside," he said.

"She did?" I frowned, trying to replay that day's events in my mind.

"You were too busy pissing off the skinwalker." Luc grinned.

"We can take her up to the roof." Tyra waved her hand between herself and the Diné warden. "We strip her clothes off, wake her up, and see what happens."

"We've got nothing to lose at this point." Hadar spoke for the first time. His normally cheerful disposition had taken a beating since the demon army surrounded us.

"You might want to chain her before you wake her," Luc added. "Our skinwalker subpersona may decide to walk Elizabeth over the edge of the roof."

"Let's do it," I muttered.

Hadar dropped his wards. Luc hobbled out of Elizabeth's room. He returned a few moments later with Yar, his own warden from Orrin who had accompanied us to Tandor, and a set of spelled manacles.

My stomach lurched. They were probably the same restraints the renegades used on Dav when they tortured him.

The giant mountain of a warden bound Elizabeth and carefully lifted her over his shoulder. Tyra and Spotted Fawn's warden merely looked at each other and shrugged. I didn't blame them. I wouldn't want to haul Elizabeth anywhere again either. Despite her thin frame and the months of torture, she was no lightweight.

Tyra pulled the blanket from the justice's bed. I couldn't fault my warden's consideration of Elizabeth's comfort. My sister priestess had suffered enough.

Spotted Fawn and her party followed Luc, me, and our wardens to the roof of Balance. Heat from the stone seeped through the thin soles of my borrowed sand boots. The dull red sun had started its downward slide.

Damn, it was that late already. I needed to get some rest before my watch on the walls started tonight, but first things first. And I hoped to Balance Luc's idea worked. Otherwise, we'd have to put Elizabeth in one of the cells in the basement of Light and put a guard on her. Our allies were stretched thin as it was after the massacre at the inn.

When Yar had picked up the unconscious Elizabeth, her hood had flipped forward to cover her head. Tyra laid out the blanket on the roof, well away from the Temple's water tanks. Yar gently laid Elizabeth on the thin wool.

Something odd happened to parts of Elizabeth's exposed skin. A shimmer I couldn't explain. Tyra and Spotted Fawn's warden began stripping off the justice's clothing. As they bared more of Elizabeth's flesh to the sun, the shimmering intensified.

"Luc?" I laid a hand on his shoulder. "What do you see?"

"A nearly naked justice," he quipped. He looked at me with sudden seriousness. "What are you seeing?"

"I'm not sure," I murmured. The shimmer didn't have a recognizable color. It wasn't like the waves of heat off desert sand either. Luc's mind entered mine so he could see the strange shimmer. His confusion melded with my own.

"Her small clothes as well, Lady Justices?" Tyra looked up at Spotted Fawn and me. We both nodded silently. Slightly back from Elizabeth's head, Hadar scribbled across the parchment. Bidzii leaned over his shoulder, no doubt relaying the Thief priest's notes to Spotted Fawn.

Once Elizabeth's flesh was totally exposed, a shudder rolled through her body. She flailed and thrashed, the motion reminiscent of a slug coated with salt. Her motions bruised her limbs since she only had the thin blanket to protect her from the sandstone.

"Hold her," Spotted Fawn ordered through Bidzii. She repeated the command herself in Diné.

Both Balance wardens seized Elizabeth's arms, and they both cried out and jerked away.

"What is it?" Alarm ran through me that Tyra had been harmed.

"She's cold." My warden stared at her hands before she looked up at me. "Colder than a mountain lake in the middle of winter."

We had our confirmation the skinwalkers were using demon magic. The question was whether Elizabeth would survive whatever the piece of skinwalker in her soul was doing to her.

Another scream erupted from Elizabeth, long and loud, before she collapsed on the blanket. The shimmer faded, and her skin returned to its normal golden color.

Except where she was injured when the fragment of skinwalker's essence struggled to remain in her.

"I think we boiled off the skinwalker bit that was clinging to her mind," Luc said.

I released his shoulder, stepped closer to the unconscious justice, and ran my hand down her left shin. "She's no longer cold." I pressed my fingers to the pulse point of her ankle. "Her heartbeat is strong."

Hadar pulled a small object from his pocket. "Tyra."

She caught the object he tossed, snapped it, and held the broken pieces beneath Elizabeth's nose. A rancid smell, worse than the most ill-kept sewer pipes I'd ever encountered, hit me and I leaned away.

"Wha-a-a," Elizabeth slurred. She tried to bat at Tyra's hands and missed.

"What's your name and rank?" I snapped.

"Elizabeth DiBalance, Chief Justice of the city of Tandor in the queendom of Issura." Her voice grew as she spoke.

"Who am I?"

"Anthea DiBalance, Chief Justice of Orrin." Elizabeth ran her hands over her torso. "Why in all of Balance's names am I naked?"

I chuckled. "What's the last thing you remember?"

"Luc truthspelled me, and—" She frowned. "I don't remember you asking me any questions. Everything is blank after that."

"Would you allow me to look?" I asked softly.

She nodded, and I extended my senses. Elizabeth was there, mostly. In her more recent memories, jagged gaps existed. Almost as if they'd been torn from her mind. It had used Elizabeth's torture to drive its claws deep inside her mind. But there was nothing to indicate the skinwalker or any fragment of it was still present.

I released her, drew a deep breath, and sat back on my heels. "Well, the good news is you are no longer possessed by a skinwalker."

"And the bad news?" Spotted Fawn prompted.

"We still don't know where that damn demon is hiding within Tandor."

Chapter 18

By the time Chief Healer Aaron arrived and dealt with Cricket's injuries and the family was released to Child to handle the emotional impact, it was nearly First Afternoon.

Shi Hua's stomach reminded her she hadn't broken her fast as she and Mateqai jogged across the street to Balance.

Nathan, Chief Justice Anthea's squire led Shi Hua and Mateqai to Balance's main receiving room. Yanaba and Balance's chief warden Little Bear were inside eating their midday meal. Two additional places had been set at the table.

Yanaba's personal squire raced out of the room as soon as Shi Hua and Mateqai entered.

"So Light finally deigned to attend to their duties," the justice teased.

"I thought you needed another day of rest, Lady Justice, before you returned to your own duties." Shi Hua grinned though her friend couldn't see it.

Yanaba snorted. "Your page said you had a rather exciting morning."

Shi Hua sat down at the table, as did Mateqai. She relayed the morning's events to a rapt audience while Mateqai tasted the food Sivan served to Shi Hua. Surprisingly, the Balance head of household didn't throw a fit like Istaqa would have.

"You actually blurted out you are with child in front of the civilians?" Yanaba stared in Shi Hua's general direction with an incredulous expression.

"Knowing I shared his fears got the man to drop his knife," she replied.

"So . . ." Yanaba stroked the rim of her cup. "Are you already carrying?"

Shi Hua sighed. "It's only been three nights. Even with mine and Chief Healer Aaron's abilities, it's too early to tell."

"All it takes is once," Little Bear said from behind his cup. Sivan whacked the back of his head. "Hey!" He glared at his partner.

Sivan glared right back. "The ladies may be young enough to be our daughters, but you will treat them to the respect of their rank."

Shi Hua and Mateqai shared a look. Despite their own head of household's idiosyncrasies, Istaqa wouldn't stoop to striking anyone.

The subject turned to the city's readiness for a battle.

"Tandor's still there, isn't it?" Little Bear asked.

Shi Hua closed her eyes and threw her senses south. The awful grating against her mind was as constant as it had been for the last two and a half days. She opened her eyes and nodded.

"DiCook's been doing his job." Little Bear waved his hand holding a slice of bread. "The city cisterns are full thanks to the heavier than usual rains we had this winter. Our staple stores are good for now. Despite the late snow, farmers are taking their herds to summer grazing grounds in the mountains early. The Smiths Guild have been running the forges from sunrise to sunrise. As for the rest—" He shrugged. "That's up to Duke Marco and Han. Will the Reverend Father of Light leave you two here since we're short-handed?"

Shi Hua frowned. She and Jeremy had been actively avoiding the subject. "I don't know. Our last communication from the home Temple was merely that he and as many priests as he trusted were coming south with the queen's army."

She pushed back her plate and leaned her elbows on the table. "I'm more worried about the civilians trapped in Tandor. If we're already having a problem with citizens giving in to despair here in Orrin at the mention of demons, how are our people doing down there surrounded by an entire demon army? Tandor lost its entire Temple of Child to the renegades. The civilians may do the demons' job for them."

Chapter 19

Our afternoon didn't get much better. One of the Plains Nations healers came to evaluate Elizabeth, but the one priest of Child never came. At some point, I fell asleep in the chair in Elizabeth's room.

Someone nudged my shoulder and I jerked upright. "I'm awake. Is it a demon attack?"

"Anthea, let's go back to my quarters and get some sleep," Luc murmured.

"I'm fine," I said. "I just needed a nap."

"No, you're not fine," Spotted Fawn said through her clerk. "Get some sleep. I'll stay with Elizabeth until our brother from Child arrives."

"Besides, you're supposed to be on the wall at First Night," Luc reminded me.

"All right, all right." They were correct, and I was too damn exhausted to argue.

A few moments later, Luc and I lay in his bed, holding each other. However, sleep eluded me due to the puzzle I couldn't solve.

"It's deliberately staying away from me, so I don't see it," I murmured.

Luc didn't need to ask what I was talking about. "Are we sure?"

"What do you mean?"

He rolled on his side and propped his head on his fist. "What if the skin-walker inside Elizabeth lied to us? Trying to get us to waste resources hunting for a phantom?"

"Technically, it didn't say anything," I reminded Luc.

"True." He stared in the direction of the door for a long moment. "However, we keep assuming the renegades and their allies would only subvert an unwilling person. What if they created a subpersonality in someone who cooperated?"

"You mean like the Tandor seat of Child did with Aduba?"

"Wouldn't the false face be easier to maintain if the primary persona wasn't fighting against it?"

I considered Luc's theory. "Your idea would keep a human ally from garnering any suspicion. They could pass a truthspell. And a human renegade could definitely help a demon evade me. Living demons don't contaminate anything."

"And despite the skinwalker's act, it would be damn near impossible for it to use Elizabeth to sabotage the water supply. Not when Tyra has accompanied Elizabeth nearly every moment since we returned to Tandor after meeting up with the Diné army in the desert."

I didn't like the conclusion Luc had already drawn. Even worse, it led me to Shi Hua and Jeremy's report of the attacks back home.

"Or we could have more than one demon in Tandor and they are wearing human skins like the demons who infiltrated Orrin."

Luc sucked in a harsh breath and released it. "There can't be too many within the wards, or they would have struck in force by now. Jeremy said there were twenty-eight in Orrin, and we have far more clergy here with the Diné, the Cliffdwellers, and the Plains Nations forces. What I can't figure out is why bother with wearing a human skin if your allies had firm control of the city already?"

"The demon may have been inside Duchess Nadine's estate with the others," I speculated. "When we defeated the other three and the second skinwalker, it could have grabbed any human in the resulting chaos, taken what it needed, and buried the rest."

"They couldn't have taken too many humans to skin without arousing suspicion. Tandor's too small."

"I suppose you're right." I sighed. "Either way, the damned things could be hiding under our noses. How in the names of the Twelve do we find them?"

"I'm waiting for you to pull the answer out of your arse." He slid his left hand underneath me and squeezed the body part in question.

I slapped his chest. "You are incorrigible!"

"And insatiable." With a kiss, he preceded to make me forget our troubles.

And he succeeded in wearing me out so I could sleep.

Chapter 20

The queen's army arrived in Orrin at First Morning on Fifth Day, exactly a week after the demons were discovered and destroyed inside the Temples of Balance and Death.

And they came much earlier in the day than anyone had expected.

Everyone at the Temple of Light, except the wardens on guard duty, were at morning prayers when the peacekeeper arrived with the news regarding their visitors from the capital.

Shi Hua watched from the corner of her eye as Magistrate DiCook's messenger whispered to Jeremy. Chief Warden Nicholas rose and joined the two men, probably more out of worry a priest he was charged with protecting might be harmed rather than curiosity.

Once the peacekeeper scurried out of the main sanctuary, Jeremy bowed to the civilians attending the dawn services. "Forgive me for our abbreviated worship once again, but Sister Shi Hua and I have been called to other duties."

She scrambled to her feet, sketched the requisite gesture of respect toward the statue of Light, and crossed the sanctuary to join Jeremy. *Are you sure the queen requested my presence?* she asked silently.

Amusement filled his eyes. *The crown princess is leading the army, and yes, she specifically asked for you. She's with Duke Marco and Prince Alika at the duke's estate along with Reverend Father Farrell.*

Of course. It would not do for the crown princess to ignore the local nobility, much less visiting royalty. She would need the locals and the Sea Peoples to augment her forces.

Nor could she meet with one Orrin Temple alone without arousing the ire of the other eleven, which was why Jeremy had been summoned though he'd be the last person to be offended by a snub. Unfortunately, the queen, Duke Marco and Orrin's chief justice of Balance were too entwined in both their personal and professional relationships to totally avoid all questions of impropriety.

A few of the Orrin Seats would make sure to stir some trouble regarding Anthea and her absence in a crisis.

On the other hand, maybe the Issuran factions would behave themselves with Prince Alika there. The renegades' attempt on his life precipitated the discovery of the demons within Orrin's walls.

I still don't know why the crown princess would want to speak to me, Shi Hua protested silently while she jogged alongside Jeremy to the stables, their wardens following as if they were second shadows. It didn't help matters that she was not an Issuran citizen, though both her own Reverend Father of Light in Jing and the Reverend Father of Light here in Issura had agreed to the temporary transfer. With the spate of demon activity over the last month and a half, Shi Hua truly wondered if she'd ever see home again.

Because right now, you are our primary contact with Tandor, Jeremy chided. *And our sister city is under a demon siege.*

But I can't reach anyone there! I've tried!

You are her best source of information before she marches south, Sister.

Shi Hua swallowed a groan at the reprimand, though she'd been the one to insist they stick to protocol outside of Jeremy's bedchambers. She'd only talked with High Brother Luc, Chief Justice Anthea, and Ambassador Quan twice, once before the demon army arrived at Tandor's doorstep and once after. Surely, the crown princess would give more weight to her own clergy than someone from a foreign empire.

This was not going to be an enjoyable meeting at the duke's estate. And she hadn't broken her fast yet.

For the second day in a row.

Who else will be there? she asked silently as she and Jeremy saddled their mounts. Nicholas and Mateqai did the same.

High Brother Han and High Sister Bertrice are already there. The other seats are on their way.

Of course. Han had been organizing the city's defenses over the last three days. And the demons had used four dead humans to infiltrate Death's morgue.

"What about Justice Yanaba?" Shi Hua asked.

Jeremy looked down at her from atop his horse. "You're the one visiting Balance every day. What do you think?"

Jeremy's gentle question was an answer in itself. Shi Hua climbed onto her own mount. Despite getting the clearance from the healers to resume her Temple duties, Yanaba would stay behind. Shi Hua prayed to Light the justice was fit enough to deal with whatever political problems the other seats would try to dump on her.

"You know High Mother Bianca will find a way to insert herself into this meeting," Mateqai said.

Nicholas shot his junior warden a warning look, but Jeremy merely nodded.

"If she is there, fine." Jeremy sounded far older than his twenty-one winters. "All of the Temples need to let go of our petty differences. We have demons on our border, and we must work together."

"Yes, sir." Mateqai nodded.

Nothing more was said on the ride to the duke's estate.

Loud voices echoed and tension thickened the air in Duke Marco's great hall when Shi Hua and the rest of the party from Light arrived. A huge map of Issura covered most of a large table. Whatever argument had been happening died as the duke's steward announced their presence.

At the sight of High Mother Bianca seated next to Duke Marco, Shi Hua glanced at Mateqai. The corner of her warden's mouth quirked, but otherwise, he kept the solemn mien the situation warranted.

However, High Mother Bianca sat on the duke's left. His sister, Lady Alessa, sat on his right. Shi Hua wondered if she'd be allowed to extend felicitations to Lady Katarina before they left. The duke's wife was Temple-born herself and had made a point of welcoming Shi Hua to Orrin. But Lady Katarina was also very aware of the politics between the orders. If she weren't so close to her delivery, she would no doubt make sure Bianca wasn't anywhere near her husband.

On the other hand, Bianca may have inserted herself between the duke and Prince Alika on purpose so she wasn't sitting next to her fellow clergy. There was still a quiet debate about whether she had been used by the traitor Gerd to remove Chief Justice Anthea by way of false accusations or whether Bianca was smarter about covering up her suspected illicit activities than Gerd had been.

It was a bit of a relief when Reverend Father Farrell's face lit up with a huge grin. "Just the people we need to speak with!"

The head of the Issuran order of Light sat at the opposite end of the table to the left of an imposing woman. Shi Hua sucked in her breath when Crown Princess Chiara turned to appraise the newcomers.

Not even Emperor Bao Chengwu of Jing gave off such an intimidating air. The crown princess's long, sharp face was almost masculine in appearance. She didn't bother with any accoutrements or insignia of her rank, other than her own gray-streaked blue-black braids wrapped and pinned in the shape of a coronet on her head. She dressed in plain black leather and steel chainmail. Her dark eyes were piercing, and Shi Hua had no doubt the crown princess missed little of what happened around her.

Following Jeremy's lead, Shi Hua bowed.

"We come to serve, Your Highness," Jeremy murmured.

A wry smile lightened the crown princess's face. "From what your colleagues have said, it sounds to me like you and your Temple have been doing more than your fair share of service, Brother Jeremy." She gestured at the two people on the other side of the Reverend Father.

To his left was High Brother Han of Conflict. The normally jovial priest was especially somber behind his bushy red beard.

Beside Han sat High Sister Bertrice of Death. Her cropped hair gleamed silver in the morning light from the manse's high windows. She didn't look any happier than Han.

"Please take a seat, Brother Jeremy. I'd like to ask both you and Sister Shi Hua some questions about the events in Orrin over the last two months." The crown princess pointed at two empty chairs between another man on her right dressed in the same military garb as the crown princess and Orrin's magistrate Malven DiCook.

Shi Hua took a longer look at the man as she took the seat next to DiCook. White threaded through his black hair. The man wore the pearl and silver pendant of a Lord General, but the stitching on the hem of his cloak was the green and blue insignia of the Duke of Standora, the title given the queen's consort.

So this was the infamous White Eagle.

Crown Princess Chiara's husband had been a Conflict Priest. There had been conjecture he would become the next Reverend Father of Conflict until the queen asked or demanded, depending on who told the story, White Eagle be given dispensation to leave his order and marry Chiara. With the death of the queen's consort a decade ago, she'd given her son-in-law the title.

The tale had even made its way to Jing. Shi Hua questioned why anyone in their right mind would leave Temple service. Her best friend Mei Wen thought the story terribly romantic.

Worry wormed its way past Shi Hua's initial reaction, and not just because the heir to the throne of Issura knew her name. She'd never feared the people here before, but Ambassador Quan had always been with her at these types of meetings. As his bodyguard, her attention had been consumed with watching for dangers to him.

But then came the discovery of renegades infiltrating Issura's Temples of Light and her temporary transfer to Orrin. High Brother Luc's irritation with her performance as a priestess would be a mosquito bite compared to the displeasure and consequences should she incur Crown Princess Chiara's wrath.

For the next candlemark, Shi Hua and Jeremy were questioned. About their first encounter with a demon egg last autumn. The abduction and recovery of High Brother Luc. The more recent discovery of demons wearing human skins. Justice Yanaba's spell to track, freeze, and destroy the demons, the one that nearly killed her. The demon eggs hidden in the corpses of Peacekeeper Dante and his family.

But when Crown Princess Chiara questioned the wisdom of Chief Justice Anthea and High Brother Luc's absence at such a crucial time, everyone at the table erupted in protest.

Everyone except High Mother Bianca and Duke White Eagle.

"Enough!" The crown princess slapped the table hard enough goblets, wine decanters, and even the parchment map jumped and shivered.

Everyone went silent until Reverend Father Farrell cleared his throat. "It was mine and Reverend Mother Alara's decision to send the two of them to Tandor—"

The crown princess held up her forefinger.

His face flushed. "I will not be silent when you question—"

"I will not tell you again, Reverend Father," she said coldly before she turned her intimidating gaze on Shi Hua. "Why aren't you defending them, Sister?"

Shi Hua swallowed hard. "It's not my place—"

"No, your place is in a Temple in Jing." The crown princess's eyes narrowed. "But you're here, and I'll use whatever resources are at hand. Now, why aren't you defending them?"

Shi Hua dug her nails into her palms to keep from retorting in kind. Quan had never been this rude, even for the short time he had been the crown prince of the empire. She lifted her chin. "Because Chief Justice Anthea and High Brother Luc don't need to be defended. They know their duty, and they have served to the best of their abilities."

Something thawed in the crown princess's icy demeanor. "Even if such service means the ultimate sacrifice?"

Shi Hua worked to keep her face impassive, but her gut clenched. Maybe it was a good thing she hadn't broken her fast after all. "Yes, Your Highness."

Crown Princess Chiara faced High Mother Bianca. "You were the only one from Orrin who didn't take umbrage at my words. Why?"

The priestess cast a sly look in Reverend Father Farrell's direction. "It's not my place to question the instructions from the heads of other orders." She turned to the crown princess. "But as Sister Shi Hua has stated, our seats of Balance and Light will defend the queendom from demons with their very lives if need be."

The crown princess blew out a deep breath. "Since we've lost contact with our clergy in Tandor, we must assume the worst." Her gaze bore into Bertrice. "High Sister, can you activate the defense spells at your sister Temple in Tandor from here?"

Bertrice's face paled to nearly the color of her hair. "Your Highness, you cannot be serious!"

Crown Princess Chiara leaned her elbows on the scarred wood, her palms pressed together, and her chin resting on her fingertips. "I fear High Mother Bianca is right, albeit indirectly. Destroying the Duchy of Tandor may be the only way to stop the demon army."

Chapter 21

Shi Hua jumped to her feet. "Your Highness, give us a chance to try to resume contact with the Temples in Tandor before we resort to such measures."

Crown Princess Chiara narrowed her eyes. "Do you always allow your juniors to speak out of turn, High Brother Jeremy?"

Now, why had she suddenly start addressing him as high brother? Shi Hua worked hard to keep her face impassive. The heir to the throne of Issura was definitely not someone to underestimate. But what game was she playing?

"With all due respect, Your Highness, it's Acting High Brother," Jeremy replied coolly. "And my predecessors Kam and Luc encouraged their juniors to find and offer solutions to problems. I follow their wise lead."

However, he tugged on Shi Hua's robes out of sight of everyone but the magistrate. She took the hint and resumed her seat.

"I must agree with Sister Shi Hua," Han said in his deep, booming voice. "If Tandor had fallen, the demons would already be here. Since the city lies at the crossroads to Diné and the Cliffdwellers, their own Temple alarms would have echoed Tandor's, not just those in Issura."

Shi Hua couldn't miss the way his avoided any mention of Cant. The demon army had come from that direction. Unfortunately, they had so few distance speakers these days no one knew the real status of the Cantish clergy, or if another demon army headed southeast to the Mecas.

And she still hadn't been able to contact Reverend Father Biming. He'd taken the *Unbridled* and sailed south to try to intercept the rest of those blasted demon eggs.

Han reached over and tapped a gap in the mountains north of Orrin on the map. "If the Diné have followed our joint procedures, they will be marching west to Tandor. They will have also sent word north and east to the Cliffdwellers and the Plains Nations. The Comanche will spearhead a force through Kulshra'jek Pass."

Crown Princess Chiara shook her head. "We're assuming the winter snows have melted enough the pass is open. According to the villages we marched through on the way to Orrin, no traders from the east have come for the Spring Rituals." She settled back in her chair. "For now, we must assume the worst—that Issura is on her own." She turned to Bertrice. "You still haven't given me an answer, High Sister."

Bertrice closed her eyes as if in prayer. When she opened them, her gaze was bleak. "I can trigger the defenses remotely but not from here. The demon spells that block communication with Sister Shi Hua also block my link to Tandor's Temple of Death from Orrin. I would need to be closer."

"How close?" The crown princess's eyes narrowed.

Bertrice blew out a deep breath. "At best, ten leagues. Possibly closer."

All the clergy at the table gasped. Acid burned the back of Shi Hua's throat. When the Death priestesses of Eire and Albion triggered their Temples, the spells not only decimated everything on those islands but all the surrounding smaller islands as well. Hundreds of leagues full of living things died in an instant of power. That was four centuries ago, and to this day, nothing could touch those islands and live. Even Duke Marco and the rest of the civilians looked queasy at Bertrice's words.

Crown Princess Chiara rose and stared at the map. Her index finger traced a path along the National Road from Orrin to a point northeast of Tandor. "Here?"

Bertrice nodded.

"But what about High Brother Nantan?" Shi Hua exclaimed. "He and his surviving priests are still in the city. Can't they override Bertrice's attempt to activate the spell?"

The crown princess looked at Bertrice who shrugged.

"Nantan could by himself," the high sister of Death said. "He's been the high brother in Tandor for ten winters."

"Would he?" Crown Princess Chiara asked.

Bertrice pressed her lips together and didn't speak for three heartbeats. "No. Assuming any of the clergy of Death are still alive in Tandor, when they realize what I'm trying to do, they won't impede it. If the demons stop me by spell or death, they will finish the task."

Crown Princess Chiara frowned. "Then we need to keep you alive to finish the task."

"But the civilians!" Shi Hua shoved her chair back and stood once again. "The Temples at least evacuated the Isles of Britannia before they launched the spell of last resort! Empress Bao De gave her armies time to escape before she and her consort ignited the trap they laid for the demon army in Jing!"

Shi Hua! Sit! Jeremy's silent command rang through her mind.

She looked down at him and forced herself not to shout her next words. "With all due respect, High Brother, I would make the same protest if I were in Jing, Toscana, or any other nation." She turned back to the crown princess. "Our duty is to protect the human race, not fling lives aside as if they are nothing more than autumn leaves."

"How do you propose to get the citizens of Tandor out from under the noses of the demons?" Chiara asked. Surprisingly, she didn't seem angered by Shi Hua's outburst. "They are my people, and it sickens me that I have to consider this action." She tapped the stylized parapet symbol for the city on the map. "This place is cursed. The entire Apache nation gave up their lives here to prevent a demon incursion from spilling into the Great Plains. Our queendom was born from the aftermath of that battle. I don't want to sacrifice my people, but do I try to rescue a few thousand in Tandor, or do I lose the hundreds of thousands more in Issura, Diné, or Pagonia who would be slaughtered if I let the demons past me?"

Shi Hua bit her lip. The question was the same type Brother Fang would have asked in one of his philosophy classes when she was a novice. Personal feelings must sometimes be set aside for the greater good.

She bowed to the crown princess. "My apologies for my outburst, Your Highness." She resumed her seat.

Beneath the table, the magistrate squeezed her hand briefly. It was good to know someone else was as disturbed at the thought of abandoning their friends in Tandor as she was.

❖

Between the preparations of the Orrin clergy, the duchy's call to arms, and meetings with the commanders from Standora about the tactics used against the demons, Shi Hua never had a chance to consume a real meal. While most of the nobles requested clergy from Conflict or Father to consecrate their men and women at arms, a few asked for her and High Brother Jeremy specifically. Her stomach growled in the middle of blessing Lord Antonio and his children.

Lord Antonio's sons snickered when her stomach burbled again. Their eldest sister elbowed them both sharply though she kept her own head bowed. Even the nobleman and several of his retainers smiled.

". . . and may the Lord of Light welcome you into his embrace for One is Twelve and Twelve are One," she finished.

"One is Twelve and Twelve are One," Lord Antonio and his people answered. They rose and drifted back to their campfires outside Government Gate, the main entrance into Orrin. Several hundred other fires dotted the darkening, grassy lawns outside of the walls. There simply wasn't enough space in the city to house everyone.

Lord Antonio paused and bowed to Shi Hua. "Sister, your stomach indicates you haven't had a chance to eat today. I'd be honored if you'd join us for the evening meal."

As if on cue, the Temple bells began pealing First Evening. And he was right. All she had eaten today was a couple of bites from a roll during the meeting at Duke Marco's estate.

Shi Hua smiled and returned his bow. "Thank you for the invitation, m'lord, but as the bells are telling me, I'm already late for a meeting with Reverend Father Farrell."

"Of course." Lord Antonio turned to follow his people.

His request for her services gnawed on her more than the hunger. "Lord Antonio, would you answer a question, please?"

He stopped. Like many in Issura, he carried mostly Chumash features except for the prominent Toscan nose. His dark eyes flickered with curiosity. "Yes?"

"May I ask why you requested me for your blessing?" she said softly, stepping closer to him. "I'm not of Issura, and I'm all too aware of how Issurans feel about female clergy of Light."

"You've survived several demon attacks, Sister. I'm hoping your good relationship with Thief rubs off on us." Lord Antonio nodded before he turned and strode off in the direction of his encampment.

Warden Mateqai, who had been waiting nearby, led their horses to Shi Hua and handed her the set of reins for her own mount.

She cocked her head as she regarded the noble's statement. "Why not ask for Thief's blessing if that were Lord Antonio's concern?"

Mateqai chuckled. "That was a compliment, Sister. It's rare for so many of the Twelve to focus Their attention on one person."

Shi Hua shivered as she mounted her horse. The vision she saw in the midst of Yanaba's spell, whether it was Balance Herself or the long dead Chief Justice Thalia, bothered her more than she cared to admit. "Honestly, I'd prefer They turn Their attention directly to the demons."

They rode toward Government Gate. Both Peacekeeper Jamie and Chief Warden Little Bear of Balance nodded and waved them through despite some grumbling from those who had been waiting for admittance most of the afternoon.

She felt a bit sorry for Little Bear. It had to be driving him and the Balance wardens insane that the crown princess ordered them to stay in Orrin, especially with Chief Justice Anthea being one of those trapped inside the Tandor city walls. And here he was, assisting the peacekeepers with basic guard duties, instead of protesting his lot.

Orrin bustled with people dodging to and fro as they went about their errands. It would normally be this busy during the week before Spring Rituals. But instead of the usual boisterous joy accompanying the holidays, everyone carried a grim expression along with their supplies, weapons, and messages.

The rear yard was crowded when Shi Hua and Mateqai reached the Temple of Light. Henry, their stablemaster, appeared harried as he directed his own staff and Reverend Father Farrell's.

"You two need to get inside," Henry snapped. "You're late."

Even Mateqai's eyebrows rose at the lack of manners in their stablemaster.

"Excuse me?" Shi Hua frowned at the man as she dismounted.

Henry's cheeks turned beet red above his beard. "I beg forgiveness, Sister. I meant no insult."

"None taken," she replied as she lowered her voice and stepped closer. "Is everything all right?"

Henry's lower jaw worked before he murmured, "We don't have enough room for this many people or animals. I've resorted to picketing some of the extra horses in the meditation garden."

In other words, their head of household was throwing a major tantrum about equines chewing on the grass and newly sprouting herbs and flowers. She glanced at Mateqai who stared at the tips of his boots. Smart man. She pursed her lips before she turned her attention back to Henry.

"Do you want me to speak to Istaqa?" she whispered.

"I don't want him sent back to Standora." Henry's expression shifted to guilt and regret he'd even brought up the subject. "Everyone's wound up over the demons laying siege to Tandor."

When Istaqa had been going on about having a woman in the Temple, High Brother Luc threatened to dismiss their head of household and send him to the capital for reassignment if he didn't behave. Such a measure would leave an indelible stain on the man's record.

And if Jeremy found out Istaqa was harassing the rest of the staff, not just Shi Hua, he'd follow through on Luc's threat.

"Neither do I," Shi Hua whispered. Despite butting heads with Istaqa over the Issuran decision to only have men serve the Temple of Light, she had to admit he was damn good at his job.

Most of the time.

"Let me try to talk some sense into him before Brother Jeremy learns of the issue," she finished.

Henry almost looked relieved when he nodded, but his jaw muscles still jerked. No doubt having the Reverend Father in residence didn't put him totally at ease either.

Regardless, she needed to have a little talk with their head of household.

Shi Hua marched into the temple. Luckily, Istaqa was right by the kitchen entrance, inspecting every dish before the kitchen boys and the drafted civilians scurried out of the kitchen with their burdens. Their cook shot her a pleading look. So, Henry wasn't the only one having issues.

"Istaqa, may I have a word with you?"

He turned to her and shook his head. "Not right now, Sister. You need to get cleaned up. The Reverend Father is waiting. Also, your new bow has arrived, and I placed it in your chambers." He turned back to the cook. "That broth needs more seasoning—"

Shi Hua dropped her voice an octave. "That was not a request, Master of the Household."

He pivoted slowly back to her. It must have finally sunk through the man's thick skull she outranked him from the expression of raw fear on his face.

"Your office. Now." She strode out of the kitchen, not waiting for any acknowledgement.

"B-but, Sister—"

She didn't look back, merely raised her right index finger. Watching Chief Justice Anthea in action had been a boon. Istaqa shut up and followed her.

When she reached his small office, she made a point of sitting behind his desk and jabbed her index finger in the direction of the one visitor's stool. Istaqa immediately sat. Mateqai silently closed the office door. He would stand guard in the hallway to make sure they weren't interrupted.

Shi Hua narrowed her eyes and stared at their head of household. Istaqa's gaze flicked everywhere but at her.

"I've put up with your behavior toward me because I realize the cultural differences between Issura and Jing are disconcerting to you," she said, keeping her voice even. "But I will not tolerate you treating the staff poorly."

A sullen expression overtook his features. "You have no standing here," he muttered.

"Until the Reverend Father assigns new clergy to Orrin, I am the acting second. Given that there is a demon army four days south of us, I will not be leaving Issura any time soon."

Obviously, neither thought had occurred to Istaqa from his expression of shock.

"Modify your behavior now, or I will relieve you of duty. Is that understood, Istaqa?"

He bowed his head. "Yes, Sister."

"And thank you for delivering my bow safely." A little bit of consideration was due. Istaqa's efficiency had never been in question. "You are dismissed."

Istaqa scrambled out of his office as if demons chased him.

Mateqai peered around the doorjamb, his black eyebrows raised in inquiry. She merely shook her head as she rose. "Keep an ear out for me."

The warden nodded. He struggled to keep the amusement off his face. He was probably not the only person in the Temple of Light who thought their head of household needed to be taken down a peg or two.

"Shall we attend the Reverend Father's meeting?" she said as she strode to the door.

"Yes, Sister."

When they approached the high brother's private dining room, two unknown wardens stood guard at the door. The one on Shi Hua's right saluted.

"They are waiting for you, Sister."

"I'll return at the end of your meeting." Mateqai started to bow to her, but the warden who had spoken held up a hand.

"Your presence is required as well, Warden Mateqai." The unknown warden knocked a certain pattern before he opened the door.

Shi Hua exchanged a look with Mateqai, but he appeared as confused as she felt. However, it would be nice to have a familiar presence besides Jeremy at this dinner meeting.

There were fewer people seated at the oval table than she expected. Reverend Father Farrell sat at the far end, opposite from Jeremy. Three of the Reverend Father's entourage of clergy were also in attendance. Chief Warden Nicholas and another warden she didn't know sat to Jeremy's left. The two seats to Jeremy's right were empty.

The smile the Reverend Father favored them with wasn't as broad as the one from this morning. From the dark smudges under his eyes and the deep lines around his mouth and eyes, he appeared to carry the weight of Issura on his back.

Between the infiltration of his order by renegades and the demon army, he probably felt as if he carried the weight of the world.

"What's the word amongst the nobles, Sister?" he asked as one of his priests poured wine for her and Mateqai. Her warden intercepted her goblet and took a drink before he handed it to her.

Reverend Father Farrell's smile fell. "You don't even trust us, Brother Jeremy?"

"How many demons and assassins have you survived, sir?" Jeremy's tone was firm despite his insubordinate words.

The other three priests glanced at the Reverend Father and Jeremy before they exchanged worried expressions. None of them would even look in her direction.

After a long moment, the Reverend Father nodded. "I apologize, Jeremy. And to you, too, Shi Hua. Reading a report is not the same as experiencing something in life."

She cleared her throat. "To answer your question, Reverend Father, the nobles and their people are nervous. It's been four generations since the last demon incursion. We need to be mindful of the spiritual needs of the queen's army."

"What do you two really think of the crown princess's plan?" the Reverend Father asked as he dug into his meal.

Shi Hua looked to Jeremy. The anger he'd held in check earlier shone in his eyes. "I think the priests in Tandor have already considered her plan on their own. High Brother Luc is probably searching for a way to evacuate the civilians as we speak."

"What would be his plan?" The Reverend Father tore off a chunk of flatbread and dipped it in his broth.

"According to Chief Justice Anthea, only two of the tunnels in Tandor are passable," Shi Hua said. "The north tunnel comes out too close to the demon army to be safely used. The east tunnel comes out in the Valley of the Lost far beyond the National Road. They wouldn't be able to move fast in the heat, and the dust raised by their passage would give them away. They'd have to find a third option."

"So how do you two propose to evacuate the civilians?" The Reverend Father's attention shifted between her and Jeremy.

"The remainder of the Sea Peoples fleet, sir, and however many ships Duke Marco can muster." Jeremy's initial anger turned to bleakness. They'd run the calculations half a night with Titus, the captain of the duke's flagship, and Captain Iakepa of the Sea Peoples. "However, there simply isn't enough ships to carry everyone out of Tandor, but we have to try."

"Do you realize the panic we'll cause when the civilians realize some of them will be left behind?" the Reverend Father said quietly. "Tandor doesn't have anyone from Child left, and if we take anyone from Orrin—"

"That's one less spot for a civilian on board." Shi Hua nodded. "We know.

There are a couple of ships still in Tandor's harbor. If we take sailors with us to crew those ships—"

"It still won't be enough." The Reverend Father took a long drink of wine before he looked at them again. "This time of year, there should be plenty of ships plying this region of the Peaceful Sea to evacuate Tandor." He shook his head. "The sinking of those trade ships and the murder of their crews off the coast hampers any rescue."

"What if we send the ships south after the queen's army marches for Tandor?" Jeremy said. "It's four days by the National Road, but only two days by sea. We could trap the demons between the fleet and the army. You only need one distance speaker to coordinate between the two."

"You'd give up Sister Shi Hua?" Reverend Father Farrell cocked his head.

Jeremy leaned back in his chair. "I thought that was why you brought Brother Elroy." He waved a hand at the priest with orangish-red hair and freckles.

"How do you know—" The priest beside Brother Elroy started to rise, but Elroy placed a hand on his friend's upper arm.

"Settle Long Wind." Elroy grinned at Jeremy. "I didn't think you remembered me."

Jeremy shrugged. "It hasn't been that long since I took my vows."

Shi Hua desperately wanted to ask what was between Jeremy and the older priest. Well, he wasn't that much older. He looked to be around High Brother Luc's age. But now was not the time or place to ask such questions.

So, she steered the conversation back to the evacuation. "A second distance speaker would definitely help with the coordination. According to the histories, the demons haven't mastered swimming. They are willing to sacrifice a small number of themselves to cross a river, but they can't handle a large body of water. If we only bring one ship at a time into Tandor's harbor, the other ships can launch spell-laced fireworks at the demon army.

"Fireworks?" Long Wind frowned. "What are those?"

"A recreational use of flash powder in Jing," Shi Hua replied. "We use them for celebrations and holidays, such as the Spring Rituals. With the right spells and ingredients, they can create pictures in the sky."

Elroy snorted. "Pictures aren't going to scare away a demon army."

"No, but Jing flashbangs can hurt them," Jeremy said. "We couple those with our Light abilities and we can extend the use of both flash powder and priests." He glanced at Shi Hua. "And priestesses."

The Reverend Father rubbed his chin. "Thief is working on flashbangs as we speak."

"Our Thieves already have the cask of powder Ambassador Quan donated before he left," Shi Hua offered.

The Reverend Father eyed her. "I like the plan, but you realize the crown princess has the final say."

"Yes, sir," she and Jeremy both murmured.

"I still like to have some of these fireworks of yours with the main army regardless of what Her Highness decides." The Reverend Father focused on Shi Hua. "Can you teach these men tonight?" He waved at the three priests who accompanied him. "The crown princess plans to leave at first light. They can teach the rest of the Light division your tricks."

"Yes, sir." Shi Hua nodded firmly.

The Reverend Father cleared his throat. He appeared totally discomfited. "The other matter I need to discuss is the recent order—"

"I've already spoken to Reverend Father Jin back home." Her words came out in a rush. "I know my duty."

An embarrassed smile appeared on Reverend Father Farrell's face. "Given there is only one Light priest left in Orrin, you have your pick of any of the priests I brought with me."

"I've made my choice, and I'm quite happy with it." She lifted her chin and made a point of laying her hand on Jeremy's arm.

"Well, then . . ." It was amazing the Reverend Father could look both mortified and relieved at the same time. Even odder was the disappointment in the other three priests' expressions. What exactly were they expecting when they came to Orrin?

"What else was on your agenda, sir?" Jeremy sounded more sure of himself than she'd ever heard him.

"Garbhan will be staying here while you and the sister come south with me."

The youngest brother in the Reverend Father's entourage took a studied interest in his food at his senior clergy's words.

Jeremy scowled, actually scowled, at the Reverend Father. "Are you sure taking both distance speakers with us is a wise course of action? That won't leave anyone to pass word to the queen if something goes wrong."

"Under normal circumstances, no." The Reverend Father poked at his stew before he stared at Jeremy. "But if we're going to make your plan to evacuate Tandor with the ships work, we'll need both Shi Hua and Elroy."

The Reverend Father took a bite and swallowed. "You and the sister are the only people I have who've actually fought any demon, much less multiples of the damned things—"

The discussion flowed into preparations for the coming battle, but all Shi Hua could think about was what would happen after this day was finished. Something was going on with their visitors, but she couldn't quite put her finger on what crawled up the back of her neck.

Chapter 22

When the sun peeked over the eastern mountains the next morning, Shi Hua's horse pranced nervously beneath her thighs as she stood in formation outside Government Gate. Jeremy's steed stood contentedly and munched on an apple from last fall. The animal's mood probably had more to do with the idiotic smile Jeremy wore.

"Would you please change your expression?" she hissed to her senior.

"What's wrong with my expression?" If anything, his grin grew wider.

"You look like a boy who's been deflowered by the entire population of Love." She glared at him.

"Well . . ." He shrugged. "The first part is true."

She rolled her eyes. "Would you like the magistrate to post a formal announcement?"

His smile faded. "Wasn't it . . . nice for you, too?"

"It was . . . fine." So she had to imagine she was with Sister Claudia of Love in order to finish. The last thing she wanted to do was to hurt Jeremy's feelings.

"Fine? It was only fine?"

"Can we not talk about this right now?" she begged.

"You were the one angry because I smiled," he snapped.

"Because someone shouldn't be smiling like a fool when they're about to march into a war!" She said the last part louder than she meant to. The priests and wardens around them stared at them.

Mateqai nudged his horse between theirs. "With all due respect, can you two save the lovers' spat until after we deal with the demons?" He backed his steed to resume their position in the ranks.

Shi Hua's face heated. Her warden was right. This wasn't the time or place to be discussing such things. But then, they shouldn't be discussing them at all. There shouldn't even be a reason to discuss them.

And here, she believed her life had become complicated when she was recruited as Ambassador Quan's bodyguard.

No pennants or banners flew like they would at home in Jing. No banter or challenges to each other's weapons prowess either. In fact, the Issuran forces were terribly quiet. To them, there was no glory in killing the enemy.

There was even less glory at the possibility of killing their own people. Surprisingly, Crown Princess Chiara agreed to Light's mad plan last night.

The clergy from Knowledge stayed up the entire night to calculate materials and trajectories for the modified fireworks. Thief drafted anyone from the other orders who weren't accompanying the army to help with the production.

Well, anyone except the priests of Light and the priestesses they took to bed.

Shi Hua glanced behind her. Her fellow clergy from Standora all had idiotic smiles similar to Jeremy's. Sister Dragonfly was right. Men did go insane when it came to bedplay.

A blast of a ram's horn echoed from the direction of the National Road. Tension rose among the people and animals at the signal. An itch tickled the back of her mind.

Bring them home, Sister.

Shi looked over her shoulder. Sister Dragonfly's height and scarlet robes stood out at the top of the watch tower. But it was the smaller black-cowled figure huddled next to her who had spoken. Chief Warden Little Bear stood on the other side of Yanaba. The young justice must have thrown a major fit for anyone to let her this near the edge of the city walls. Dragonfly and Little Bear probably were there to make sure not even Yanaba's fingertips extended past the outer edge of Orrin's wall.

We will, Shi Hua assured her friend. She didn't have to ask who the justice meant.

The troops in front of them began to move, and Shi Hua nudged her horse into motion. She sent up a silent prayer to her patron deity she hadn't just lied to Yanaba.

Chapter 23

I awoke alone once again. Without the Temple bells or my personal assistant Sivan, I had no idea how long I'd slept. Luc's side of the bed didn't hold his body heat, which meant he'd been awake for at least a candlemark. I tried not to draw a deep breath as I dressed. The last true bath I took was the evening before we left Orrin. Tandor's heat only accelerated any body odor.

When I entered the sanctuary, Brother Bumblebee waited on a bench. He jumped up when he spotted me. "I have your morning rations, Chief Justice."

"Morning rations?" I stared at the cloth-wrapped bundle in his outstretched hands. "You mean evening? I'm supposed to be on watch at Neighbor's Gate at First Night."

"High Brother Luc suggested you needed the extra rest, and Reverend Father Nizhé'é' concurred." The young priest gave me a cheeky grin. "The Reverend Father sent me to escort you to Knowledge when you rose."

His good cheer lashed at my bad mood. "Wipe that smile off your face, or I'll let every woman in the city have their way with you."

"Yes, m'lady." His smile dimmed a bit, but it remained.

"Thank you for my meal, Brother." I accepted the cloth-wrapped food. "I'm sorry. I'm not truly awake until I've had my first pot of tea."

"So High Brother Luc warned me."

Of course, he had. I unwrapped the light bundle. A piece of Cantish flat bread and a dried fish. With our water situation, the cooks couldn't even stew meats or vegetables too often. And with the demon army camped at our doorstep, no one could fish beyond the breakwater without disrupting the city's wards.

I didn't realize how much Deborah, our cook at Orrin's Temple of Balance, had spoiled me. She even found a way to make clams palatable, and I detested the things with a passion.

I quickly ate, wishing for some of Luc's Cantish sauce to wash away the salty fish flavor. I hadn't met any Issuran clergy of Knowledge yet who didn't go mad over food or drink inside their precious libraries. This may not be her library, but I had no doubt the Diné sister would react the same way if I brought my morning meal, meager as it was, into her ostensible realm.

Bumblebee escorted me next door to the Temple of Knowledge. A wash of excitement bumped against my mind, though the brighter colors of the citizens' flesh passing by would have given them away.

"What's going on?" I whispered to Bumblebee. "Everyone seems to be in a better mood today."

"Word's gotten out that we have a plan," he murmured. "However, the citizens do not have the details. The Reverend Father was most displeased with our brother of Child, but he spilled the secret to keep a mother from slicing the throats of her four children."

My soul ached with Bumblebee's news, but I wasn't sure how much was the terror the demon inside the walls might know our plan, or how much was a mother in such despair she would foolishly give the demons a possibly way into the city.

"We have a vague idea that might get everyone killed in the execution," I growled.

He shrugged as we climbed the steps to Knowledge's entrance. "A little hope will keep order for a bit longer, Lady Justice. Perhaps that's more important. Fear of the demons, of what they will do to people, can be more dangerous to us than the demons themselves.

The younger priest spoke truly, no matter how much his cheer and faith galled me. Or maybe it was the possibility my own Goddess had appeared to Shi Hua and Bertrice back home, but never to me, that triggered my foul mood. I could use some reassurance, but it was not to be.

Once again, wardens guarded the doors of the Temples on Tandor's main thoroughfare. Unlike our original visit a fortnight ago, all the guards appeared alert. While none of them appeared friendly, neither did they carry the bored, aggressive stance of the disguised renegades.

Our wardens were probably doing the same duty in Orrin. I prayed they supported Malven and his peacekeepers, and in turn, the magistrate bolstered both the Temples and Duke Marco in keeping order. Otherwise, Orrin's civilians could suffer from the same despair as the woman who thought the only way she could save her children was by killing them.

Reverend Father Nizhé'é' waited for us in the same room within Knowledge as before. Luc was seated across the table from him, staring at the map.

And between them sat a steaming pot. The sweet odor of Jing tea permeated the air. I couldn't help salivating at the delicious scent.

The Reverend Father laughed. "You weren't joking, High Brother. She does crave that particular drink."

I swallowed the extra saliva in my mouth. "Brother Bumblebee said you requested my presence, sir."

"Luc said you haven't pulled a plan for flushing out the demon or its human assistant out of your arse yet." The Reverend Father gestured at the red pot. "He suggested some extra sleep and your favorite beverage might help."

I glared at Luc. "You actually told him that?"

His smile mocked me. "Are you suggesting I tell a falsehood to a superior, Chief Justice?"

"Where did the tea come from?" I crossed my arms.

"It was thoughtfully donated by Ambassador Quan." An edge laid underneath Luc's words. After everything we had been through, he was still jealous of the Jing emissary. And Quan's only interest in bedding me was due to my surprising resistance to his rather minor Thief talent of luck.

"And who brewed it?" I couldn't help teasing Luc. Not when he acted this way, even though I knew the ambassador would never perform such a menial task if he could help it.

"Brother Hadar," Luc bit out.

"And does the Diné sister of Knowledge know you brought a pot of tea into the library?"

The Reverend Father laughed again. "I've already taken full responsibility on Luc and Hadar's behalf. As I pointed out to Sister Lizard, we're planning on destroying everything within Tandor by one means or another. Some spilled tea will not make a difference."

I dropped my arms and laughed as well. "You haven't met High Sister

Mariana. She'd beat demons over the head with her cane if they dared to bring a beverage into the Orrin Knowledge library."

I took the chair between them while Brother Bumblebee sat across from me. When I offered tea to the three men, they all refused. I wasn't in a generous enough mood to push the matter.

The first sip sent a trill of pleasure through me. Part of me thought I'd never taste Jing black tea again. I eyed the map as I savored my tea. Twelve markers formed a large circle in the middle of the parchment.

I looked around the room to ensure we were alone before I spoke. "What are you two planning?"

"Putting yours and Nantan's idea into practice." The Reverend Father tapped the map next to one of the markers. "He and Aduba are at the Queen's Gate with Elizabeth, attempting to set up the Balance spells."

"Justice Elizabeth?" I paused in taking my second sip. "After what we had to burn out of her yesterday?"

The Reverend Father shrugged. "She was awake and willing. I took her up on her offer of assistance since you were still asleep and Spotted Fawn had just retired for some rest."

I ignored his implication Spotted Fawn and I were derelict in our duties. "The brother from Child and the healers said Elizabeth is physically and mentally capable?"

"Yes, Anthea," The Reverend Father said. "In fact, yours and Luc's idea regarding sunshine to purge the remnant of the skinwalker out of Elizabeth's system was a blessing in disguise. It lodged itself in her memories of her torture, and the memories themselves died with the skinwalker fragment. Without those memories, she's in much better spirits."

"But she does know what happened to her, doesn't she?" I asked.

"In as much if I told you I had three brothers and one sister, you would then know that fact, but you would not know the actual experience." The Reverend Father shrugged. "Elizabeth knows the facts, but she doesn't feel the experience since that portion of her memory has been destroyed. You and Luc probably saved her sanity."

I finally put my finger on what was bothering me about his speech pattern. "Is there a reason you've dropped titles, sir?"

His attention shifted from the map back to me. "Because all our pomp and posturing doesn't matter as much at this moment. Not if we all die here."

"We may just do that yet," Aduba grumbled from behind me.

I turned in my seat to see him step aside while Nantan guided Elizabeth into the room. Greenish-yellow sweat trickled down her face. Bumblebee jumped up and dragged a chair over for her between Luc and me.

"What happened?" the Reverend Father asked.

"It's one of those things our predecessors probably believed was common knowledge and didn't bother writing down." Elizabeth cocked her head. "Is that Jing tea I smell?"

"Yes," I answered. "Would you like some?"

"You have no idea how much." She chuckled as I poured another cup. I took her right hand and wrapped her fingers around the ceramic.

She took a drink and sighed. "Balance bless you."

"What happened?" the Reverend Father said again. From the impatience in his voice, he wasn't a man who repeated things often.

"Since I was helping her, Balance's defensive spells pulled on the energy residing within the walls of the Temple of Conflict," Aduba said. He crossed his arms and scowled. "It would have dangerously depleted the latent magic in the building itself and compromised the seal to the tunnels, not to mention the city wards."

"Therefore, we decided not to complete them without consulting with you," Elizabeth added.

From the emphasis on the word the Reverend Father spat, the red, nearly pink, glow of his face and hands, and the shocked expression on Bumblebee's face, it was an epithet of epic proportions.

"If the charging of the spells do that with a fully functional Temple, we might as well open the tunnel entrance in Balance ourselves," Elizabeth said bitterly. "The results will be the same."

Open the tunnel entrance in Balance . . .

"Oh, I am such an idiot!" I set aside the cup and placed my palms over my face.

"I've heard there's a first time for everything," Luc quipped.

I dropped my hands. "The damn demon is hiding in Balance."

Chapter 24

Everyone in the Knowledge meeting room stared at me.

"How can you be sure, Anthea?" the Reverend Father asked.

"It's the one unoccupied building in Tandor—"

"And the only Temple that has its demon alarm spells depleted, not just de-activated." Elizabeth waved her hands in her excitement. Tea sloshed over the edge of her cup, ran down her fingers, and dripped on the tile floor. She didn't seem to notice. "The demon's magic would blend in with the background sensation of the damage to the Temple building."

"How could it remain in there?" Nantan gestured in the direction of the Temple of Balance. "Much less how could it meet with its possible human ally? The rear of the structure is unstable."

"If you could change your density so something could pass through you, why would you worry about being crushed?" I pointed out.

"The demon with the renegades who abducted me slipped through the stones of the cave-in Anthea and Shi Hua caused in Orrin's tunnel system," Luc added.

"And a demon is not an egg or an artifact, so it's not going to contaminate its surroundings," I finished.

"Not to mention, the wardens are either keeping an eye on the demons outside the gates or the humans on the main thoroughfare to keep the peace," Luc said. "No one's watching the back gates of the Temples. Its ally could meet the demon out of anyone's sight." He turned to me. "But how do we know for sure the demon is in Balance?"

The Reverend Father's hand slashed through the air. "None of it matters if we can't set up the Balance spells to kill the beasts without killing the civilians."

"Sir, with all due respect—" I stood. "—this is the opportunity we needed." I looked at Aduba. "How much power did you drain from Conflict?"

"None." He shook his head. "Once I realized what was happening, we stopped."

"Do you think it will totally drain the Temple?" An eagerness shone on the Reverend Father's visage. He must have realized the destination of my logic.

Aduba shook his head. "Not totally, but the city wards depend on the amassed power within all twelve of the Temple structures. We've already lost Balance. The clergy and handful of civilian Talents left in Tandor won't be able to keep the wards up for long if we drain the rest of the Temples, sir."

"We're going to run out of water before the wards collapse." The Reverend Father rose and tried to pace in the tight confines of the meeting room. He whirled and faced me. "If we leave the direct Balance spell until last—"

"—it will be a race to get everyone out in time and the demons inside the walls before we set off the defensive spells." I learned over the table and tapped the edge of the map. "Are we still heading for Diné?"

"Not my first choice." The Reverend Father came over to stand next to me. He crossed his arms, but his right hand stroked his chin. "Orrin is much closer, but . . ."

"Diné is the wiser course for the civilians," Luc said. "The last thing the queen's army needs is a panicking populace caught between them and the demons, assuming Issuran forces are headed south."

"We're still going to need clearing parties to go out both tunnel exits." Aduba indicated what I assumed were the markings for the underground system on the map. "If the demons leave behind some of their numbers at the exits, we could find ourselves trapped in the tunnels. It will be a total and complete massacre if that happens."

"And you know the civilians will panic," Bumblebee said.

"By the Twelve, even some of our own will panic," Luc commented.

"To be honest, if it weren't for our late high brother of Child's spell, I'm sure I would have urinated in my leggings the first time I saw a demon," Aduba said with a laugh.

"That still leaves the question of how do we pack and spread the word without alerting the demon's helper," Elizabeth said.

I grinned even though she couldn't see it. "If someone would allow me a second pot of tea, I'll see what I can pull out of my arse."

Chapter 25

At the command to halt for the night, Shi Hua eased down off her horse. Everything between her shoulders and knees ached. She hadn't ridden this much since High Brother Luc was abducted at midwinter. A group of renegades had given her and the Wildling clergy a merry chase through the foothills of the Gray Mountains in their efforts to distract Chief Justice Anthea from finding a demon grimoire before they did.

A royal page raced up to Jeremy and bowed. "The crown princess and your reverend father wish to see you immediately, High Brother."

"It's just 'Brother.'" Jeremy's kind smile to the girl was much better than the idiotic grin he wore earlier.

"I beg your pardon, sir, but you are the acting high brother of Orrin, therefore the correct address is 'High Brother.'" The girl wasn't acting cheeky. In fact, her expression was all earnest seriousness.

Shi Hua busied herself with her gear to keep from laughing outright. Mateqai did the same. Even the mouth of the somber Chief Warden Nicholas quirked beneath his moustache.

Jeremy, Light bless him, took the unintended reprimand with good humor. "I stand corrected." When the girl didn't move, he added, "Is it safe to assume you were ordered to escort me to this meeting?"

"Yes, High Brother."

Jeremy waved a hand in Shi Hua's direction. "What about Sister Shi Hua?"

Her breath caught for an instant. While she didn't relish coming under the crown princess's scrutiny again, it was good to know she hadn't irreparably damaged her personal relationship with Jeremy by this morning's outburst.

The page frowned at her before she turned back to Jeremy. "I'm sorry, sir. The crown princess did not specifically request the sister."

"Are you going to deny a warden accompanying the high brother?" Nicholas's voice rumbled over the general cacophony of the army setting up camp for the night.

"No, sir." The girl's chin jutted forward, as if she were insulted at the chief warden's implication she would do something improper.

"We'll take care of your horses, High Brother." Mateqai stepped forward to take the reins.

From the sour look Jeremy gave the warden, he would have yelled at Mateqai about his choice of titles if the royal page weren't watching the whole scene. "Thank you."

Both he and Nicholas handed over their mounts. The chief warden clapped Mateqai's shoulder and gave a slight shake of his head, no doubt at his needling of Jeremy. The two men set off after the page.

"You really shouldn't tease Brother Jeremy," Shi Hua murmured as they led the mounts to an unclaimed area along the ridge the crown princess had chosen. Having lived in Issura for the last five years, she understood the dangers of a flash flood though the weather oracles hadn't predicted any more storms for the length of the march south.

"He might have to get used to the title of high brother," Mateqai replied.

"Don't say that," she snapped.

Mateqai lowered his voice. "You're forgetting I was at your meeting with the crown princess." Worry shown in his eyes, the same worry she felt. He didn't want to lose Luc any more than she and Jeremy did. If the evacuation of Tandor failed . . .

No, she couldn't think like that. Shi Hua turned away from Mateqai and focused on her tasks. The Twelve were watching over them. She had to cling to her childhood faith, else she would go mad. Then, she'd be of no use to anyone.

They had fed and watered the four horses when two wardens in Love insignia approached. Mateqai stepped between them and Shi Hua. He didn't reach for his sword, but he kept a hand on the handle of his knife. The two from Love were of the same height, but the thing that stood out to Shi Hua was the female warden's light eyes.

The other two wardens stopped several strides away, and the female warden cocked her head.

"A little paranoid with old friends, Mateqai?" she asked.

"If you'd been assigned to Orrin for the past two years, you'd be a little paranoid as well, Catherine." But his weight stayed on the balls of his feet. "What were the last words you said to me?"

"That you should switch to Love because you're very talented at bedplay." She grinned at him. "What village did we grow up in?"

"We didn't," Mateqai said. "You grew up in the capital. I grew up in New Roma." He still hadn't released the handle of his knife.

Warden Catherine noticed and grimaced. "So things in Orrin are even worse than the reports said." Her attention turned to Shi Hua. "This is Warden Hototo. We're here for your additional protection, Sister. We understand if you need to truthspell us, but Crown Princess Chiara doesn't want a diplomatic incident with Jing on top of everything else going on."

"Diplomatic incident?" Shi Hua frowned. Such a thing should be the least of their worries.

The male Love warden made a disgusted sound in the back of his throat. "A minor noble's son from the Pana Valley allowed his pride to get in the way of our priestesses' focus on the clergy from Light. He often worshipped with High Sister Imala, and he became . . . physically aggressive last night."

"Oh, Blessed Light!" Shi Hua swallowed a groan. "Please tell me she's all right."

"The sister is fine," Catherine said, but the hesitancy in her voice meant things had gone too far.

Mateqai stared at the female warden with raw disbelief. "He wasn't executed?"

"Lashed and sent home." Catherine shook her head. "And that was after Sister Imala threatened to unman him."

"She's *berda*?" Mateqai finally released his knife handle, and Shi Hua breathed a prayer of relief.

"No." Catherine grinned. "She's a very powerful mover. If it weren't for Reverend Father Farrell, she probably would have ripped the boy's balls off with her talent."

"A sister of Love who's a mover?" Shi Hua asked.

Catherine shrugged. "Strange times, Sister. Orrin's chief justice is sighted. A *berda* is about to be confirmed to a seat of Love. And I heard through the fishwives that Balance Herself appeared to you when you were fighting demons in Orrin."

The warden's statement was so matter-of-fact it relieved Shi Hua. It was nice not to be subjected to another round of suspicion, disbelief, and fear over her vision that occurred inside the Temple of Balance when Justice Yanaba activated its defensive spells.

"You are correct in that we live in strange times. Demons walk our world again." Shi Hua shrugged. "Let us get the truthspelling out of the way so we can set up our campsite before Brother Jeremy returns."

The two Love wardens exchanged embarrassed looks.

"What's really going on?" Mateqai's hand rested on his knife handle again.

"High Brother Jeremy will be spending the night with High Sister Imala," Catherine said softly.

"Doesn't he have a say in this?" Shi Hua crossed her arms. She and Jeremy had an arrangement. Or had he changed his mind after this morning's tiff?

"One of you needs to answer her," Mateqai said gruffly.

"You're Light." Hototo shrugged. "Would you disobey a direct order from your Reverend Father?"

The Love warden's statement was like a punch in the gut. Reverend Father Farrell knew she had chosen Jeremy. If the crown princess were truly worried about a diplomatic incident, well, one of her people had just caused such an incident.

Shi Hua strode in the direction of the Love pavilion.

"Sister, wait!"

She ignored Mateqai as another suspicion occurred to her. What if the renegades or the demons had replaced Reverend Father Farrell, and he planned to kill the last of Orrin's Light priests?

Fear gave her feet wings as Shi Hua raced for the bright red banners fluttering under the setting sun.

Chapter 26

Shi Hua ran for the Love pavilion as if Jeremy's life depended on it. For all she knew, it did. She arrowed for the largest tent where she sensed his presence.

The wardens at the entrance flap reacted to her racing full tilt toward their high sister. Steel hissed against scabbards.

Shi Hua skidded to a stop. "Let me pass," she snarled.

"The high sister is not to be disturbed for the rest of the night," the man on her right answered.

"How does your order apply to my high brother?" Shi Hua gripped the handle of her knife. The idiots had let her get too close. The swords would be more of a hindrance, and they'd be dead before they knew what was happening.

Mateqai and Catherine joined her. Mateqai closed his hand over Shi Hua's and gave a slight shake of his head.

"Are you two idiots by birth, or did you get kicked in the head by your horses?" Catherine snapped. "You do not draw against any priestess!"

The two exchanged sheepish glances. "It was merely a misunderstanding, Chief Warden," the one who originally spoke said as the two guards sheathed their weapons.

Chief Warden? Shi Hua blinked. Catherine hadn't mentioned her rank when she approached their campsite. Did Mateqai know? It made her all the more suspicious.

"Where is High Brother Jeremy?" Shi Hua tried to draw her knife again, but Mateqai kept his hand clinched over hers. Part of her realized his head was cooler in this matter. Another part wanted to flip him on his backside and rush through the flaps to find Jeremy.

A feminine voice called from inside the tent. "What is going on out there?"

The warden who hadn't spoken ducked inside. More words were exchanged, but Shi Hua couldn't make them out.

When the Love warden came out, he held aside the flap. "The High Sister will see you now, Sister." His emphasis on ranks was obvious and petty, and Shi Hua really didn't care.

She charged inside the tent, Mateqai and Catherine on her heels. Only two other people were inside. Both Jeremy and the high sister rose from the pillows they sat upon. Musky incense burned in a brazier, and a decanter of wine sat on the low table between them. The scene, the odors and the lighting was exactly how Yin Li had taught her to seduce and distract a man.

However, she'd never seen a sister of Love dressed for war, other than the times her aunt had been demonstrating disguises. Even then, Yin Li had dressed as a man.

High Sister Imala had dispensed with the belled veil and robes of her order. She wore a scarlet tunic under a mailed shirt similar to those worn by the clergy of Conflict. Vambraces and knee-high grieves of scarlet-dyed, boiled leather matched the layered short leather skirt constructed in the style of the Peloponnesian city-states.

Imala frowned at Shi Hua. "May I ask why you demanded an audience at this time of the evening?"

On the other hand, Jeremy looked relieved by her sudden appearance.

"Because Chief Warden Nicholas isn't here," Shi Hua spat as she edged closer to Jeremy. "The renegades have been actively assassinating the clergy and wardens in Orrin, and we've become quite used to watching each other's backs." Her hand slashed the air of its own accord. "*No* priest or priestess goes anywhere without a guard. So where is Nicholas?"

"He's with me."

Shi Hua turned to see Reverend Father Farrell duck through the tent flap. Nicholas followed him inside, an odd look on his countenance.

"And my personal affairs do not concern you, Sister," Imala said.

Shi Hua gathered every little bit of patience, understanding, and diplomatic poise she possessed, though it may be too late. "They do when you conspire to deliberately separate me from my chosen at a time when demons have been trying to kill us."

In the space of a heartbeat, a myriad of emotions crossed the Love priestess's beautiful features. Imala glared at the Reverend Father. "You neglected to mention our sister of Light made arrangements with the High Brother of Orrin."

"Acting High Brother," Jeremy corrected.

Shi Hua ground her heel on the toes of his right foot. His sharp intake of breath was his only sign of discomfort.

"He's young," Reverend Father Farrell replied. "He needs to spread his seed as far as possible."

Shi Hua wasn't sure if anger or embarrassment caused the flush on the Reverend Father's face and neck. Mortification definitely flowed from Jeremy as he finally realized his superior had used him, though Light only knew the reason. It wasn't like Farrell hadn't known of their agreement.

"However, I have not conceived a child yet," she said mildly. "I'm sure High Sister Imala wouldn't want to stress my high brother, and as a result, neither of us can conceive."

"The odds of a child with Light talent would be greatly increased if both parents have those abilities." While High Sister Imala's words were conciliatory, the anger in her eyes was aimed solely at the Reverend Father.

"Yet, Sister, you announced that you were already with child before I arrived in Orrin," the Reverend Father countered.

"I lied to keep a distraught father from harming his son over demon fears. Sir," she added belatedly.

Imala turned to Shi Hua and gentled her countenance. "I beg your forgiveness, my sister. I hope my gift of Chief Warden Catherine and Warden Hototo were not offending to you as well."

"Ambassador Quan would be quite pleased at your concern for my safety." Shi Hua smiled. "And I beg your forgiveness as well. After the last several months in Orrin, I have become paranoid about my senior priests' safety. I should not have accused you of planning to harm High Brother Jeremy."

At least, not without more evidence. However, given the renegade infiltration of Issura's Light order, why would Farrell want to cause additional schisms within his priesthood? It bore further consideration.

High Sister Imala inclined her head toward Shi Hua. "Of course you should retire to you own tent for the evening. However, I would like to invite both High Brother Jeremy and yourself to the evening meal at my tent tomorrow night when we camp."

"We would be pleased to accept." Shi Hua bowed.

"Until tomorrow night then," Jeremy murmured and bowed to the high sister as well.

Reverend Father Farrell said nothing as they filed past him, nor did he try to stop them. It took all of Shi Hua's will not to confront him. However, she'd learned some diplomacy during her service to Ambassador Quan. Now was not the time to question the Reverend Father's motives.

Not without getting herself lashed or executed.

Neither Shi Hua, Jeremy, nor any of the three wardens spoke a word as they returned to the area where they'd left their horses and gear. Belatedly, Shi Hua realized that was a misstep on their part. Someone could have sabotaged their equipment or poisoned their provisions.

Maybe she was becoming paranoid. If it weren't for all the attempts to kill her . . .

"Thanks for the rescue," Jeremy murmured as they set up their tent.

"I apologize for overstepping my rank, High Brother." She hammered the support peg into the ground with her mallet, imagining it to be the Reverend Father's head.

For once, Jeremy didn't argue about his title.

"You didn't." He laid his hand over hers that held her mallet. "I'm sorry he put all of us in that position."

"All of us?" Shi Hua frowned.

"The High Sister didn't pick me if that's what you're worried about, nor I her." Jeremy tied off the line he held onto the peg.

"Then what was the Reverend Father up to?" she whispered.

Chief Warden Catherine crouched next to them. "He's embarrassed he can't perform since the decision was made to lift the restrictions on Light and Balance."

Shi Hua and Jeremy stared at her.

The warden shrugged. "Why do you think she sent us to you, Sister? She was concerned about your safety if High Brother Jeremy was with her."

"But the Reverend Father knew about the sister and high brother's arrangement before we left Orrin," Mateqai said.

Shi Hua glanced around their little encampment. From the expressions on their faces, all the wardens had heard hers and Jeremy's exchange.

Chief Warden Nicholas cleared his throat. "The Reverend Father stated he was concerned Ambassador Quan may try to lay claim to any child Shi Hua bore."

"That's illegal," she muttered. "He would never have the audacity to interfere in Temple matters such as this."

Catherine nodded as if she expected such an answer from Nicholas. "What happens with the audits of our Temples if the clergy performing the audits are renegades?"

"Are you accusing High Brother Luc—"

"Not him." Catherine stood and shook her head vigorously. "I've been reading Acting High Sister Dragonfly's reports to the home Temple. Someone's trying too hard to eliminate the Orrin clergy. I swear in all the names of Love my high sister would not have harmed you or High Brother Jeremy. We have reason to believe the attack on her last night was not what it appeared."

"What do you mean?" Shi Hua prayed what she suspected was wrong. She and Jeremy stood as well.

"The noble who attacked her had no memory of the event," Catherine said.

"Surely, the Reverend Father truthspelled him," Jeremy protested.

"He appeared to." Catherine's light eyes reflected the fire Hototo had started to prepare their dinner. "She had a friend of hers from Thief truthspell the noble again the next morning. She would not presume to be an equal to those in Balance when it comes to logic, but the answers were not the same under the two different casters." She glanced around, but no one was close enough to hear them.

Shi Hua extended her senses. No one hid in the nearby brush. No sense of magic anywhere.

"This is what she wishes to discuss with us tomorrow night," Jeremy stated.

Catherine nodded. "It will be done under the guise of you two asking her for advice."

Despite the seriousness of the situation, a giggle burbled out of Shi Hua. "You have no idea how much advice we've already received."

The warden's eyebrow lifted in question.

"Don't worry, Chief Warden," Mateqai interjected. "The sisters of Love in Orrin have made quite sure everyone in Light and Balance are educated in regards to the recent changes."

Catherine shook her head. "I'm sorry you have been put in this position."

The three male wardens laughed at her double entendre. Even Shi Hua had to smile at it. Poor Jeremy looked positively mortified.

He cleared his throat. "Why would someone want High Sister Imala injured or dead?"

Catherine shrugged. "My guess is the rumor that she's considered most likely to succeed our Reverend Mother."

"She was sent with the army on purpose," Shi Hua guessed.

"Much the same way the Reverend Mother of Balance sent Chief Justice Anthea to Tandor," Catherine said.

"Are you saying High Brother Luc is—" Jeremy checked their vicinity again. No one paid attention to anything but their own meal. Still, he lowered his voice. "Are you saying someone suspects Luc as a renegade?"

"No." Catherine shook her head. "We suspect Luc was sent to Tandor to get him out of the way of the renegades."

"You mean Rev—" Shi Hua started.

Catherine held her forefinger to her lips and shook her head. "No more discussion about this. Not until you speak with the High Sister at tomorrow night's camp."

Shi Hua exchanged a look with Jeremy. She didn't need silent speech to see her own worry and fears mirrored in his eyes. But Chief Warden Catherine was correct, this was not something to be discussed in the open.

And if High Sister Imala refused to ward her tent or let Jeremy truthspell her at the next evening meal, then they'd have an answer about who to trust.

Chapter 27

Despite the chill in the night air on top of the wall and my sitting position, I was drenched in perspiration. I folded my fingers together, palms out, and stretched them above my head. Beads of yellow sweat dripped down Sister Lizard's forehead. She blinked rapidly and swiped at the offending moisture.

On the other hand, Nantan looked positively composed compared to me and the Knowledge priestess.

I groaned, stretched out my legs and reached for my toes. "How can you not be tired?"

He chuckled. "I've reached the point where exhaustion is my normal state." He faced Sister Lizard and repeated my words and his in Diné.

She smiled and nodded at me. I think it was agreement that she was tired, too.

I stood and looked out at the demons surrounding us. Unlike the still, huddled positions they took when not attempting to breach our defenses, they stared at us. I couldn't tell for sure though since I couldn't detect their eyes. My impression was based on the fine hairs on my neck and back standing up as if I were being watched by a predator.

Which they definitely were. They'd consume our entire world if we didn't stop them.

A shudder ran through me at the memory of the demon who wanted to eat me when I'd been captured by the ones Samael DiRoy summoned. It was the first time I'd truly felt my mortality.

Nantan's psyche brushed mine when he extended his senses. "The power in the buildings is half of what it was, but the wards are holding."

"For now," I murmured. "They know something is happening."

Sister Lizard spoke as she gestured toward the demons.

Nantan answered in Diné before he turned back to me. "She wants to know if you think they're aware of exactly what we're doing."

I considered her question while I gazed at the black figures below us. "They're aware of the magic drain. They simply wait for the wards to weaken to the point their own power can bring them down." I turned back to Lizard and shrugged. "Hopefully, they believe their agents within the city are continuing their mission of eliminating us. And that the wards are fading due to the lack of reinforcement."

Nantan reported my words to her, and she nodded thoughtfully before she spoke again. This time, her words sounded more like a statement. He turned back to me.

"Lizard thinks we should drain the wards a little each day, then rebuild them a little—"

"Make them look like they're failing, so when we take them down, the demons will assume we couldn't keep them active. They won't hesitate coming into the city," I finished.

"Yes." Nantan didn't need to translate. Lizard nodded vigorously at the excitement in my voice.

"Do not speak of this to anyone. I will inform the Reverend Father of your plan."

Nantan repeated my words. Once again, Lizard nodded and asked something.

"Will you be needing more tea?" Nantan translated.

I cocked my head and smiled. "You're the first clergy of Knowledge I've met who doesn't go into fits over food or drink in their Temple."

She shrugged and gazed in the direction of Knowledge's four spires, her face dimming to a pale yellow. "We cannot save the collection of Tandor. It seems rather petty to chastise you or anyone else concerning a pot of tea," Nantan translated.

After Nantan and Lizard climbed down from the wall and headed toward their respective Temples for some rest, I walked along the battlements to Neighbor's Gate. As I expected, the Reverend Father stood at the tower parapet and stared at the demons as if he could force them away by the sheer power of his will.

I halted beside him. "May I speak to you privately, sir?"

"Of course."

When I rested my palm on the back of his hand, his smile died. His psychic walls slammed into place.

I hadn't pushed any further into his mind than the surface layer in order to use silent speech, so his defensive reaction surprised me.

Is there something wrong, sir?

You startled me. That is all. Some of his tension eased, but somehow, I knew if I tried to probe him, he would react poorly. Or even violently.

He was definitely hiding something from me though. It could be as inconsequential as his own fear. Showing insecurity would not bolster his troops' esteem, and for now, I was merely a member of his forces.

I apologize, sir. It's best that the fewest possible people know about Sister Lizard's idea. I quickly laid out the Knowledge priestess's addition to our main plan.

The demons will take the lure and enter the city, believing they have the upper hand. The Reverend Father nodded.

We believe so, sir.

That leaves the problem of clearing the tunnels in order to get the capable adults out.

I frowned. *Why only the capable adults?*

The Reverend Father's smile returned. *Reby and Luc are going to load the ships with children, the elderly, and those whose health or condition would not allow them to make the trek to Diné. Hadar has scrounged enough people to man both ships. He's created rigging inside of Thief for them to practice.*

They can't sail to Diné.

No, but they can head north for Standora. He shrugged. *If Issura has been taken, they'll head for Pagonia.*

Before I could ask another question, a high-pitched scream shattered the night.

Chapter 28

I automatically looked toward the demons, but they didn't move.

Shouts of men and women filtered from the direction of the initial scream.

Aduba's mind entered my link with the Reverend Father. *We've found a body, sir.*

Poison? I asked.

Surprise at my presence filtered through the connection. *Skinned. We could use your insight on the cause of death though, Chief Justice.*

"Go." The Reverend Father inclined his head toward the ladder.

"You're not coming?"

"I'll keep an eye on our friends." He scowled at the demons.

I glanced at the black forms sitting at the base of Tandor's walls. Again, I had the impression of them watching us attentively.

Whatever they were trying this time was beyond me.

I jogged in the direction of Aduba's essence. My path ended at a warehouse by the harbor. He waited by the doorway and led me inside.

Instead of packed dirt, flagstones covered the floor. The warehouse was so full of Light balls the magic tingled along my skin from every direction. The smell of pitch filled the area. Spools of rope sat next to spools of chain, all in various sizes and materials. I followed the Conflict Priest to the back of the warehouse, which was crowded with stands holding giant rolls of oiled canvas.

A Cliffdweller healer knelt beside the half-eaten corpse. Flies, maggots, and rats consuming the flesh were to be expected. He reached out to the body.

"Don't touch it!"

My alarm caused him to pause, thank Balance. He withdrew his hand and stood, a knowing expression on his face. Inclining his head, he murmured something in his own language.

"We already detected the curse." Amusement laced Aduba's voice. "As Healer Kotori says, some of us have paid attention to the reports of the demon and renegade encounters in Orrin. He was trying to find a way to remove it."

Aduba danced around the naming of the skinwalkers, renegades with magical talent who learned demon spells. They were rarely spoken of aloud in Diné culture, though the Reverend Father had apparently given up on honoring that particular taboo.

I couldn't rip my gaze from the green form on the canvas. "Has anyone been reported missing?"

"No, m'lady." Aduba shrugged. "But then, someone could have been reported missing to our former magistrate prior to the assassinations of the personnel from the other Temples, and he didn't bother to record it since he knew who took the person."

Aduba didn't sound quite as furious about the betrayal by their magistrate as he had been a few days ago. In fact, he sounded resigned to the horrible reality of skinwalkers and demons.

On the other hand, I was probably too pleased with my role in causing the deaths of those in Tandor who sided with the renegades.

I approached the corpse and crouched to examine it. Not even the barrels of pitch could cover the reek of death. Not that the warm weather here in Tandor hadn't helped with decomposition. Canvas had been pulled back to reveal the body.

"How was the corpse found?"

"The smell," Aduba said dryly. "Brother Hadar sent a couple young men here to fetch some material for the *Wave Dancer*'s foremast. The brother didn't trust the current one since the duchess's flagship has been sitting at the dock for nearly a year, and he can see rips in it."

I looked up at the Conflict high brother. "How can Hadar examine the ship when he can't get to it?"

"Through my distance-view glass." Aduba smirked. "We're all praying the bilge pump and rudder are intact, else it will be a very short trip."

I turned back to the body. Unlike Brother Jon's corpse we discovered near midwinter, the rats, insects, and the creatures so tiny they were invisible to other humans weren't bothered by this curse. I checked the visible bones.

"I'd say the woman has been dead two days. Three maximum. No obviously broken bones, though I can't be certain since most of her finger and toe bones are missing." I shook my head and looked at the two men. "With the rats having eaten her internal organs, it will be difficult to determine the cause of death." I watched the healer as Aduba translated for me.

Kotori nodded, then asked a question of his own.

"He wants to know how you came by your knowledge of medicine and anatomy," Aduba said.

I sighed and pushed to my feet. "Chief Healer Aaron assigned some of his staff to assist me in murder investigations. We've had far too many over the last year in Orrin. Master Devin and Journeywoman Bly have been most gracious in sharing their knowledge."

Kotori's eyebrows rose as Aduba repeated my words to the healer. He muttered something that made Aduba chuckle.

"What is so amusing?" I asked.

"Kotori said the main reason the Healers Guild broke from the Temple of Death was due to the clergy's seeming callousness to those severely injured or ill. It never occurred to the Guild their knowledge regarding the means of death could assist Balance."

I smiled at the healer. "It is something to consider. I've found our relationship useful."

Kotori nodded and asked another question.

"How did you get your Death seat to cooperate?" Aduba translated.

I laughed. "She used to be a healer herself until she burned out her talent saving my life. However, High Sister Bertrice acknowledges the politics between the Temples and Guilds. Either I or her second needs to be present during Master Devin's inquiry of a body."

Again, Kotori appeared surprised. He didn't ask anything else, but he seemed to be considering our arrangement in Orrin.

I looked at the present body again. "We need to find out who she was."

Aduba grimaced. "Sisquoc and the Tandor Wildlings are already searching based on the scents here. Is there any reason I shouldn't salt the body so we can move it to Death?"

The exhaustion I'd kept at bay since this morning's tea rushed through me all at once, and my shoulders sagged. "I'd like to know the difference between this curse and the one they placed on Brother Jon's corpse."

"The renegades were attempting to perfect their trap." Aduba stroked his beard.

"Perfect it?"

He nodded. "Your people in Orrin recognized the oddity in regards to the Light priest's body."

"You mean the lack of decomposition?"

"Yes. None of you touched the body because of the inconsistency. Therefore, none of you triggered the curse before discovering it." He stopped playing with his facial hair and waved at the corpse. "Our demon friend was obviously hoping to kill more priests by making the deposit of the body look more natural. Thankfully, the two young men who discovered the body were startled enough they didn't touch it either."

"The deposit?"

"She wasn't killed here." He made a disgusted sound in the back of his throat. "Not enough blood."

A chill ran through me despite the residual heat inside the warehouse. "So what is the demon using the blood for?"

Chapter 29

After giving Reverend Father Nizhé'é' my report on the corpse discovered in the warehouse, he stared out towards the demons again, though I didn't think he could see them in what was for him a moonless night.

"Can you tell if a demon is wearing a human skin?" he asked softly.

"I don't know." I leaned against the parapet and watched the demons, too. "I know I can see them when they only pretend to be something else, like a sash or a tree limb. I can see a skinwalker wearing a human skin since the human is dead and the skinwalker has been corrupted by the demons' magic. I can see when a person is directly possessed by a skinwalker." I snorted. "And I learned yesterday when a person, possessed by a fragment of a skinwalker's essence, is exposed to direct sunlight, I can see the possessed person's skin shimmer.

The Reverend Father flinched at my mention of the renegade sorcerers who used demon magic, but he said nothing. Maybe he wasn't as immune to the taboo subject of skinwalkers as I had thought.

I shook my head. "All I can tell you is neither Nantan nor any of the clergy I worked with this afternoon is a demon. From my research, they can't perform our type of magic themselves."

The demons' heads were still raised as if they watched or listened to us. They hadn't moved from their huddled positions since I left to review the body the young men found at the ship supply warehouse. Maybe Sister Lizard was right. Maybe they detected magic in ways we couldn't. Even the constant buzz in the back of my head from the active city wards was softer with the drain from the Temples to build our trap for the damned things.

"If the demon took a skin, it wants or needs to move among us," the Reverend Father murmured. "But why?"

"Unfortunately, there isn't a tea that allows me to read their minds," I said sourly.

"I wouldn't ask that of anyone..." He hesitated before he said, "Thank you, Chief Justice. Head back to Light and get some sleep."

I couldn't help the irritation that crawled through my blood. His tone reminded me too much of the one Kam used when he thought I was being ridiculous. "Someone needs to keep watch on the demons. I'm the only one who can do it in the dark."

"I need you alert over the next few days, especially with the extra strain on the wards," the Reverend Father said. "We can manage one more night without you, Chief Justice."

I understood the game he played, but I didn't like the way he singled me out for special treatment. After the last fortnight, resentment at his behavior bubbled to my surface.

"Chief Justice Elizabeth can recharge Balance—" I bit out.

"She's still not in the best of physical condition, nor will I risk her life." He lowered his voice. "Not when you've tried so hard to save it. And I need you and Spotted Fawn in the best condition you can be for us to pull off your plan."

"Sisquoc and his team are still searching for the murderer—"

"And he will no doubt inform Aduba, who will in turn inform me."

"But—"

"Anthea." The Reverend Father turned away from the parapet. "Do not make me carry you to your bed."

I jerked at his patronizing tone. "I beg your pardon. You will not speak to me—"

"I will continue to treat you like a recalcitrant brat if you continue to act like one." He took a step closer to me. The same maneuver I used against those who questioned my authority. "Is that understood?"

This wasn't a battle I should win. There were too many lives at stake. Retreating at the logic of the situation didn't make the blow to my pride any easier to accept.

"Yes, sir. Permission to leave?"

"Granted."

Despite his scowl, I still had a sense of amusement beneath his irritation as I pivoted and stalked toward the tower's ladder.

Brother Bumblebee had graciously left an activated light globe in Luc's quarters. Not that I needed it. A light globe didn't affect my eyesight because it didn't give of any heat. But since Luc wasn't here, he would need it when he returned.

I stripped off my damp clothing and nearly choked on my own odor. For the love of Mother! I took more baths in cold mountain streams while I was a circuit justice than I cared to remember, but at the very least, I could bathe regularly.

A different, smaller jar sat next to the ceramic container with my water ration on the table acting as Luc's desk. I crossed the bedchamber and lifted its lid. Citrus and sweet almond almost covered my own vile smell. A scraper sat on a piece of parchment between the two jars.

The raised writing of Balance met my fingertips. A note from my counterpart:

> *Bumblebee traded Love for some cleaning oil. Luc told me about*
> *your previous experience, and he tested it to make sure it was safe.*
>
> *Elizabeth*

A warmth spread through me that had nothing to do with Tandor's heat. This simple kindness in the midst of our disastrous situation meant I would, at the very least, die relatively clean.

I took the two jars and scraper into the bathing room. Seated at the drain end of the empty pool, I smoothed the oil over my body. I ran the scraper over every inch of my skin and flicked the detritus toward the drain.

The sewers emptied into a pit in the desert, but with the wards up, all exits had been closed and locked. Normally, I would be more concerned about stopping up a water drain with oil, but odds were Tandor wouldn't exist in a few days.

A bit of my drinking water and a clean cloth rinsed the dust from my hair and the grime from my face. My efforts weren't as good as my imported Aleppo soap, but they made me feel and smell cleaner than I had in over a fortnight.

The outer door opened and closed. For an instant, I realized I hadn't brought any weapons into the bathing room before Luc's essence registered.

"Anthea?"

"Coming." I gathered my accoutrements and returned to the main chamber.

Luc blinked, and a broad grin split his face. "Did you clean up for me?"

"Actually, I'm surprised you haven't kicked me out of your bed from the way I smelled." I set the jars and scraper on a small bench one of the Light brothers had found for our use.

"I can't complain. I've been merely stewing in my own sweat. I haven't been running all over the city the way you have." He propped his crutches against the table and pulled me into his arms.

The material under my chin didn't feel like the silk of a Temple uniform shirt. I ran my hands over his back. "What are you wearing?"

"Civilian clothes." He chuckled. "You weren't the only one who couldn't stand their own smell."

I took a deep breath and pulled back to look at him. "You took a bath with water."

He laughed at my accusation. "Healer Kotori justified it due to my recent injury. He claimed he didn't want a secondary infection ruining Devin's work."

"You know the Cliffdweller tongue?" I cocked my head.

Luc shrugged. "Father insisted my sisters and I have a working knowledge of the languages where he traded. Unfortunately, I've forgotten a lot of it from lack of practice. However, after my so-called bath, I wanted some clean clothes. This was the closest to Light colors one of the merchants could find in her stores."

He leaned back and grabbed a bundle from another chair. "Speaking of which, here's some for you."

The leggings were leather, but the shirt was cotton like Luc's. In the spring heat, most of the clergy had given up wearing their formal robes out in public during the day.

"Thought you might want something cleaner than your borrowed uniform while you're on guard duty tonight," he added.

"Tell her thank you for me." I set the bundle on his desk before I faced him. "However, I've been ordered to rest."

Luc laughed again. "Why do you sound like a child who has misbehaved?"

My body stiffened at the similarity to the Reverend Father's words. "Who told you what happened on the tower?"

"No one." Luc smiled faded. "Did you have words with the Reverend Father?"

"You could say that," I bit out.

He grabbed his crutches. "Let's lie down, and you can tell me about it."

Luc crossed to the bed and perched on the frame to strip off his own clothing. I merely laid on top of the sheet covering the padding. It was still too warm for a blanket, though that would change before dawn.

He extinguished the light ball, and I cuddled against him, the need for contact overriding the heat. I told him about the progress on our trap for the demons and the finding of the body.

"Why didn't you meet me at the warehouse?" I asked softly.

"Did you rewind the timeline?"

"No. I was concerned about the reaction to the spells we've planted on the walls if I tried." I sighed. "We're attempting things I've never read about, much less conceived."

"Then you didn't need me to interpret." It was a statement, not a question.

"Do you believe I made a mistake by not rewinding?"

"No." Luc stoked my belly. "We want the demon in the city to feel safe, don't we? If you had done the rewind, whether I was there or another Light priest, we would have known for sure who the demon was disguised as. If it were present in the warehouse—"

"I would have seen it," I protested.

"You can see through huge bolts of canvas?" He chuckled. "If it was simply hiding behind one of those racks, it would have listened and known you discovered it or its ally. Our plan for using it to lure the other demons into the city would have been ruined."

"It has to know something is up if Hadar is scavenging the warehouses for ship supplies."

"Does it matter if we get the two ships seaworthy?" Luc shifted to his side and cupped my cheek. "The demon has to know we can't possibly get ten thousand people out of Tandor on two ships."

"True."

He kissed me before he said, "Now, are you going to tell me what happened between you and the Reverend Father that angered you?"

"Leave it to a Light Priest to dig for the truth of a matter," I grumbled. However, I spilled the story of the Reverend Father's threat and insult.

Despite Luc's willpower not to laugh either physically or mentally, I could still feel his amusement trickle from behind his shields.

"Have you noticed you're the only one he tolerates insubordination from?" Luc finally said.

"I beg your pardon?" I pushed up on my elbows and glared at him though he couldn't see my expression.

"If any of the rest of us spoke or acted—"

"How was I disrespectful? He keeps asking for my opinion!"

"I was going to say before you interrupted me . . ." Luc waited for me to yell again. I didn't. However, I clenched my fists in an attempt to rein in my frustration.

". . . he almost treats you as an equal. He respects your opinion, even though you met less than a fortnight ago—"

"He is also constantly amused by me," I bit out.

"So was I when we first met," Luc said.

"I don't think it's quite the same," I muttered.

"By the Twelve, I hope not!"

"You can be quite incorrigible at times."

"I do it to keep you on your toes."

I lay on my back and cuddled against Luc's chest once again. "He reminds me too much of Kam," I said softly.

After a long while, Luc whispered, "I miss the old man, too."

Chapter 30

I woke to find myself alone in Luc's bedchamber.

Again.

Maybe he was simply used to not sleeping past sunrise anymore since he became the high brother of the third largest city in Issura last year. Many civilians attended the dawn services at Light, and he was required to attend to their needs.

I scrubbed the sleep from my eyes and donned the loaned clothing Luc had procured for me. From the tightness across my hips and rear end and the looseness in the waist, the leggings had been made for a very young woman or a man. The shirt was light and comfortable though. What I hadn't noticed last night was a tight-fitting leather vest in the pile of clothing that would keep my breasts in place while running or fighting.

When I entered the sanctuary, Bumblebee was once again waiting for me with my morning meal.

"Luc said you would need to examine the warehouse where the body was found, and you would need some assistance." The young priest appeared thoroughly enthused despite our predicament.

"Don't the Diné members of Light ride circuit with the justices as part of their training?" I asked between bites of dried fish and flatbread.

He laughed. "We don't have the number of permanent structures you do in Issura, so clergy travel with the clans during their seasonal migrations. So, I've rode circuit as you would say since I was a novice. During the Spring Rituals, all the clans come together at our home Temples. Matches are negotiated and made among the clans, and half the clergy rotates to a different clan. But four justices and their staffs serve primarily the trading outposts along our borders."

"Like Spotted Fawn?" I asked.

Bumblebee nodded. "That's part of the Light and Balance rotations." He chuckled. "The home Temples make sure no pair spend longer than two years together. Can't have us misbehaving."

I considered the concepts he presented. If Luc and I were in Diné, we would have been separated years ago. Sadness swept through me, so I quipped, "The recent edicts make that worry irrelevant. However, it would keep individual priests and priestesses from creating a power base in one place."

Bumblebee shook his head. "The Chumash used to be a little more like us and the Plains Nations. When the Toscans came to what is now Issura, the Chumash ideals changed."

For some reason, the thought of such a radical switch made me sad. But then, if my great-grandmother hadn't traveled from Diné to Issura for trade while pregnant, I might have been born in Diné.

A chuckle burbled from me. "Maybe that's why I enjoyed riding circuit so much. The Diné wanderlust from my mother's side."

"Could be," Bumblebee said agreeably.

I ate the rest of my meal. "Let's go find Aduba. I have some questions for both of you."

The three of us entered the warehouse. Magic didn't buzz against my psyche like it had last night. The odor of decomposition still lingered in the air long after the remnants of the corpse had been salted and burned.

"Has anyone found the spot where the woman was killed?" I asked as we walked back to the area where the body was discovered.

"No," Aduba said. "And it worries me. She wasn't randomly selected. The demon wanted her for a purpose."

"What makes you say that?"

He waved at the spot where the corpse had been last night. Nantan's people had taken the canvas that had hidden the body as well as the dead woman herself after both were salted to remove the curse. The oiled material would have ignited without much help.

"She was hunted, drained and skinned," Aduba said somberly. "The rest of the corpse was used to lay a trap for us. The demons remind me of how the Plains Nations hunt and use bison. Nothing goes to waste."

A shiver ran through me. Was that why demon skin was used for their grimoires? They wasted nothing?

I turned to Bumblebee. "Are there any Diné legends regarding skinwalkers using blood?"

The Light priest thought for a moment. "Not directly according to my teacher from Knowledge. She claimed our stories were offshoots of the originals that had been lost."

"What do you mean?" I frowned.

He shrugged. "Nearly every civilization has a few common tales."

"Like the Great Flood?" Aduba said.

Bumblebee nodded. "One other tale refers to creatures that drink blood to survive or to remain young."

"That would account for your basic mosquito," I said dryly.

"There are some areas of the world where bats drink blood instead of nectar," Aduba offered.

I raised my eyebrows at the Conflict priest, unsure if he were teasing or not. "But do the bats deal in demon magic?"

"Not that I am aware." Aduba grinned at me.

"What if the demon needed the blood to maintain its spells on the skin it's wearing?" Bumblebee suggested as he poked through boxes of pulleys.

"The blood would congeal soon after leaving the body." Aduba shook his head. "There's no method of preserving the blood without mixing it with something else."

"But if the demon did have some elixir it mixed with the blood to keep it in liquid form . . ." An awful thought occurred to me. It must have occurred to Aduba as well from the expression of horror on his face.

"No." He shook his head vigorously. "Nantan is not a traitor!"

"It wouldn't have to be him directly," I said. "It could be anyone with access to Death's morgue. Does anyone else use ice in their cold rooms?"

Aduba shook his head. "It's too expensive to ship all the way down here, even in winter."

"Excuse me, Chief Justice, High Brother," Bumblebee began. "Getting in and out of Death would be too much of a risk for a single demon. We chill jars of sheep milk and butter in mountain streams in the summer. Given our foe can access the clever methods of storing hot and cold water in Tandor without anyone seeing it, the best place to hide a container of blood would be one of the cold-water tanks we couldn't test for poison."

I stared at the younger priest. "Of course. You are brilliant, Bumblebee!"

His face turned a dark orange at my compliment. "It just seemed to be the logical conclusion."

"So what now?" Aduba said. "We start checking tanks?"

"Not yet." Purpose wove a rope around my psyche. "I'm going to double-check the warehouse to make sure our demon isn't here, and then I'm going to find out who our victim is."

Chapter 31

Shi Hua's thighs and rear end ached as she followed Jeremy toward the Love pavilion shortly after First Evening. She'd definitely grown too soft in her masquerade as Ambassador Quan's concubine. Thankfully, Nicholas and Hototo volunteered to set up everyone's tents while Mateqai and Catherine accompanied them, but no one else gave their little group a second look as they passed by.

Everyone in the camp was jittery and preoccupied. Shi Hua couldn't blame them. The Sea Peoples and Issuran fleets should be leaving at the next tide. Until one of the distance speakers left in Orrin confirmed the ships' departure, the queen's army faced the distinct possibility of a total rout. There would be little to no cover from the demon army around Tandor.

The two wardens standing guard at High Sister Imala's tent nodded to Catherine as she led Jeremy and Shi Hua through the flap. Once again, the high sister was dressed as a warrior, not a priestess of Love. She looked up from the scroll she perused at her tiny camp desk and smiled.

"Welcome, Sister. High Brother." Imala set aside her scroll and rose to her feet. "Please have a seat." She gestured at the pillows once again arranged around a low table.

"I hate to request this, but—"

Imala held up her hand to stop Jeremy. "I plan to ward my tent once our dinner is delivered." Another smile graced her face. "And I fully expect you to truthspell me."

"It's unfortunate matters have come to the point where we cannot trust each other without spellwork," Jeremy murmured with a slight bow.

A somber expression chased away Imala's initial good nature. "True. I've read the reports from my sisters in Orrin." She turned to Shi Hua. "Once again, I tender my apologies to you, Sister. I never would have intentionally overstepped your choice at this time."

"I accept your apologies, High Sister." Shi Hua inclined her head. The Love priestess was being terribly gracious given Shi Hua's own abominable manners last evening. "And thank you for loaning us your own wardens. Ambassador Quan will be most pleased with your consideration for my safety."

"It is my honor," Imala replied.

Shi Hua and Jeremy removed their weapons and harnesses. While the Temples in Orrin had thrown normal etiquette to the winds given the problems with renegades, assassins, and demons over the last several months, it wouldn't do to alienate a potential Reverend Mother by wearing swords and daggers at the dinner table.

In the meantime, two women wearing the uniform of Temple household brought in trays of light fare. Catherine made a point of tasting everything, as did Mateqai, before the women placed the contents of their trays on the table. However, neither the serving women nor the high sister looked offended. In fact, Imala appeared pleased the wardens took their duty to protect the clergy seriously. The Love priestess's assistants left, and she warded her tent and joined them at the table.

Mateqai and Catherine took positions at opposite ends of the interior. Shi Hua would have been nervous if her personal bodyguard hadn't vouched for his counterpart from Love. And it said something about how much High Sister Imala trusted her own protector given the delicate subjects of this meeting.

"You've read the reports from Orrin . . ." Shi Hua prompted.

"After what happened to our sisters there, none of my sisterhood or our wardens have been taking any chances." Imala sipped her wine before she added. "I want you to truthspell me so there are no more misunderstandings between us."

Shi Hua looked at Jeremy. He nodded.

She whispered the spell to counter any blocker the high sister may have cast, then the truthspell itself. "Do you mind if we ask why the Temple of Love developed the truthspell blocker?"

Imala smiled over her cup of wine. "Yes, I do."

Shi Hua's face heated at her misstep. She cleared her throat. "Why did your sisterhood develop the truthspell blocker?"

"To protect our worshippers' secrets." The high sister waved a nonchalant hand. "Prior to the start of the demon wars, those of us who served high officials within the Temples, the royals, the nobility, often found themselves in dangerous situations not of our making as enemies tried to use us against those we served."

"Such as the Assassins Guild?" Jeremy asked.

She nodded and let out a deep sigh. "However, any spell is a two-edged sword. It shames me Gerd used it to further her own devices."

"High Sister, I am deeply sorry to have to ask this," Jeremy said. "How long have you been worshipping with Reverend Father Farrell?"

"Not until the edict came down." A rueful smile crossed Imala's lips as she ladled their dinner into individual bowls. "It's not for lack of trying on his part since I first became a novice. My own Reverend Mother is very protective of our sisterhood. She often ran interference when it came to Light priests not willing to adhere to their own vows."

"So High Brother Dav isn't the first?" Shi Hua asked.

Imala's laughter reminded Shi Hua of her mother's wind chimes back home in the village of Yintze. The Love priestess shook her head. "Of course not, my dear. Light priests have been breaking their vows for millennia. So have the justices of Balance for that matter." Her humor died. "As long as they drew no attention to themselves, the heads of the Temples turned a blind eye, if you will. All humans are subject to Love's whims whether we like it or not."

"That explains why nothing was done about High Brother Kam and Justice Thalia." Jeremy dipped his flat bread into the thick porridge flavored with bits of dried meat and vegetables.

"That's assuming anyone knew about them," Shi Hua added.

"No clergy would admit to knowing about their affair after it had gone on so long. Not without repercussions to their own position." Imala grimaced. "The only reason Gerd admitted to knowing her parents' identities was an attempt to incriminate Kam after she'd been caught in her own schemes."

"About Reverend Father Farrell—" Jeremy began, but Imala held up her hand.

"Before we broach that subject, do you two have any concerns regarding lovemaking?" She grinned. "That way, if we are truthspelled, we won't set our guts on fire."

Shi Hua's cheeks flamed at Imala's question. A quick glance at Jeremy showed he was as embarrassed as she was. She gulped some wine and cleared her throat. "How long could this take, and how will I know when I'm carrying a child? The sisters in Orrin were more concerned with the . . . act and not the results."

"Are you two having problems with the act?" Imala's manner actually came across as truly concerned, which helped Shi Hua's nerves immensely.

Jeremy shook his head far more vigorously than she did though.

Imala cocked her head and regarded Shi Hua. "I can drop the wards and kick Jeremy out if you need to talk privately."

"It-it's, well, um—" Shi Hua gulped more wine. "I'm more interested in women—which he knows. He's been very attentive and understanding . . ."

"But no matter how much you like and respect him, you're wondering how long you have to do this?" Imala said softly.

Shi Hua nodded. Her eyes blurred, but not from the drink. The last thing she wanted was to hurt Jeremy's feelings.

"It depends. That's Mother and Father's purview." Imala shrugged. "Love can only stir the desire." She tore her flat bread into tiny pieces. "I would suggest you don't try any more after —"

"But I'm supposed to—" Shi Hua protested.

"I'm not asking you to stop," Imala held up a hand. "But anticipation of the upcoming battle will affect your bodies. Conceiving might be next to impossible for the next few days with the stress we will all be under. Which brings me to another issue we need to address."

She inhaled sharply, as if she were worried about their reaction to whatever she was about to say. "Shi Hua, when we reach Tandor, Princess Chiara wants you to drop back and ride with me at the rearguard."

"No!" Shi Hua jumped to her feet. "That's ridiculous. Light rides in tandem with Conflict and the civilian forces—"

"Take your seat, Sister!"

She looked down at Jeremy. The last time she seen such fury was when High Brother Luc accused her of lying. Or Reverend Father Chen of Conflict after she bested him in a contest during the Spring Rituals after her fourteenth winter.

Slowly, she lowered herself back to the pillow on which she'd been sitting and lowered her gaze. "I beg forgiveness, High Brother."

"Why does the crown princess want Shi Hua with the rear guard, High Sister?" he asked.

"She'd rather have you both with me."

Shi Hua's head shot up at Imala's dry tone.

"But she can't do that without arousing your Reverend Father's suspicions," the Love priestess continued. "As the Reverend Mother of Balance pointed out to both Princess Chiara and the queen, we can't prosecute him as a renegade without proof."

Jeremy frowned. "The crown princess thinks Chief Justice Anthea and High Brother Luc are close to that proof?"

"As are you two and Justice Yanaba, which is why she ordered the Orrin Balance wardens and the rest of your Light wardens to remain behind." Imala stared at her untouched bowl of porridge. "Finding the facts is like constructing a puzzle box, but all the pieces are the same length with the exact same notches on them." Frustration filed her voice.

Shi Hua took a deep breath and glanced at Jeremy. He nodded.

She swallowed the lump in her throat. "What does the Issuran Reverend Father of Thief say?"

Another rueful smile crossed Imala's lips. "Not much of anything these days. He's become very tight-lipped, but he agrees with Reverend Mother Alara that proof is needed."

"Catherine mentioned you were attacked the evening before we left Orrin. Is this true?" Jeremy asked.

Imala lifted her chin. "Yes."

"What time was this?"

She hesitated and pursed her lips, but it wasn't from pain. "The Temple bells had rung Second Evening shortly before Lord Aquilus's son Scipio appeared at my tent."

"What was Reverend Father Farrell doing so close to the Love pavilion?" Jeremy continued.

"I don't know." Imala scowled. "He claimed he would send another Light priest to me when he failed to perform." She sighed. "Please do not repeat that. It can happen to men as they grow older."

Shi Hua blinked in surprise. "But there are certain herbs and foods that can increase blood flow. He did not try those?"

Everyone inside the tent stared at her. Heat seared her cheeks. "My aunt belongs to the Temple of Love. She mentioned these things during my private lessons with her."

Imala nodded. "Yes, he did. To no avail unfortunately." She dipped a chunk of flat bread into her porridge before she popped the tidbit into her mouth.

Jeremy continued his questioning. "Did you truthspell Scipio?"

The Love priestess shook her head and swallowed. "Reverend Father Farrell truthspelled Scipio immediately after the attack. Brother White Wolf, a friend of mine in Thief, questioned him the following morning before he was sent home."

"Were you present for both interrogations?"

"Yes."

"What did Scipio say the reason for the attack was when the Reverend Farrell questioned him?" Jeremy asked.

"He said the brothers of Light had no right to spread their seed when they failed to protect to the human race." Imala frowned. "He then claimed I'd been mistakenly assigned to a Temple, I was his wife, and he had a right to my body. None of it made any sense. It was like we weren't speaking to the real Scipio."

Worry squirmed up Shi Hua's spine. Imala's description sounded too much like Anthea's version of the skinwalker possessing High Brother Dav of Tandor.

"What did Scipio say when Brother White Wolf truthspelled him?" Jeremy continued.

Imala shivered. "He said he didn't remember coming to my tent. He didn't even remember the lashing from the previous evening. However, he acted more like himself than he had the night before."

Everyone in the tent remained silent for a long time. Shi Hua forced herself to eat. This might be the last hot meal she had for the next few days.

"Do you sympathize with the renegades, High Sister Imala?" Jeremy asked.

"No!" Dishes and cup rattled in response to her anger. The camp furniture trembled, and the fabric of the tent itself rippled as if caught in the grip of a stiff wind.

The high sister's magic slammed against Shi Hua's, but Imala couldn't break the truthspell. Catherine hadn't been joking about the priestess's power. Shi Hua reached for her knife. Even the two wardens placed their hands on their sword pommels.

"I-I'm sorry." Imala struggled to pull her magic into herself. Most of her furnishings stopped moving as she tried to regain control of her gift, but the wine skin still shivered. "I know you have to confirm my allegiance."

"Have you had any dealings with renegades, either directly or indirectly?" Jeremy continued with what had become standard questions in Chief Justice Anthea's repertoire.

"No."

"Do you believe the Twelve Temples need to be destroyed?"

"No."

"Have you had any dealings with demons, either directly or indirectly?"

"No."

"Have you knowingly had in your possession any demon artifact?"

"No." Imala took a deep breath and released it. The wineskin stopped dancing along the tabletop.

"Do you know of anyone who has knowingly had possession of any demon artifact?"

Imala's lips quirked. "Sister Gerd, Sister Gretchen, Sister Dragonfly, Chief Justice Anthea, and Reverend Mother Alara of Balance had possession of a demon grimoire at one time or another until Reverend Father Farrell destroyed it in Standora a fortnight ago."

Jeremy turned to Shi Hua. "Did you have any additional questions, Sister?"

"Did you actually see the destruction of the grimoire Chief Justice Anthea once had in her possession?"

"I . . . no." Imala pursed her lips. "He burned what looked to be the same book, but I did not examine it prior to the burning.

Shi Hua inclined her head. "Thank you for your cooperation, High Sister."

Jeremy frowned at Shi Hua. "You think the Reverend Father swapped the grimoire for something else?"

She shrugged. "Anthea did to fool the demon you killed in the Orrin tunnels."

"Honestly, I'm not sure how you two have kept your sanity through all this." Imala shook her head.

"Probably because we never had any to begin with," Jeremy joked.

The rest of their meal passed with Jeremy and Imala gossiping about people they both knew in the Issuran capital. Shi Hua smiled, nodded, and asked questions where appropriate, but something about the noble attacking the Love priestess didn't sound right. And for the love of Light, she couldn't put her finger on it.

As Mateqai and Catherine escorted them back to their campsite, Shi Hua brushed the back of Jeremy's hand with her own. *Do you really think the high sister is telling the truth?*

About the Reverend Father?

Yes.

Jeremy glanced around them to spy for eavesdroppers even though they used silent speech. *She was truthspelled.*

I know but— Something gnawed on Shi Hua's mind, something elusive and it was driving her mad.

What reason does she have to lie to us? Jeremy asked.

I guess I'm worried I'll take her at her word simply because my favorite aunt serves Love. Shi Hua chewed on her lower lip.

The fact that you asked that question means something else has sparked your instincts. Jeremy's face was cloaked in shadows despite the torches and campfires surrounding them. She couldn't tell if he really believed his reassurance. *It will come to you.*

I hope the revelation comes before it's too late.

Chapter 32

Shortly after First Evening, I took a deep breath to calm myself before I entered the Sea Wolf. Across the inn's great room, Reverend Father Nizhé'é' waved to get my attention. He was the only one who knew the truth besides Aduba and Bumblebee.

And Aduba asked that I block his memory so he didn't accidentally reveal it to anyone. I think his request was more due to his fear he would do something rash considering the losses the renegades and their allies had inflicted on his city.

The deaths of his friends. The deaths of people he considered family though he'd never admit his vulnerability.

I strode across the flagstone floor. No one so much as looked in my direction. It was an odd sensation. I'd gotten used to people staring at me.

I wasn't sure if I liked the lack of attention or not.

At the table by the dark fireplace, I took the empty seat next Luc. Nantan sat next to the Reverend Father. Luckily, the Reverend Father had been taking his meals here since the Diné army arrived in Tandor. And he often met with other ranking clergy while he ate.

Luc and I had been in this particular inn twice, only because he demanded we go. He claimed he wasn't hiding in the Temple of Light all the time during this stupid siege.

I could sympathize. He had been going stir crazy when he was recovering from the loss of his left foot prior to our mission to Tandor.

"Find anything that might lead to our poor unfortunate's identity, Anthea?" the Reverend Father asked while he poured me a tankard of light ale. All the inns had started serving their various brews with our rations, partly to extend the water supply and partly because we couldn't carry the damn barrels across the desert as we fled.

"No, sir." I accepted the tankard from him. "I have to agree with Aduba. The demon merely moved the body to the warehouse, hoping the curse would delay us refitting the two ships we have available."

The wife of the innkeeper who'd been poisoned along with so many of the clergy and wardens approached. She set a steaming bowl in front of me. It was all I could do not to vomit in terror or run my sword through her.

"Thank you—forgive me, but I forgot your name." I smiled at her, or rather it.

It smiled in return. "It's Gray Sparrow, m'lady."

"How's your son doing?"

It made the appropriate sorrowful expression. "He's still under the care of the priest of Child. His father and the staff's horrible deaths were too much for him."

"I'm so sorry. I'll pray for him." I poked at the dish in front of me. "What is this? It smells wonderful!"

"Steamed dumplings and chicken. Some of the families have donated their fowl to the cause." It shook its head. "We no longer have enough grain to feed all the animals."

"Then I'll say a prayer for their sacrifice. Thank you, Gray Sparrow."

It shuffled away, and I continued to poke at the reddish mass in my bowl.

"If you don't want your dumplings, I'll eat them," Luc offered.

I looked at the Reverend Father. He leaned his head to his right. I shook mine slightly.

Maybe, we'd pinned too much hope on my odd eyesight detecting anything out of order. But my rewind of time in the warehouse had been pretty damn conclusive. The poor innkeeper hadn't even known he'd been sleeping in the same bed with a demon before he died in such an awful manner.

But the demon wearing the skin of Gray Sparrow looked totally human to me. I wanted to scream in frustration. There could be dozens of disguised demons in the city.

I shoved the bowel over to Luc. "Go ahead. I don't think I can eat right now."

"Anthea," the Reverend Father said softly. "You need to keep up your strength. We only have three justices in Tandor."

From the corner of my eye, I could see the demon in human skin clean off a nearby table. Close enough to hear us speaking.

"That's the problem, sir." I shook my head. "There's only three of us. We took out most of the magic embedded in the Temple of Balance to kill the first skinwalker and a huge number of the renegade humans. There's only so much of our power we can infuse every day, and with the imbalance from one weakened Temple, the wards are draining the other eleven faster than they should."

"What can we do to shore up the Temples' magic reserve?" the Reverend Father asked.

"We do exactly what Anthea and the other justices are doing to our own Temples," Luc stated. "Recharging the reserves."

"The problem isn't just Balance," Nantan added. "The imbalance grows because we don't have the same amount of clergy for each of the other Temples. For example, we only have one person each for Mother, Vintner, Child—"

The Reverend Father held up his hand. "I get the gist. How long do we have?"

Luc shook his head. "Two, maybe three, days before the wards fail."

The demon pretending to be Gray Sparrow approached us. "F-f-forgive me for eavesdropping, m'lord." It looked around to see if anyone else was listening and lowered its voice. "There's a rumor you had a plan to get everyone out of the city."

The Reverend Father closed his eyes, a sorrowful expression on his face.

"Y-you lied to your own people?" the demon said incredulously.

He opened his eyes. "You cannot tell anyone, Mistress Gray Sparrow. People will panic and do awful things to each other."

"B-but the ships . . ." The demon searched each of our faces.

"We can only get the children out, Mistress." Luc shook his head. "Surely, you want your son to live?"

It hesitated just a fraction too long before it nodded vigorously. "Of course, b-but . . ."

I grabbed its wrist. For an instant, demon cold penetrated its skin. "For the love of all you hold holy, you cannot breathe a word of this. Else, your son and all the children will perish with the rest of us."

It nodded, a little slower this time. "I understand, Justice. Would you like me to bring you something else to eat?"

I released its wrist. "No, thank you, Gray Sparrow. You've done enough for me."

The demon collected the tray of dirty dining ware and toddled toward the kitchen.

The Reverend Father's gaze met mine. *Do you think it believed us?*

We'd better pray to the Twelve it did, I said silently. *Or we are all lost.*

Chapter 33

Shi Hua sat cross-legged on the bedroll she shared with Jeremy. He sat across from her, his palms hot against the backs of her hands as they rested on her knees. Reaching out with her mind, she found Yanaba awake and reading in the main reception room of the Temple of Balance in Orrin. The junior justice still didn't feel complete, even though Brother Turtle of Child had warned Yanaba might not make a full recovery. She'd stretched her very soul to the breaking point in trying to track the demons who'd infiltrated Orrin and trap them.

However, the junior justice wasn't alone. Balance's Chief Warden Little Bear, Magistrate DiCook, and Brother Xander of Death filtered through the connection.

Yanaba laughed silently, a warm feeling despite the late hour. Shi Hua wondered how much of the justice's mood was due to Xander.

How's the trip to Tandor?

Sore backsides, Shi Hua replied. *Has the fleet left?*

Evening tide. DiCook's mental essence was prickly compared to the Temple personnel. *Brother Elroy relayed the message to Reverend Father Farrell as they left. Why are you independently confirming this?*

Because we're having our own issues during the march south. Jeremy quickly relayed the attack on High Sister Imala, the Reverend Father's odd behavior, and Imala's warning.

That doesn't make sense. Even with our current emergency in Tandor, Scipio should have been turned over to Orrin's Temple of Balance. Yanaba's concern regarding the breach of judicial protocol overrode any hint of her ego. *I can't hear Princess Chiara condoning a noble being short-changed in this manner.*

We're assuming she even knew, Little Bear commented. *It sounds like Lord Aquilus may have been threatened or bribed into silence.*

The last thing the crown princess needs is Temple machinations in the middle of a battle. DiCook's anger sparked against Shi Hua's mind.

Have you told High Sister Bertrice of these incidents? Xander asked.

No, Jeremy admitted.

I agree with Xander. Little Bear wasn't as furious as the magistrate, but he was rightly concerned, and Anthea depended on her chief warden's counsel. Shi Hua felt a little better knowing he was as troubled as she was. *Let Bertrice know what's going on. She may have knowledge you lack at the moment, or she may have some insight. In the meantime, I'll have Gina check with the sisters of Love here in regards to Imala's reliability.*

Shouldn't we inform Lady Alessa? DiCook asked. *Lord Aquilus may not be one of her brother's vassals, but she may have knowledge we are lacking as well.*

Are you going to throw a fit if I request to send Little Bear with you? Yanaba's amusement danced along their link.

DiCook laughed despite his anger. *Thank you for having some decorum to ask, Lady Justice. Your senior would simply charge up to the duke's estate and demand answers.*

As I said, consult with High Sister Bertrice, Xander said. *We will investigate from this end.*

With that advice, Shi Hua broke the link. She blinked to orient herself.

Jeremy stretched his arms over his head. "Well, that wasn't a bit helpful. There's no way we can get near the Death pavilion without the Reverend Father knowing."

"Yes, there is."

"Intercepting a farspeaking message in nearly impossible." Jeremy shook his head. "Silent speech this close could be overheard."

"You're right." She reached into the bottom of her pack. Silky material met her fingertips. "That's why I'm going to tell her in person." She pulled out the dark gray clothes High Brother Biming had given her years ago.

Jeremy grabbed her wrist. "You can't go sneaking around the camp."

"No, you can't sneak around the camp because you couldn't sneak if your life depended on it."

"If you're caught in a Thief uniform—"

"It's not a Thief uniform." She held up the shirt to show the lack of insignia.

"You're arguing semantics—"

"Keep your voice down," she hissed before she yanked her uniform shirt over her head. "I'll be there and back before you know it. We'll still have time for intercourse."

"You think that's what I'm worried about?"

She looked pointedly at his pants before she met his eyes again.

"That's not what I'm worried about," he muttered. "If you accidentally get yourself killed—"

"I won't." She slipped on the gray shirt and started wiggling out of her leggings. "I snuck in and out of Balance back in Orrin several times without getting caught."

"You did what?"

Shi Hua yanked her uniform leggings off her feet and pulled on the gray ones. "At least, I don't have to worry about ice this time." The thin gray slippers and hooded jacket completed her ensemble.

She glanced at her weapons and hesitated. Her sword or bow would identify her, so there was no point in bringing them. Throwing knives in wrist holders would have to do.

"Watch yourself," Jeremy murmured as she strapped on the knives.

Shi Hua nodded. She pulled her sleeves straight and flipped up her hood. The fact that he didn't question her choice to carry any weapons while sneaking through the camp meant he was as uneasy as she was about the Reverend Father's manipulations and High Sister Imala's story.

When Nicholas and Hototo set up hers and Jeremy's tent, they set it back, not just from their wardens' tents but from the rest of the army as well. No doubt, they thought they were being considerate in giving the clergy a bit of privacy for their recently sanctioned activities to produce children with Light talent. Shi Hua doubted the men realized how easy it was for someone to slip out beneath the oiled canvas walls.

Of course, they didn't. No one from Light thought that way. No one but her. To her knowledge, she was the only Light clergy who had also trained with Thief. Maybe that was the problem. Light was too open. Too honest. Too easy to infiltrate because their clergy so rarely questioned each other.

Shi Hua waited for her eyes to adjust to the darkness before she crept between the picket lines and the outer tents. None of the troops stayed awake past the evening meal. Not with a day and a quarter of marching and a demon battle ahead of them.

But the sentries, both Temple and civilian, were hyperalert. It took more time than she anticipated to reach her goal. The black and white flag of Death hung limply from the post, the only indication of the high sister's rank. She slipped under the canvas of Bertrice's tent.

The high sister sat at a camp table, peering over a scroll beneath a glowing globe. She jerked at the appearance of a hooded figure. The senior priestess's sword was halfway out of her scabbard before Shi Hua flipped back her hood.

"I beg your forgiveness for interrupting your evening, High Sister." Shi Hua bowed. "Brother Xander suggested I relay some news to you and ask your opinion."

Bertrice exhaled and her shoulders relaxed. "Sneaking around like that is a good way to lose your head, Sister. Especially these days." She slid her sword back into its scabbard. "What does my second need that couldn't wait until morning?"

Shi Hua quickly laid out the events with Reverend Father Farrell and High Sister Imala, then the conversation with the parties in Orrin. "Jeremy and I find ourselves in the odd position of not knowing who to trust."

Bertrice propped her cheek on her fist. "Should I be impressed you feel you can confide in me?"

"You've been inside my mind, High Sister."

Bertrice's mouth pursed at the reminder of Shi Hua's visions during and after the demon battle inside Orrin's Temple of Balance. The worst part had been when the vision form of the dead Justice Thalia addressed Bertrice directly through Shi Hua's mind.

The high sister waved at a camp stool, and Shi Hua took the offered seat.

"I heard about the incident with High Sister Imala several candlemarks after we left Orrin." Bertrice frowned and shook her head. "Yanaba is correct. Even if the matter with this Scipio wasn't referred to her, it should have been referred to Justice Clymene within the army for dispensation."

"I do not wish to speak ill of another clergy member, especially a reverend father, but does the crown princess know—"

The tent flap rustled, and two people entered. Both were dressed in the same non-descript gray Shi Hua wore. The first figure pushed back its hood to reveal the crown princess of Issura.

A sardonic smile graced Chiara's aquiline features. "Do I know what, Sister?"

Chapter 34

I paced in Luc's quarters after we returned to Light. Now, I understood Aduba's reasoning for the memory block. He was someone after my own heart. The need to right a wrong was nearly overwhelming.

"I should have trapped and questioned it," I muttered.

"That defeats the purpose of the plan for the demon to tell his friends outside the walls that it's safe to come in." Luc sat on a chair and sharpened his sword. "Not to mention, how do you plan on holding it?"

"Spelled manacles."

The whetstone paused in its slide. Luc gave me the look he did when he thought I was being totally ridiculous. "Are you sure a pair would hold one? Your time-freeze spell only slows down the damn things."

"Well, wards then!" I threw my hands in the air.

"And you would be trapped inside with the demon," he pointed out.

"Water. We can hold it under water."

"And how do you prevent yourself from drowning?"

I whirled to face him. "You are not helping!"

"You're just angry you have to depend on Bumblebee to do your spying."

"He's by himself." I crossed my arms. "He should have taken backup."

"Reby's with him."

I snorted. "Was that your brilliant idea?"

"Yes." Luc resumed sharpening his sword. "I defy even a demon to escape her stench if she sprays it."

"Just because you got sprayed by her doesn't mean a demon can be," I shot back.

"You told me she did when you confronted the skinwalker and Ural DiSand."

"Like you listen to everything I say." Anger made my skin itch.

He remained silent. The rasp of the whetstone was worse than the buzz of the city wards.

"Why are you even bothering with your steel?" I snapped. "It's not like you're going to be using that blasted pig sticker!"

As soon as the words flew out of my mouth, I realized I'd crossed the one line I swore never to cross.

Luc's hand with the whetstone paused again. "I know you are frustrated by your inability to act, Chief Justice, but I do not appreciate you taking your bad mood out on me." His voice was calm. Too calm. Which meant he was beyond furious.

I walked over and knelt by his chair and rested my forehead against his thigh. "I'm sorry, Luc. I'm so, so very sorry." Tears pricked my eyes. "I should never have said that."

"No. You shouldn't have." From the clatter, he set his sword and whetstone on his table cum desk. His fingers stoked my hair. "Why are you working so hard to drive me away?"

I sniffed and looked up at him. "I don't want to lose you."

His right thumb wiped away the tears. "Don't you think I have the same fear? If our plan succeeds, you're going to be trapped in one of those lighthouses when Nantan sets off the last resort spells."

"Unless I jump into the sea," I murmured.

He shook his head. "Not to be morbid, but the Peaceful Sea and your family do not have a good relationship."

"One time," I muttered. "And no one really knows what happened to her in that blast of power onboard the pirate flagship."

"We can't do anything until Bumblebee and Reby return. Hopefully they will have some good news," he said. "So relax and read something to pass the time."

"I can't." I grimaced at the memory. "I destroyed everything inside Balance, including Elizabeth's library."

Luc shuffled through some things on the table before he handed me a thick volume. "Here."

"What's this?" My fingertips drifted over the leather binding and found the raised writing of my Temple. "*A History of the Apache?*"

"Sister Lizard found it in the stacks of the Tandor Knowledge library." Luc grinned. "I thought I might need to distract you at some point."

I sighed. "You know me too well." I rose and claimed another chair before I began reading the history.

Chapter 35

"I-I-I—" Not only couldn't Shi Hua get a word past her lips, her heart threatened to choke her at the sight of the crown princess. If the heir to the Issuran throne took offense at Shi Hua's words to the high sister, the best scenario would be sitting in a cell until a ship could take her back to Jing.

The worst was her neck at the wrong end of a justice's sword.

High Sister Bertrice rose and bowed to Princess Chiara. "The sister was merely requesting my counsel, Your Highness. No insult was meant."

The second figure pushed his hood back. More shock hit Shi Hua at the appearance of Talbert, Orrin's high brother of Thief.

He grinned. "If Sister Shi Hua is sneaking around the camp in my Temple's colors, my guess is she's here to discuss the same subject we are."

The crown princess grimaced. "I'd hoped not to drag High Brother Jeremy or Sister Shi Hua into this matter."

Shi Hua found her voice and lifted her chin. "We're already in the middle of the chaos, Your Highness. While I appreciate your concern—"

"You're an adult, and you know your own mind?" The princess chuckled. "By the Twelve, you remind me too much of myself at your age."

"Actually, I was going to say we need to help each other rather than trying to protect each other from uncomfortable realities," Shi Hua said. "I approached High Sister Bertrice first because she has been inside my mind. She knows me, and I trust her counsel."

"And you weren't as likely to be stabbed to death by her before you completed your investigation?" A wry smile crossed the princess's face.

"I'd prefer not to be a target for anyone," Shi Hua replied. "However, it is an uncomfortable reality that I am one."

Chiara claimed another camp stool. "So, you two have noticed Reverend Father Farrell's odd behavior as well?"

Talbert circled the tent, laying wards so no one would interrupt or overhear them. Embarrassment hit Shi Hua that she'd forgotten such a simple precaution. She glanced at High Sister Bertrice who had resumed her seat.

"Tell Princess Chiara everything you've just told me, Sister," Bertrice said.

Sucking in a deep breath, Shi Hua retold her and Jeremy's encounters with both Reverend Father Farrell and High Sister Imala.

"Why didn't High Brother Jeremy come along on tonight's expedition?" Chiara asked when Shi Hua finished.

Talbert snorted. "That boy couldn't sneak if his life depended on it."

Chiara gave Shi Hua a questioning look.

While she didn't like speaking ill of anyone from her order, especially those she called friend, Shi Hua shrugged. "As the high brother says."

The crown princess chuckled. "Then you both smarter than I expected."

"I beg your pardon?" Shi Hua wasn't sure if the princess's words were a compliment or an insult.

"Can we drop the diplomatic pretense?" Chiara eyed Shi Hua.

She nodded. Even Bertrice and Talbert appeared curious to where the crown princess was going with her thoughts.

"According to High Brother Talbert, you were specifically trained by Temples other than Light to be Ambassador Quan's bodyguard and advisor, correct?" Chiara tilted her head.

Shi Hua nodded again.

"Brother Jeremy has also absorbed far more lessons than his opponents realize." A smile curved the crown princess's mouth. "He has plausible deniability to Farrell if you are caught skulking around the camp, especially with you being non-Issuran."

Shi Hua kept her face still as she worked through the situation. That wasn't what happened in their tent. Or was it? Or was this another attempt to separate what was left of the Orrin Light Temple?

No, she trusted Bertrice. There was no hint of deception in the older woman when Shi Hua had entered the high sister's tent.

Shi Hua released her pent-up breath and smiled at the crown princess. "You see truly. If I were caught, he would be free to continue."

Her partial admission took the crown princess aback. "To continue what?"

"To find out why Chief Justice Anthea and I are on the top of the Assassins Guild's list of people to remove from the playing board."

Chiara blinked slowly as she processed this information. A scowl followed. "I was not aware of this." She turned to Talbert.

He merely shrugged. "As I told the chief justice, neither she nor Sister Shi Hua has needed our assistance. In fact, their continued survival has led to the opportunities I spoke of earlier."

"You're dangling us like bait?" Part of Shi Hua was highly incensed by his attitude. Reverend Father Biming was never this callous.

Talbert chuckled. "That's exactly what our chief justice said. However, it has been necessary for my order to keep silent on a number of matters."

"If you're finished being furious with the high brother, yes, I do want you in the rear guard with High Sister Imala," Chiara said lightly. "If I had more of a say, I'd want you and Jeremy both with rear guard. It would be too easy for someone to kill you both in the heat of a battle." The princess leaned forward and rested her elbows on her knees. "High Sister Bertrice will also be with the rear guard, and she's the one who recommended you. Can you show her the same devotion you've shown Ambassador Quan?"

"You-you want me to be her bodyguard?" Shi Hua's attention shifted to Bertrice and back to Chiara.

"Don't become too excited about the prospect," Bertrice said dryly. "Once the demons realize what I'm doing, we will become the center of their focus."

"But the plan we presented to you . . ." Shi Hua's heart beat so hard she feared it would break through her ribs.

"Your plan to get the civilians out on the fleets is still in effect," Chiara said grimly.

Fear and hope warred in Shi Hua's mind as she realized the crown princess's true intention. "The ships aren't the distraction for the army. We're the distraction for the ships."

Chapter 36

Banging on the bedchamber door jerked me out of a nightmare. For once, I didn't wake alone in Luc's bedchambers.

However, we'd both fallen asleep at the damn table.

Luc blinked and called out, "Enter!"

The door opened, and Reby's acting second Sisquoc stepped inside the room. He shook his head. "With all due respect, High Brother, you should lock your door when you're asleep."

Luc swiped his face with his right hand while I surreptitiously wiped away my drool from the history I'd been reading. At least, I didn't have to worry about smearing the ink.

"If a demon wanted in here, all it has to do is slither through the gaps between the door and the frame," Luc said. "Is there a particular reason you're here, Sisquoc?"

"High Sister Reby confirms a signal has been sent to the demon army from inside Tandor."

Alarm trilled through me. "Why isn't she reporting? Is she all right? What about Bumblebee?"

Sisquoc smiled. "They are both fine. They've enlisted a few more Wildlings to observe our prey. In the meantime, they are searching the untested cold-water tanks for an item Bumblebee says the demon hid."

I swore one of Luc's favorite Cantish oaths. "He went beyond the task I assigned him."

"As if you have never done so," Luc teased.

"Maybe I did some foolish things when I was his age—"

Luc merely lifted his right eyebrow.

I ignored his unspoken comment on my more recent behavior in favor of addressing the Wildling. "Tell them not to touch the object. It probably has a curse laid on it to protect it."

Sisquoc nodded, but he asked no questions. Reby made a good choice in trusting him.

"Is there anything else?" Luc asked.

"People are packing gear and food in the thought we will be evacuating." Sisquoc hesitated. "I normally would not question my superiors, but I would merely suggest that false hope can be more detrimental than the most damaging lie."

"Let them pack, but only what they could carry across the desert to Diné," I said softly. "Encourage those who aren't preparing to do so. Frankly, this may be a desperate gamble on our part, but I would appreciate your silence for now."

The Wildling considered my words for a moment. I could almost see the moment when it registered inside his mind we knew who the demon was masquerading as and what his senior priestess was doing. He inclined his head to me.

"Is there any other way I may be of service?"

"What hour is it?" Luc asked.

"It's just past Third Night, sir," Sisquoc responded.

I groaned. "Thank Balance. I could use some additional sleep in a more comfortable position."

"That's all for now, Sisquoc," Luc said.

The Wildling inclined his head once again before he departed, closing the door behind him.

"Well?" I peered blearily at Luc.

"All we can do is keep up the bait." He shrugged.

I stood and started peeling off clothing. "Then I'm sleeping so I don't say anything more idiotic than I already have today."

"Want some company?" Luc's heated look at my bare chest said I wouldn't be getting any rest for a bit.

Chapter 37

The third day's march started much as the last two days had, except this time Chief Warden Catherine and Warden Hototo fell in behind Nicholas and Mateqai. Shi Hua knew it was too much to hope the Love personnel would go unnoticed, but Crown Princess Chiara had spoken with High Sister Imala after questioning Shi Hua. In turn, the Love priestess had ordered her wardens to stick with Jeremy and Shi Hua.

The sun was a fingertip above the mountains when Reverend Father Farrell and two of his own wardens trotted along the sandy berm of the National Road back to the middle of the column. The Reverend Father's cheeks flushed above his neatly trimmed beard.

"Why in the many names of Light are you two out of order?" he barked.

Heads turned toward them among both the Temple and civilian ranks at the Reverend Father's outburst.

"Crown Princess Chiara was concerned about the safety of Sister Shi Hua," Catherine replied evenly.

"Crown Princess Chiara has no authority over Temple personnel," Farrell hissed. From the way his eyes darted, he didn't want the audience, but it was too late.

"High Sister Imala has offered the service of her wardens as recompense for unintentionally insulting Sister Shi Hua," Jeremy replied smoothly. "The crown princess does not wish to damage Issura's relationship with Jing, especially since both Ambassador Quan and Sister Shi Hua have been instrumental in helping us ferret out renegades."

"For all we know, Jing is behind those blasted demon eggs that were hatched in Cant," the Reverend Father spat.

"The first egg brought into Issura was aboard an Issuran vessel and was intended to kill Sister Shi Hua." Jeremy guided his horse between Shi Hua and the Reverend Father's party.

In her peripheral vision, she was aware their wardens and the Love personnel had taken defensive positions around her. The surrounding troops stopped marching. This was quickly getting out of hand.

"Gentlemen, let's hold our enmity for our real foes, not each other." Shi Hua used a bit of magic to amplify her voice.

A wave of motion ran from the front of the army. Horses and people parted to reveal Lord General White Eagle astride a black stallion.

"I must agree with the sister," he said. The general didn't bother with magic to be heard. His voice would carry over the insane noise of a battlefield. "Let's save our energy for the demons."

The Reverend Father's chin jutted out. "With all due respect, Your Grace, this is not a royal matter."

"It is if we don't reach Tandor in time." The general tilted his head. "Ride with me, Reverend Father," he said more softly before he reined his horse around to reach the edge of the road. "The rest of you, move out!"

Neither of his statements were a request. The ranks hurried to catch up with the rest of the troops while the Reverend Father joined the general riding parallel with the army.

Unsure of what to do, the two wardens who had accompanied Farrell spurred their horses back to the head of the Light division.

Shi Hua's little group fell back into their positions. No one's face indicated anything untoward had happened. She glanced at Jeremy. He gave the slightest shake of his head.

She chewed on the tip of her tongue to keep from saying anything untoward. After Chief Justice Anthea's descriptions of the skinwalkers, Shi Hua had to wonder if one had stolen the Reverend Father's form.

Once again, she found herself wishing she had the chief justice's peculiar form of sight so she could know for sure.

Chapter 38

Once I'd broken my fast, I reported to the Neighbor's Gate for guard duty. Reverend Father Nizhé'é' was still atop the tower, watching the still forms in their alternating rows.

I frowned and examined them more closely. They seemed to be sitting a little straighter.

"How long ago did they change position?" I asked.

"Around Second Night," he replied.

About the time our disguised demon sent its message from Duchess Nadine's manse. From a spot no one could see it unless they were a Wildling clinging to the tiny space between a roof gutter and the outer wall.

We couldn't talk openly on the tower, and I wasn't about to touch his mind again without permission. However, he didn't seem inclined to want to discuss last night's events.

Maybe that was for the best. I didn't like the sudden, but necessary, need to learn espionage as the chief justice of Orrin. Sorrow filled me at the simpler years when Luc and I rode circuit.

"I'm going to retire," the Reverend Father murmured. "Send a messenger if they change positions again."

"Yes, sir."

As he strode toward the ladder, he shoulders stooped as if he were far older than his forty-eight winters.

I sighed and stared at the demons again. He was carrying the weight of his army and the entire populace of Tandor. I doubted I could handle the burden as well as he did.

Reby waited for me at the Temple of Light when I returned after my watch on the tower. Bumblebee was nowhere in sight. I gestured for her to follow me into one of the consulting rooms.

I closed the door and warded the room. My first question for her was, "Is Bumblebee all right?"

"He's fine." She gave me a tired smile. "He went to get some sleep. We were up all night."

"We got your message via Sisquoc." I leaned my elbows on the table. "You're sure Gray Sparrow didn't see any of you?"

"Absolutely." She slouched in her chair. From the dull yellow of her complexion, she was barely awake herself. "Jumping Mouse lived up to her name and her second form. Gray Sparrow used a lantern to flash signals towards the surrounding demons. Only someone in the north desert could have seen unless they were flying outside of the city wards."

"Anything else?"

"Hadar's got most of Thief helping him and Luc with ships, so I have Wildlings keeping an eye on Gray Sparrow. A wicked smile lit Reby's face. "The demons don't seem to take us as seriously as they do Light or Conflict. Or even you justices."

I cocked my head. "What makes you say that?"

"That's not Gray Sparrow inside her skin."

"You're changing the subject, but again, what leads you to that conclusion?"

"Because whatever she is, she smells like a demon."

"Demons smell differently?"

Reby nodded. "We kept detecting it for years here in Tandor and in the surrounding desert, but we couldn't figure out what exactly it was. Not until our cook tried to poison us. We thought the scent had to do with the skinwalkers until we found those demons in Duchess Nadine's manse. Of course, with the siege—" She waved her hand to encompass the city. "The smell's so strong we're having trouble differentiating a single entity within the walls. At least, not until Jumping Mouse got close enough to the thing pretending to be Gray Sparrow."

"Twelve bless you!" I jumped up, raced around the table, and hugged the Wildling woman.

"Uh, Anthea, neither of us are the hugging type." But my embrace muffled Reby's voice.

I pulled back and grabbed her shoulders. "Don't you understand? We have a way to check for demons before we leave Tandor!"

"Wait a moment." She laid her palms on top of mine. "Then why didn't High Brother Jax and his people detect the demons that infiltrated Orrin?"

My initial joy ran headlong over a cliff as the import of Reby's words sank in. I released her and stepped back. "No, not Jax, too."

"I don't want to throw accusations at anyone, Anthea." Reby shook her head. "For now, this is staying between us. And Luc because I know you tell him everything."

"But how do I warn Yanaba?" The panic sent my heart hammering so hard I feared it would pound its way through my ribcage.

"When we drop the wards," Reby answered with a surety I no longer felt. "You and Luc start screaming to get your distance speaker's attention. Because if your insane plan doesn't destroy the demons, the two ships we do have may not make it to Orrin before the demons do."

Chapter 39

Shi Hua grimaced as she watched the setting sun. Crown Princess Chiara had ordered the march at a five-four beat at dawn, the same as she had the last two days. The extra leagues gave them less than a day's march from Tandor.

Less than a day from the demon army.

Wildling and Thief scouts had been surging even farther afield than the main troops. So far, the Wildlings hadn't caught the scent of their foe, nor had those from Thief detected any signs of alien magic.

When the last sliver of orange disappeared, the hand signal to stop for the night came down the ranks. Shi Hua swallowed a groan of relief. Everyone moved with unnatural quietness, as if worried the demons surrounding Tandor might hear them.

No fires were laid, nor did she or any of the Light priests create balls so the soldiers, wardens, and clergy could see. No sense in alerting the demons to their presence through magic or the scent of burning wood.

After giving their horses long drinks at the manmade oasis on the edge of the desert, the troops picketed their mounts. The fighters quickly pitched tents and laid out their bedrolls some distance away from the water hole by the last reflection of the sun. They munched on a mix of dried venison, dried fruit and nuts while the various Temple and guild wagon masters watered their beasts.

The support personnel, their animals, and equipment would remain here. While some people would die in the battle because of the lack of immediate care, support staff could do no more on the rear lines than serve as extra food for the demons.

And Light help them, if the battle went against the queen's army, the support staff and a few Wildling scouts would have a head start up the mountain trail to the fortified town of Cliff Edge while the rest of the Wildlings would race back to Orrin, spreading word to the scattered farms along the National Road. All those people could die if the army lost. It also meant the fate of the citizens trapped inside Tandor's walls would be sealed.

Shi Hua stopped chewing the dried plum in her mouth. So that was the second reason Crown Princess Chiara wanted her with the rear guard. Bertrice would order Shi Hua to warn Yanaba and the rest in Orrin if the battle went against them. Right before Bertrice triggered Tandor's Death last resort spells. Why else would the princess put one far speaker at her side and the other as far from the immediate fighting as possible?

"Are you all right?" Jeremy asked quietly.

Shi Hua chewed the last bits of fruit and swallowed them. "I'm concerned about tomorrow's battle."

"You and every other person here."

She could hear his humor in the darkness and imagine the smile on his face.

"No, I mean keep an eye on the Reverend Father," she reiterated Bertrice and the crown princess's order.

"I will," Jeremy said solemnly. "You keep those demons off Bertrice, or all of this will be for nothing."

"I will," she said with equal graveness. She pulled the string tight on her bag of trail mix. "Would you mind if we sleep together?"

"Just sleep, right?" He almost sounded afraid she meant the other thing.

"Yes." She hesitated a moment before she blurted, "I need some human contact before we're neck deep in demon carcasses tomorrow."

"I'd like that, too," he admitted.

She helped him spread his blanket across the ground cloth of their tent before she shook out her blanket over them. His body warmth felt good beneath her cheek and arm.

"I've never had the luxury of thinking about the possibility of dying before," she murmured.

A sharp bark of laughter erupted from him.

"This isn't funny," she muttered.

"The closest I came was that demon in the tunnel you and the chief justice collapsed. Of course, I merely had to finish all the damage you had inflicted on it, but I agree—fighting for your life is better when it happens and you don't have time to think so much about the possibilities." He tightened his arm around her shoulders briefly. "I'm sorry you've had so many brushes with Death Herself. But you know you can share the burden once in a while. Like when you and the Temple seats ganged up on me when we didn't know we had demons in Balance's gaol."

"If we get High Brother Luc back, he can send you on all the demon-associated jobs," she teased.

"*When* we get the high brother back," Jeremy said sharply.

"I apologize." She tried not to let her smile filter through her voice. "I misspoke. When we get High Brother Luc back."

"That's better."

After a while, Jeremy's breathing deepened, and his heartbeat slowed beneath her ear. Despite her edginess over tomorrow, sleep took Shi Hua more quickly than she expected.

Scratching on the tent wall jerked Shi Hua from an odd dream. It was still dark, and she automatically reached for her knife. Jeremy silently moved beside her, reaching for his own weapons.

"Sister? High Brother?" Nicholas's voice penetrated the fog of sleep.

"We're awake, Chief Warden," Jeremy called.

"Yes, sir," came the muffled reply.

Shi Hua quickly dressed before she folded and rolled her bedding. It took a few moments for the entire army to strike their shelters and load their gear into the empty wagons. If things went well, the survivors could reclaim their belongings this evening.

She tried not to think about the alternatives while she checked the saddle on her horse.

"Shi Hua?"

She looked up at Jeremy.

"Don't take chances." He grasped her hand. "Keep yourself and Bertrice alive."

"Yes, sir."

He kissed her on her forehead. She swallowed hard. There was nothing else to say. They both knew their assignments and their duty. He pivoted and strode over to where Chief Warden Nicholas held the reins to both of their horses.

They mounted, and Hototo fell in on Jeremy's left.

A lump grew in her throat. If there was nothing more to say, why did so many words threaten to choke her?

Mateqai nudged his horse closer to her. "Shi Hua, we need to join the high sisters."

"Yes, of course." She grabbed the pommel of her saddle and hoisted herself astride. With a gentle tug of the reins, she guided her horse toward the rear guard.

Shi Hua was grateful Mateqai and Catherine ignored her wiping at the excess moisture impeding her vision.

Chapter 40

Reverend Father Nizhé'é' finally called a city meeting in front of Government House at First Evening. Light balls filled the plaza and tingled across my skin. The Reverend Father used magic to amplify his voice so everyone could hear him explain tomorrow's plan.

Surprisingly, none of the civilians protested evacuating the children in the ships.

"What about the rest of us?" the head of the Smiths Guild called out.

"Our wards will fail about tomorrow at mid-morning," the Reverend Father said. "About the same time as high tide. It'll be a fight to keep the demons contained long enough for the ships to leave the harbor."

A fearful murmur ran through the crowd.

We need more clergy from Child, I said to Luc.

Seeds in one hand and scat in the other . . .

He was right. All my wishing wouldn't change our situation, but for the love of Balance, I would never discount my fellows from Child ever again.

". . . each report to your assigned Temple after breaking your fast," the Reverend Father finished.

"What about Balance?" Another man I didn't recognize shouted. "Part of the roof has fallen in!"

"We can't use Balance for that very reason. The justices can't seal it from attack. The other eleven can still be warded individually."

"But Reverend Father, we were told there was a plan to evacuate everyone from Tandor!" At the familiar voice, I spotted Bathilda from the Weavers Guild near the front of the crowd.

He took a deep breath. "The only way any of us are getting out of Tandor is by killing all the demons. If we succeed, we are going to have to leave. The demons' agents have already tainted half of our water supply. The clean water will be their primary target tomorrow." Regret at having to lie filled his voice. "Therefore, regardless of how tomorrow's battle ends, we are going to have to leave Tandor."

Another rumble ran through the crowd, but this one was sadness, not fear. The loss of their homes would hit them even harder once they discovered what Nantan would do tomorrow. I prayed they weren't inside the city when that spell was launched, but the odds weren't looking to be in our favor.

The Reverend Father turned away from the front of the crowd. Nantan stepped forward and began reading off which neighborhoods would report to which Temple in the morning. Various guild leaders stepped forward offering their assistance.

Groups were sent in different directions. Some to collect water from the clean tanks, some to collect food we could carry through the desert, and others to distribute weapons.

Bumblebee stepped beside me and nodded. Good. He found the jar, and we had Light priests he trusted for my special task tomorrow morning.

Luc gently shook me awake. "It's time Anthea."

I flung back my covers, and a shiver ran through me that had nothing to do with the predawn air. Luc and I dressed, but before he opened the bedchamber door, I seized his cheeks and laid a very thorough kiss on his mouth.

"Stay alive," he whispered.

"The same goes for you."

I swallowed hard. The odds were too great that one of us would die today, but nothing we could do could change the arithmetic. Luc and I didn't even look at each other as I collected Bumblebee with his three compatriots and head for the Sea Wolf.

Chapter 41

Shi Hua grimaced behind the scarf covering her mouth and nose. Heat wasn't a problem yet, but the dust stirred by the thousand or so horses and troops raised a cloud everyone in Tandor would be able to see.

According to the weather oracles, there was nothing to be done. The winter storms were over, and there wasn't a lick of moisture for them to draw from until the army reached the aqueduct. By then, it was too late to suppress the dust.

Even in the brown-gray swirl of fine sand, the fighting garb of Love, Mother, and Child stood out. Red, blue, and green surrounded duller browns and black that covered Light and Death.

It was an even rarer occasion for the Love priestesses to show their faces and discard their bells. Their order selected for their physical beauty as well as their talent. But every woman here had the same fierce mien as Aunt Yin Li did during their unarmed combat practices so many years ago.

"Shi Hua, as soon as the princess engages the demons and the forward clergy bring down their interference spells, warn Anthea that loyal ships will be coming into port," High Sister Bertrice said from behind her own scarf.

"How do you know she's still alive?"

Bertrice laughed. "Neither the Assassins Guild nor any demon has killed either of you yet. I'd lay three gold crowns she's alive and still inside Tandor. I think Thalia would have mentioned it if Anthea had crossed."

The subject of Shi Hua's vision inside Balance when Justice Yanaba activated the last resort spell made Shi Hua squirm in her saddle. Especially since Anthea's dead predecessor said she would be seeing Bertrice soon. Her horse pranced away from Bertrice before Shi Hua regained control of both herself and her mount.

"What if the demons hear me?" she asked.

"Just don't tell Anthea what I'm doing in case they can hear you." Bertrice scarf fluttered with her sigh. "If High Brother Nantan or any of his order are still alive, they will sense what I'm doing and warn the other Temples."

"But there's no cover from the seawall to the lighthouses at the opening of the harbor. The demons will—"

"Ignore the citizens of Tandor once they realize what I'm up to," Bertrice finished.

Hitari, the only warden from Orrin's Temple of Death the high sister brought with her, laughed from behind her mask. "Don't worry, Sister. There will be plenty of demons for you to vanquish. The Chief Justice won't slaughter them all before we arrive."

"Frankly, I'd be perfectly happy if she did, Warden," Shi Hua said dryly.

The order to halt flowed back from the front of the column. It felt as if ants crawled under her skin. This was the last rest break before they engaged the demons. And with the sun fully above the mountains, their foes would know they were on the way.

Chapter 42

The four Light brothers and I entered the Sea Wolf. Bumblebee carried the jar of blood he'd retrieved from one of the cold-water tanks. We'd added a little Jing flash powder to the jar before we headed for the inn.

Only a handful of Conflict priests and wardens had arrived for the morning meal, all of them hand-picked by Reverend Father Nizhé'é' and Aduba. None of them had eaten the food before them, though they'd torn bread and stirred the leftover chicken and gravy in their bowls.

The woman who kept the inn smiled at me, but her eyes darted back and forth nervously. "A table for all of you, Chief Justice?"

"Yes, please." A trill of anxiety ran up my spine. No one was supposed to have warned her and the rest of the staff. Had she been told, or was she simply that intuitive?

As the men sat at the table she indicated, I grasped her hand. *What's wrong?*

Gray Sparrow wouldn't let my youngest daughter go to the ship this morning with the rest of the children. I think she's mad with fear. The innkeeper's eyes were wide with her own panic at the impending demon attack.

Go to your assigned Temple. We'll make sure your daughter is on one of the ships before they leave the harbor.

The innkeeper nodded and scurried through the main door.

I relayed what she said to the other priests. Bumblebee handed the jar to one of his fellows from Light before he picked one of the Conflict priests. The two men silently exited the front door to circle around to the kitchen entrance.

"Gray Sparrow?" I called out as I drew my sword. I didn't need to be in Conflict to know that battling the demon in the narrow confines of the kitchen was an idiotic idea. The rest of the priests drew their own weapons as well.

"I suggest you leave now, my darling Red Justice. I know how distressed your kind becomes at seeing its young dead." The voice coming from the kitchen didn't sound human. Had the demon dropped its pretense because it knew its game was done or because it believed it would win and could resume its human disguise somewhere else?

"You mean as distressed as you become when we smash or cook your eggs?" I mocked.

A gargled cry came from the kitchen. "I will kill the young if you do not leave!"

"No, I don't think you will," I answered as I infused my weapon with my magic. "You'll keep the girl alive to stall until the city wards come down in a few candlemarks."

It made the odd chittering that was a demon's laugh. "You will die either way, Red Justice—"

I nodded to the Light priest as the demon continued its speech. He set the jar on the floor planks and ignited the flash powder. He jumped back at the unusual burst of flame from the contents.

The demon's threats ended in a screech of pain. My skin itched with the flare of Light magic, and I leveled my sword at the door.

The demon slid through the gap between the door and the doorframe. I thrust my sword into it.

The demon exploded into black powder. Before it could reassemble itself, two of the Light priests launched their power at the demon dust. The remnants flared pink before they settled on the floor and turned red.

Bumblebee peered around the edge of the door. "It's over?"

I cocked my head as I stared at the cooling particles. "That was rather anti-climactic compared to my previous experiences." I looked up at the Light Priest as he, the Conflict priest, and the little girl entered the main dining room.

When Bumblebee spoke in Diné, he apparently repeated my comment from the laughter of the other priests.

"Excellent call on the blood, Bumblebee," I said.

His cheeks turned deep red at my compliment.

"Can you have one of your brethren escort the girl down to the warehouse where Hadar and Luc are assembling the children and sailors?" I added.

Bumblebee spoke in his own language to the Conflict priest who had accompanied him to the kitchen. The Conflict priest nodded.

I knelt before the little girl. "Can you go with this brother? He's going to take you to a safe place."

"I want my mommy!" She looked on the verge of tears.

"I know you do, but I've already sent your mother to a shelter," I murmured. "And I promised her that I and the brothers with me would make sure you were protected, too. Please don't make a liar of me." I smiled at her.

After a moment, she nodded and grasped the hand of the Conflict priest.

"Go—"

Before I could finish my sentence, the Temple alarm bells started clanging. I extended my senses. Alarm trilled through everyone inside of the walls of Tandor.

Reverend Father Nizhé'é"'s mind intruded in mine. *Anthea! Get your arse up to the Queen's Gate. We've got parties approaching from the north. Both land and sea.*

Yes, sir. On my way.

"That doesn't sound good," Bumblebee muttered. Of course, he'd eavesdropped.

My heart thumped from the real fear coursing through me. "Pray to the Twelve it's not another demon army. If the rest of Issura has been lost . . ."

"Go." Bumblebee waved toward the door. "I'll catch up."

I raced out of the inn and toward the northern gate as if the demon we'd just killed was chasing me.

Chapter 43

Shi Hua watched Bertrice's eyes above her scarf. Worry clouded the senior priestess's brow. Until she could reach the Tandor Temple of Death with her power, the army would march forward. But they were already closer than the ten leagues Bertrice had estimated.

A darker yellow splotch appeared over a rise as the National Road curved back toward the coast. It grew larger with every heartbeat.

The sensation of demon magic grated against Shi Hua's psyche, larger and stronger than her experiences in the Temple of Balance in Orrin and in Death's morgue. Anticipation and fear ran thick through the men and women of the queen's army as others with talent were also affected.

She turned to Bertrice again. "Anything?"

The older woman shook her head. "Not with whatever demon spells are sealing off the city."

"Not sealing it off," Imala said from the other side of Bertrice. "Those damned creatures are trying to bring down the city wards."

Shi Hua relayed the information to High Brother Talbert who rode with Crown Princess Chiara.

A long horn blast signaled their forces to halt. It was followed by three short blasts, the order to form up.

Shi Hua was the one spot of brown in an island of black. In turn, they were surrounded by a sea of women in red. More clergy and wardens in the blue of Mother and the green of Child flanked the sisters and wardens of Love on each side.

Before them, pennants denoting the various nobles rose. The flag with the crest of Orrin fluttered in the light breeze next to the Great Bear of Issura.

Another long horn blast, a short one, then finally a long one.

Almost as one, horses went from walk to trot, canter then galloping.

Instead of drawing her sword as the rest of the Death clergy, Shi Hua grabbed her recurved bow. She pulled the first arrow from her quiver and muttered the spell to charge the projectile.

Imala signaled for the rear guard to slow just as a resounding crash echoed across the desert. The front lines had found the demons.

Chapter 44

When I reached the top of the Queen's Gate tower, Aduba was already there, peering through his distance-view glass.

I ran to his side and looked down. The demons no longer huddled near the base of the outer wall. A league out from the city, a riot of color stood out against the orange-red earth and empty black of the demons. The clash of weapons and the shouts of humans resounded across the desert floor.

"The queen's army?" My heart refused to beat until Aduba lowered the steel and glass cylinder.

"Finally!" He turned and grinned down at me. "It's definitely the Great Bear on the front flag. But this is better."

He dragged me over to another section of parapet before he handed me his distance-view glass. I peered through the smaller opening of the tube.

Ships. More ships than the Duke of Orrin owned.

"Do you see any demons?" Aduba asked.

"N-no. Wh-what flags are they flying?" My voice shook. I prayed to Balance I wasn't seeing things.

"Issura. The Sea Peoples. Jing. Pagonia."

My eyes burned as Aduba recited his list. I lowered the tube.

He latched onto my arm once again and urged me to the south side of the tower. "Look there." He pointed to a gap in the sea cliffs past the city.

Once again, I raised the tube to my right eye and squinted. More ships. "I don't see any demons from this angle."

Aduba relayed my insight to the Reverend Father.

My arms dropped, and I faced Aduba. "Who . . . ?"

"So far we've counted the colors of Cant, the Mecas, Iberia, and the Wari Empire in that southern fleet."

Iberia? Was it the *Unbridled*? Had Reverend Father Biming succeeded in his mission and brought additional help? I was afraid to hope. Ambassador Quan would be crushed if anything happened to his close friend.

"If we can get the civilians out of the city through the eastern tunnel—" I started.

"They'll be behind our lines," Aduba finished. "But the demons will swarm the fleets if they try to enter the harbor."

The demons are swarming the Issuran army, the Reverend Father said silently. *Aduba, we need their attention back on us. Anthea, you and Spotted Fawn need to clear those tunnels.*

I ran for the ladder as Aduba began bellowing orders. When I reached the bottom, Bumblebee stared up at the tower and back at me.

"The girl is with the children at the warehouse," he reported.

"Good. You and I are sticking with the plan to clear the tunnels." I ran for Balance, Bumblebee at my heels.

Wardens and clergy were layered at each of the corridors within the Temple as we raced for Elizabeth's former bedchambers. Spotted Fawn, Bidzii, and their warden waited in front of the sealed opening to the tunnels.

"About time you got here, Anthea," the justice said through her clerk.

"Everyone wants a piece of me this morning," I quipped as I knelt beside her.

In the back of my mind, I could hear the Reverend Father's count until the city wards would be dropped. The orders in the other nations' languages were easier to ignore. In front of us, demon magic scratched at the token Balance seal Elizabeth and I had erected.

"Ready?" Spotted Fawn said.

"Ready," I affirmed.

Together, we unsealed the opening. The stone rolled back as if we were rolling a bolt of cloth.

But we weren't greeted by the pale lavender light of invisible creatures that lived underground or even the dark blue-green of the raw bedrock. The empty blackness of demons filled my sight.

Twelve help us. There wasn't just a small guard as we hoped. The tunnel was literally full of demons.

Chapter 45

Shi Hua's muscles twitched with the need to take action. The training exercises back home in Jing were nothing like this roar of sound. And in those, she had been in the front line, not back here.

Movement caught her eye to her left. A demon had gotten past the Vintner priests. The gray-scaled creature skipped along the heads of civilian soldiers, its long claws penetrating skulls, even those who wore the Old Continent-style steel helms.

Shi Hua took careful aim. The demon still shrieked though her arrow penetrated what should have been its throat. It tumbled to the sand. The Child Priestesses summoned the tiny scavengers of the earth, and they made short work of the demon.

"Good shot," Bertrice said above the din.

Before Shi Hua could answer, a low rumble came from the city. Tandor's wards faded. The demon spells collapsed since they had nothing to resist them. The massive buzz in her head disappeared.

Shi Hua!

The familiar voice brought tears to her eyes. *Reverend Father Biming!*

Tell the survivors in Tandor to stay clear of the north and south sides of the city. We're going to keep the demons busy while the longboats retrieve the civilians.

The rumble grew louder, and she realized the massive gates were opening.

Wait a moment, sir. The Diné Reverend Father of Conflict is doing something. She slung her bow over her shoulder. Balancing on the rumps of her horse and Bertrice's, she stood straight to see what was happening.

Humans in red, brown, black, and gray on top of horses poured through the opening. Whoops and shouts floated over the troop lines. They weren't even in any formation.

A shout of joy erupted from High Sister Imala. She was also straddling the rump of her horse and another sister of Love's mount.

"Who?"

"The Comanche, one of the Plains Nations." Imala's grin was fierce. "Doing what they do best. Their cavalry is coming to our rescue."

Chapter 46

My heart threatened to choke me. The tunnel didn't contain a few demons standing around waiting for something to happen. They were literally packed on top of each other. The demons surged toward the access into Balance.

A light ball whizzed past my cheek and ignited the bottom-most demon. White light flared, blinding me, as the damn thing burned. Comforting warmth flowed over my skin, but it wasn't my magic. The demons slammed into Spotted Fawn's ward. They shrieked their outrage.

"Light help us," Bumblebee murmured. "How do we get the passage shut?"

"You don't," Bidzii said. He placed his hands on his justice's shoulders. "Take my energy, m'lady."

It was the first time he'd spoken as himself in my presence. The dichotomy shook me out of my shock. Spotted Fawn couldn't hold the opening for long. Like the builders of an arch, wards relied on three dimensions to support each other.

I slapped my hands on the stone, pouring my will into the closing spell. The awful sharpness of demon magic penetrated Spotted Fawn's ward. Slowly, oh, so slowly, the sandstone folded back into place, magic keeping the damn creatures from slipping through the cracks in the blocks.

Both my sister justice and I sagged, but our relief was short-lived. The demons pounded on the stone itself and the residual magic of the Temple. Neither would resist them for long.

"We'll guard this entrance," Spotted Fawn said through Bidzii. "Once you, Bumblebee and the other wardens leave, I'll ward the room. I can hold that spell long enough for you and the Reverend Father to come up with a new plan."

"You can't—" I began.

"I can, and I will." Spotted Fawn snapped. "I know my duty. Do you know yours, Justice?"

She was right. As much as the situation galled me, she was right.

"The fine line between wisdom and madness," I said.

She smiled, and Bidzii said for her, "We may not be of Vintner, but it does apply."

Bumblebee relayed the order to leave Balance. I couldn't meet the grim looks of the other clergy and wardens. We'd counted too much on being able to clear the tunnels.

Down on the street, civilians crowded around the other Temples, waiting for their orders of what to do next.

Anthea!

I stumbled on the steps of Balance at the familiar presence. If Bumblebee hadn't caught me, I would have landed on my face in the street.

Shi Hua? Where are you?

With the queen's army on the north side of the city.

What—

Shut up and listen! Issura and Cant have ships coming in to rescue the civilians.

The city wards don't extend to the lighthouses—

We know. Shi Hua's impatience filtered through the link. *The ships will help keep them off your backs, but you need to pick off the stragglers.*

Reverend Father Nizhé'é' needs those damn demons inside the city.

A glimmer of resignation came from Shi Hua. *Bertrice is here with us.*

My stomach threatened to rebel, though I hadn't broken my fast. There was only one reason for our own high sister of Death to be with the queen's army.

We have something else in mind. With the city wards down, I was afraid the demons might actually be able to hear us. *Warn Yanaba. Now! Jax and the Orrin Wildlings may be compromised.*

With Bumblebee's arms around my waist, he heard our discussion and relayed everything to the Reverend Father.

Jax? Shi Hua's shock was quickly followed by fury.

Is one of the ships the Unbridled? I needed to know before I faced Ambassador Quan again.

If I ever faced him again.

Yes, Reverend Father Biming is with the Cantish fleet.

Relief at that small grace flooded me.

The buzz of the wards snapped back in place. *Talk to you on the other side, Sister.*

Bumblebee realized he still held me and abruptly let go before he stared at me and asked, "Now what?"

"We need a new conference with the Reverend Father." We pushed past confused and frightened people as we made our way to the Temple of Conflict.

Chapter 47

The giant gates had closed, and Tandor's city wards had been re-established, but they felt far weaker than before. The Comanche priests and wardens continued their hit-and-run tactics against the demons while the queen's forces pressed their advantage with the distractions.

Shi Hua lowered herself back to her saddle and turned to Bertrice. "Can you reach the Temple of Death?"

The older priestess nodded and closed her eyes. Her forehead wrinkled between her brows before her eyes popped open. "Something's been changed."

"What?" High Sister Imala demanded. She dropped back to her saddle as well.

"The last resort spells have been altered." Bertrice shook her head. "They're linked with spells from Balance and all the other temples on top of the city walls."

"Anthea said they had a plan, but they needed the demons inside the city," Shi Hua offered.

"Oh, Sweet Death!" Bertrice swore. "They're planning to blow the last resort spells, but use Balance magic to keep the reaction within the city and harbor."

"Why would—" Imala stopped herself. "Of course. They planned to evacuate the civilians through the city tunnel system."

A shrill scream came from a horse to Shi Hua's left. The animal had dropped its rear end, throwing off the Comanche Conflict sister from its back.

No, the poor animal's rear legs were simply gone.

To her horror, gray tentacles erupted from the sand. They wrapped themselves around the screaming horse and priestess and dragged them down into the earth.

Only a few bloody spots of sand remained.

Chapter 48

We found Reverend Father Nizhé'é' near the altar inside the Conflict sanctuary, apparently talking to himself since no one else stood near him.

He cursed as we approached and said something in Comanche before he switched to the Peaceful Sea trade tongue. "Send the group at Father down to the warehouse."

The Reverend Father caught sight of us and waved us over to him. As we approached, he said something in Diné.

He grinned at me when he finished. "Hadar and Luc got our ships out of the harbor and well out of the experienced sailors' way. Your Light distance speaker with the fleet, Brother Elroy, confirmed it."

"Thank the Twelve!" Elizabeth said fervently. Tyra guided her to us, followed by Reby and Sisquoc.

"Unfortunately, not without some problems." The Reverend Father's mien turned grim. "We lost one civilian."

"But the ships were seaworthy with only the repairs we knew about?" I couldn't believe we'd been that lucky.

"Seaworthy enough to reach the Issuran fleet. Which brings us to our next problem."

"We can't go out the tunnel system," I said.

"From Aduba's report, the damn creatures are using the eastern tunnel to attack the queen's army from below the ground," the Reverend Father said.

"If we lose the queen's army . . ." Reby whispered.

"But we need time to get the civilians out before we open the gates," Bumblebee protested.

"What if we sped up time in the harbor?" Elizabeth said.

Everyone stared at the justice. We already knew she had literally lost part of her mind.

"Are you insane?" I shouted. "My junior nearly killed herself pulling a similar stunt. Not to mention, you and I would each have to get to one of the lighthouses to expand the spell."

"We're planning to go to the lighthouses anyway to set the last spells for Death. If we work together, and some of the other clergy feed the remaining power from their Temples into the spell, it's possible." Elizabeth's face lit with an odd, nearly maniacal, glee. "We can use the sea chain to extend our third dimension like Aduba originally suggested."

"But the chain is lying on the sea bed." The Reverend Father frowned.

"And such a spell would prematurely age the chain, plus anyone on those ships that enter the harbor," I protested. "Not to mention, we'd have to bring the wards back down."

"From my understanding of Balance magic, you won't be able to limit the effect to the harbor." The Reverend Father's face twisted, as if Elizabeth had just given him a piece he hadn't realized he needed to solve a puzzle.

She sagged. "No, you're right. The spell would affect everyone within Tandor's walls as well."

"That's exactly what I was hoping to hear." His expression turned even more gleefully maniacal as Elizabeth's had been a few moments before.

"It would speed up everyone, not just the ships . . ." Balance, help me! I couldn't have been more dense. "Those fighting the delaying action would be as fast or faster than the demons."

"Until the demons cross the barrier," the Reverend Father said. "But it gives us a fighting chance to get the civilians out. Go!"

Sisquoc shed his clothes and shifted to his panther form. Reby helped Elizabeth onto the Wildling's back. Tyra came with me and Bumblebee as we ran for the northern lighthouse.

Part of me wondered how much longer I could outrun Death Herself.

Chapter 49

"Demons are in the tunnel!" Shi Hua shouted. In the fighting, the army had shift to the east from the National Road. Their left flank was now overtop foes who could ooze up through the rock and sand.

More tentacles thrust up through the earth. The damn things seemed to know exactly where their prey stood. Horses shied and screamed. Humans shouted and cursed. For every tentacle that popped up and was sliced off, two more seemed to take its place.

And the demons on the surface were working hard to force the bulk of the army over the tunnel.

Shi Hua turned to Imala. The Love priestess's skin had a greenish cast as she watched the slaughter.

"You're a mover, High Sister! Pull the roof down on those damned things!" She knew shouting orders at her superiors was the way to a good lashing, but Imala seemed frozen in place.

"But the civilians!" she cried. "They'll be trapped down there!"

"They can't get out that way!" Shi Hua shouted over the cacophony. "Not with the demons down there!"

Imala nodded. "Form up! The rest of you, get back!" Another priestess and a handful of Love wardens surrounded the high sister and pushed toward the tentacles.

Shi Hua swung her horse around to Bertrice's right side and nocked another arrow. Sure enough, a demon charged literally through one of the priestesses from Mother. The woman fell out of her saddle. Her body broke into several clean pieces when it hit the ground, the blood frozen solid.

A warden tried to stab it to no effect. Shi Hua whispered her spell and released the arrow. With a screech, the demon hit the packed dirt and sand. The sisters of Love made quick work of it.

A strange quiver flow beneath them, and Shi Hua's mount pranced to his left, despite his Temple training. The sensation reminded her too much of how seasick she became every time she sailed.

Bertrice and the heads of the Child and Mother factions shouted for everyone to move right. The motion left Imala and her little group exposed, but Comanche and Issuran riders hacked at the tentacles to keep them from the Love contingent.

The shaking beneath their feet grew stronger. Imala's hands were raised. The forward sections of the army surged back toward the National Road. Red swirls of magic penetrated the earth. As one, the Comanche and Issuran riders raced from the tentacles.

With a roar, the ground shattered and fell into the giant trench Imala caused.

Chapter 50

I ran across the city, Bumblebee and Tyra on my heels. The ground shivered beneath my feet. It almost felt like a ground tremor, but it didn't last long enough. So, I kept racing for the north side of the harbor. A moment later, the wards fluttered and fell.

People lined the streets when we reached the warehouse district. Men rowed the long boats from the harbor to the docks. Thank the Twelve, the civilians were boarding the long boats in an orderly manner, though the crowd stared at us as we ran past.

We reached the narrow walkway from the sea wall to the prominence. Another Diné Conflict priest and two of his wardens waited with one of our wardens. I slowed long enough to say to the Tandor Death warden guarding the walkway, "Cut the ropes as soon as we're across, and get back to Nantan."

The six of us pounded across the planks. A splash behind us said the Tandor warden had followed my orders.

We were halfway to the lighthouse when the thunderous noise of huge amounts of Jing flash powder igniting filled the air. Giant red and pink balls arced over us. A duller thunder as they hit on the north side of the city.

More of the balls, white and charged with magic from the raised hairs all over my body, flew along the same trajectory. These were eerie since they made no noise, but the ground beneath my boots shuddered when they landed.

The projectiles stopped on the north side, though the ships continued to launch them toward the south side of Tandor. Over the crash of sea waves and the pounding of my heart came a roar.

It was a sound of the size of which had been unheard for a century. I glanced over my shoulder to confirm my gut. Beneath the hot yellow haze of dust, de-mon black mixed with the yellows and oranges of humans and animals.

And Shi Hua and Bertrice were in the middle of that maelstrom.

Chapter 51

The tentacles disappeared in the cloud of dust from this section of the east tunnel's collapse.

Imala's hands dropped, and she started to slip from her saddle. One of her wardens managed to catch her before she hit the ground.

Shi Hua turned her attention back to the trench caused by the collapsed tunnel. The clergy of Child and their wardens, as well as the Comanche riders, fell upon anything still moving in the debris. Those from Mother shifted to cover the left side of the rear guard.

The rest of the demons had retreated toward the city gate. She knew in her gut it would be only a momentary reprieve.

Lord General White Eagle called out orders she couldn't hear. A moment later, Duke Marco's flag and the colors of Father split from the main body and headed west.

"They'll collapsed the other tunnel," Bertrice murmured.

As Duke Marco led his contingent toward the sea cliffs, a huge fiery object trailing smoke flew toward the main army. It landed with a deafening boom halfway between the humans and the demons. The ground shuddered beneath Shi Hua's mount.

A few pats on his neck reassured him, but the civilian forces had trouble controlling their panicked horses. The Wildlings paced through the ranks and reassured the animals. Between the clergy and the behavior of the Temple mounts, the horses calmed in time for the next fireball.

The crown princess aimed her horse through the ranks. "Shi Hua, tell Elroy to stop firing on the north side. They're landing too close to us!"

Shi Hua closed her eyes and relayed the message, but not before the fleet launched two balls composed of Light magic in their direction. "Everyone shield your eyes!" she screamed with voice and mind.

These made no sound when they landed, but the earth still shook.

When Shi Hua opened her eyes, Crown Princess Chiara gave her a pointed look.

"They've stopped," Shi Hua said sheepishly.

"Your Highness," Bertrice called and edged her horse closer to the princess. "Our allies have set up a trap within Tandor. We need to drive the demons into the city."

"Are they insane?" Chiara cocked her head.

"No, Your Highness, they've rigged the last resort spells so they won't affect the land outside of the walls."

"And it'll work?" Chiara's expression was skeptical at best.

"Chief Justice Anthea knows her dimensional spells better than Justice Yanaba," Shi Hua blurted. "This will work."

"It had better." The princess's expression was somewhere between irritated and amused. "I'm gambling my army on your word." She wheeled her horse around and headed back to the vanguard.

Three short horn blasts followed. The lines formed again, adjusting for those who had been lost. Lord General White Eagle shouted the order, and the army marched forward.

The clash of arms was even louder the second time. Shi Hua just hoped she lived long enough to appreciate her hearing loss.

Chapter 52

The demons figured out we were up to something. Five of them bounded over jagged stones on the north prominence. And unlike us, they had climbed a sheer rock face first to reach the stones that provided some cover for the path to the lighthouse. The effort didn't slow the damned beasts one iota.

The Conflict personnel whirled to face the demons. The rest of us kept running. I tried very hard to block the sounds behind us. Those people were going to die defending us.

Defending me.

I had a choice to turn around and fight with them. Or set the spells that would save thousands of civilians. Hatred of my position and rank filled me in a way it hadn't for nearly a decade.

A stitch in my side made it hard to breathe when Bumblebee and I entered the stone lighthouse. Tyra drew her sword and watched the pathway.

Inside, jars lined the right wall. A ladder at the far end went up to the floor above us, which held the main lamp and reflector. To our left was something that looked like a spool a giant would use for her thread.

The brother and I knelt next to the gigantic winch, and I laid my hand on the shiny end of the chain fused to the metal on which it would spool. Like Luc suspected, not a spec of rust marred the steel's blue finish, and the metal tingled beneath my hand from the spells protecting it. The winch itself was spelled to make the turning of it easy for one person

I pulled the talisman Nantan had given me last night out of my bodice. The icon of Death made of onyx vibrated in my palm with his power. Bumblebee laid his hand on top of my left hand holding the icon. As I set the spell to speed time in Tandor and its harbor, and the one to contain Death's last resort spells,

Bumblebee fed magic from the Temple buildings through me and into the chain. My magic and Elizabeth's met in the center of the harbor entrance and twined around each other and the time spell snapped to life.

The cries of the gulls outside ceased. The crash of the waves against the cliff a hundred feet below us went silent. But the rumble of people clambering into the long boats continued.

"It worked." Bumblebee's voice was full of wonder, and he released my hand.

"For now," I answered. "We need to keep any demons from entering the lighthouse."

We were now committed to our mad plan. There wasn't enough residual power within the Temple buildings to raise the wards again.

Chapter 53

"What in Light's many names?" Shi Hua stared up at the walls of Tandor. The city wards were gone once again, but men and women darted to and fro along the parapet. Much faster than humans should be able to move. Their motions remind her of dragonflies darting around the farm pond on a lazy summer afternoon.

The demons realized something was happening in the city as well. As one they tore away from the queen's army and charged the northern gates. Between the loss of the wards and the demons' ability to change their mass, the beasts acted as one giant battering ram. They hit the massive iron doors with a re-sounding *boom*.

The Comanche clergy and wardens raced after their foes, picking off those on the fringes. Meanwhile, the defenders rained down magic enhanced arrows and crossbow bolts.

The demons ignored their casualties. They backed up as a group and ran toward the Queen's Gate again.

Another *boom* was accompanied by a screech of metal.

The horn sounded again. The standard of the Duke of Standora broke away from the main army. The colors of Light and Conflict accompanied the units heading for the demons.

Shi Hua's knees dug into her horse's ribs at the signal and movement, but Bertrice grabbed the loose reins of Shi Hua's steed.

"Your assignment is with me, Sister." There was no bite in the High Sister's reprimand, but heat flooded Shi Hua's face.

"I beg forgiveness."

I fear for Jeremy's safety as well, Bertrice said silently. She closed her eyes. "Nantan's in Death's sanctuary. If all goes according to the justices' plan—"

"Justices?" Shi Hua cocked her head.

Bertrice laughed. "I've met Chief Justice Elizabeth a few times. She's just as crazy as Anthea." She shook her head. "I have no doubt the justice with the Diné army is equally as mad as those two."

Shi Hua chuckled, but a shout behind them interrupted her short-lived humor. She guided her horse in a tight circle.

In time for a demon to land on top of her.

Chapter 54

Bumblebee and I exited the lighthouse. Below us on the path, the Conflict priest was putting up a valiant struggle against three foes. The bodies of his two wardens lay on the sandstone walk along with two of the demons.

One of the demons leapt up on the stones that kept anyone from accidentally falling from the path and into the harbor. The Conflict priest whirled and knocked the beast into the water below.

However, his action gave the other two demons the opening they needed.

Tyra let out a gasp as they ripped the Diné man apart.

I drew my sword as did the other two. The last two demons raced up the path. For a moment, I wished we hadn't sped up time in the city and harbor. However, we couldn't let them reach the spells we set inside the lighthouse.

There was no more time to think. I slashed at the oncoming demon's head as Tyra swung at its waist. Both of our swords passed through as we expected. I flooded my steel with my power. Tyra ducked beneath its claws, and I brought my sword down on its limb.

The demon shrieked in pain. I didn't move fast enough, and its backhanded blow knocked me into the lighthouse wall.

Tyra jumped between me and the demon. I must have injured it enough that it couldn't change its mass. She scored its torso twice. Black demon blood spattered along the stones of the paths. The rocks hissed before they cracked and broke with sharp reports.

The demon fell on its back. I shouted a warning, but Tyra seized the opportunity.

Or tried to.

The demon's rear limbs lengthened and sharpened with a speed that defied belief. It impaled my warden.

Rage burned in me as it yanked its limbs free and Tyra collapsed. It chittered despite the injuries we'd inflicted on it.

I slowed time in a narrow space around the demon and launched a running kick at its midsection. The instant I made contact, I broke the spell. The demon flew backward until it passed over the land side of the path. It seemed to freeze in mid-air, its fall taking forever from the speed of my perspective.

I whirled to find Bumblebee hard-pressed by the last demon. Infusing my sword with a bit of power, I thrust the point into the demon's back. Despite his injuries, Bumblebee launched one last light ball in the blasted creature's face.

It screamed as it burned. I yanked my sword out of its body and backed away from the heat and squinted at the blinding white light.

"Bumblebee . . ." I pointed at the demon still floating in midair with my free hand. He launched two Light balls just below the demon's trajectory.

I sheathed my sword and stumbled over to Tyra. She needed a healer. I glanced at the harbor below us. The healers were probably evacuated already. Only a few hundred people remained on the docks. The Sea Peoples' ships moored at the larger piers. Their sailors could handle the unusual behavior of the wind and tide caused by our time change.

Kneeling beside my warden, I gently rolled her over. Pink blood spurted from her wounds, but it was slowing because her heart had emptied it all from her body. Her eyes stared sightlessly at the sky. All I could do was hold her as she passed to Death's realm.

"Lady Justice . . ." Bumblebee sat heavily on the ground next to me. Only then, did I realize how badly he was injured. He brushed blood from the cut on his forehead that had run into his eyes. "What now?"

The last of the long boats pushed away from the docks. Priests and wardens retreated from the incoming demons toward the remaining outriggers. Most of the blasted creatures were in the city. A small number still harassed the queen's army beyond the northern gate.

I turned to Bumblebee. "Can you make it down to the harbor?"

He shook his head. His hair had come loose and spilled down his back. He pressed the slash in his left side with that same hand.

"Not before the demons reach it." It was a statement. Even if I left Tyra and the spells to help him, we couldn't get down the path in time.

Spotted Fawn?

Yes, Anthea.

Where—?

Still inside Balance. Even her and Bidzii's combined mental voices sounded exhausted. *As I told the Reverend Father, our lives are not worth everyone else's. It has been a pleasure knowing you, Anthea—*

Her and her clerk's presence abruptly disappeared from my mind.

I laid Tyra's body on the ground and stumbled to my feet. The ultimate blackness formed a slash through the middle of Tandor. The demon's swarmed all over the Temples, ripping apart the symbols of their hated enemies.

A familiar scream from the other lighthouse distracted me. I turned in time to see Sisquoc, in panther form, run and launch himself from the cliff edge, Elizabeth clinging to his neck and ribs for dear life.

Reby turned and saluted me before she performed the same stunt. Her shout actually sounded gleeful as she disappeared from my sight.

I turned to Bumblebee. "Care to try the same stunt? It could be fun."

"Or we will be dashed upon the rocks below." Bumblebee shrugged on his right side. "But I'm willing to take the chance if it means the possibility of surviving."

A disconcerting thought occurred. "Do you know how to swim?"

"No, but today's a good day to learn, don't you think?" He grinned at me.

The low-level link I'd been maintaining with Nantan flared to life.

Demons are in Death—

I fell to my knees and choked on blood. No, not my blood. Nantan's.

If he were gone, how in the Twelve did we set off the last resort spells?

It wasn't fair. None of this was fair.

I screamed in rage, cursing Balance with every filthy word I know. "How could you abandon us now!"

White light flared, so bright I had to bury my face in my elbow. "I didn't," a soft voice said.

Chapter 55

Shi Hua rolled as she fell from her saddle. Her hands met something solid and colder than any ice she'd ever touched. She landed hard, driving the air from her lungs. Gathering the few wits that hadn't been knocked out of her, she launched light balls point blank. The demon screamed and threw her off it.

She landed on her side as Bertrice drove her sword and power into the creature. It crumpled into dust.

Shi Hua clambered to her feet. "Thank you—"

Bertrice's face contorted, and she toppled from her saddle. All Shi Hua could do was cushion the other woman's fall.

"Gone. They're all gone," Bertrice said.

"Who?"

"Nantan. Everyone defending Death. They're gone."

High Sister Imala pushed through her surrounding sisters. The crown princess was right behind her.

"Can you activate the last resort spells from here?" Chiara demanded.

Bertrice seemed to gather herself and nodded. "Give me some space."

Someone tickled the back of Shi Hua's mind. *Everyone who we could get out of Tandor is out.*

She repeated Elroy's words to the others.

Chiara nodded in acknowledgement. Imala barked at her people to give Bertrice some room.

Shi Hua shivered despite the bright afternoon sun. If the justices' crazy stunt didn't work, Death would be escorting them all to Light sooner than they thought.

Magic crackled around Bertrice. Around them, demons shrieked and tried to fight their way to her. Exactly as the high sister of Death said they would.

Shi Hua pulled an arrow from her quiver, whispered a spell, and nocked the projectile. Imala grabbed her crossbow from another of her sisters and stood against Shi Hua's back. The rest of the army flowed into an additional protective circle around the Death Priestess.

Kneeling beside Shi Hua, Bertrice chanted.

The demons tried a flying wedge, their desperation almost as palpable as the power that prickled Shi Hua's skin. She sought target after target. Demon bodies burned in front of her.

Someone gently pressed her hand down.

The crown princess smiled. "You did your duty, Sister. Stand down."

An awful sensation came from behind her, but it was nothing like demon magic. Shi Hua looked over her shoulder. Silence reigned inside the massive walls. A gray dust blew eastward from the city.

Tandor was gone.

"You did it, Bertrice!" She looked down.

Orrin's high sister of Death lay on her side, her blank eyes staring at nothing. Dead, as her vision of Balance foretold.

Shi Hua fell to her knees, and tears rolled down her face.

Chapter 56

Beside me, Bumblebee stood, frozen in place.

"What did you do to him?" I screamed.

"Nothing," the blinding white figure said. "I sliced you out of your timeline so we may speak."

"Who are you?"

"Demanding little thing, aren't you?" Humor laced her voice, totally inappropriate for what was about to happen to Tandor. To Issura. To the world.

"Answer my question!" Tears streamed down my face from the pain of the light.

"Stop lying to yourself, Anthea. You care about these people. This place. Or you wouldn't be here."

"What does that have to do with anything?"

"Sometimes, we do give a direct answer to a plea or a question. You want to save your brother's life, don't you?"

My brother? Well, of course. Bumblebee was a fellow human, and terribly young, and he didn't deserve dying in this stupid war.

I cleared my throat. "Yes, I do. But why won't you tell me anything?"

"I'm here as you requested, and I'm giving you a direct answer. Take your brother's hand and jump!"

"Tyra's dead! That's not an answer! It's an order!" I screamed.

"Jump!" The woman in white's voice thundered through my mind. I whirled and did as she commanded.

As we hurtled toward the crashing waves below, I realized I was going to drown defending a city from attack.

Just as my grandmother Thalia had.

Chapter 57

I was dimly aware when hands plucked me from the sea. My last memory was fighting to keep both mine and Bumblebee's heads above the waves as we struggled to keep from being dashed against the rocks.

Someone rolled me onto my side and pounded on my back. I coughed once before a gout of sea water sprayed from my mouth. My stomach continued to heave until it clenched and ached. More coughing tore at the fiery pain my throat had become.

Additional hands helped me sit up though I continued to gag and choke. Someone pushed a cup into my hands.

"Take a small sip, rinse your mouth, and spit it out."

I did as ordered though part of me wanted to drain the cup of clean, fresh water. We repeated the process until my hacking eased.

"Still with us, Chief Justice?"

I blinked at the familiar voice. "Reverend Father Biming?"

His smile was bright as he crouched next to me. "Welcome back aboard the *Unbridled*, m'lady."

"Bumblebee, the Diné Light priest who was with me?" I looked around the deck.

"I made it," he called and waved. Reby, who was just as wet, was attempting to dry him off in order to deal with his wounds.

"I still have your clothing in my cabin if you wish to change." Biming stood and helped me to my feet.

"And you might want to dry out your sword and knives before they rust."

My heart skipped a beat. I turned to find Luc. "Aren't you supposed to be on another ship?"

He laughed. "The Reverend Father pointed out my sailing skills are only marginally better than Bumblebee's swimming skills."

"I'm definitely a desert boy," Bumblebee added.

"Your first lesson should not have been a justice dragging you off a hundred-foot cliff into rough surf," Reby snapped.

I didn't have the energy for a rejoinder.

Reverend Father Biming helped me to his cabin. Luc trailed along behind us. Once inside, Biming said, "I've let Shi Hua know you two are all right."

My heart seized again, but it was Luc who said, "What about Jeremy?"

"She hasn't found your second yet, but she did not feel him die. She's still—"

"Bertrice?" I said softly.

Biming shook his head. "She couldn't withstand the overload when she activated the Death spells."

I closed my burning eyes. Once again, Bertrice saved my life at a terrible price. I should have stayed on that damn cliff.

"No, you shouldn't have," Luc said fiercely. "Nantan already knew he'd die in that damned city. And Bertrice did the right thing when he fell."

"Did we get all the civilians out?"

He nodded. "Everyone except a couple of dozen helping to hold the Queen's Gate."

"I'll see about arranging something to eat for you," Biming murmured.

"Wait!"

He paused at the door and looked back at me. "We didn't reach Rambla in time." Guilt filled his voice. "So we raced to Tiwan. Luckily, since none of my crew were Issuran, the king of Cant took us seriously." He shrugged. "The Temple alarms ringing when the demons took over Rambla helped convince him, too."

Rambla had been the first large city past the Cantish border. It was approximately the size of Tandor. So, now we had a wasteland between Orrin and Tiwan.

Holy writ didn't feel comforting at the moment, so I merely inclined my head.

Once he left, I stripped off my soaked clothing. Luc wrapped me in a spare blanket and held me while I wept for my dead friends.

Chapter 58

Shi Hua marginally paid attention to the surrounding troops as she helped the clergy of Death prepare for the funerals. They couldn't risk taking any of the bodies back to Orrin. Not with all the demon activity. Everyone from Orrin already knew what happened when a demon egg hatched in a human body while inside a morgue.

Most of the queen's army still standing were surprised to find themselves alive. Even those without talent could see the spectacular energy discharge when the Balance spells fought to keep the destruction contained within the city walls.

Thief and Wildling scouts tracked down the few demons who never made it into Tandor before Bertrice set off the last resort spells. Anyone with moving talent brought down the remaining sections of the city's tunnel system. As Crown Princess Chiara said, there was no sense inviting curiosity seekers to their deaths by leaving them open.

And this way, she made sure no demons were lingering beneath their feet.

Lord General White Eagle had Shi Hua give the all-clear to the support wagons at the oasis. They arrived close to sundown. All of the wagons carried scrub wood in whatever space they had. Half the support staff began preparing a meal while the rest joined in building the funeral pyres.

As Shi Hua tied a warden's body wrapped in his cloak, a hand gripped her shoulder. She looked up to find Jeremy. His eyes were haunted. Somber. This day had changed them both.

She reached up and squeezed his hand.

He knelt at the foot of the corpse she worked on, and he helped bind the rest of it. Neither of them said anything more the rest of the night as they worked, and she was grateful for the comfortable silence.

Chapter 59

A week later, I sat with Little Bear, Gina, Donella, and Sivan in the Balance main receiving room. There was a great deal of paperwork and dispatches to go through from the nearly three weeks I was gone. And of course, nothing got done over the Spring Rituals.

There had been an edge to people's moods over the holiday. Maybe it was a good thing Crown Princess Chiara had ordered the bulk of the army back to Standora, instead of spending the holidays in Orrin. Our gaol, Light's, and the magistrate's were unusually full for this time of year.

Balance bless her, Yanaba had tried to keep up with Temple matters while I was gone, but between the injuries she suffered in the demon attacks here and the start of her morning sickness, there was no way she could.

I paced while I recited my report for Donella to send to the Reverend Mother of Balance. "... and Reverend Father Nizhé'é' of the Temple of Conflict, Diné Nation, has tendered an offer—"

"Wait. What did you call him?" Gina looked askance at me.

"Reverend Father Nizhé'é'." I frowned "He's the head of the Diné Temple of Conflict."

My warden still looked confused. "Exactly how did he introduce himself to you?"

Even with the years of Balance training, it took me a moment to recall his exact words after everything that had happened in Tandor. "'I am Nizhé'é', Reverend Father of Conflict, Diné Nation. We're here to rescue you," I recited.

Gina snorted and slapped a hand over her mouth. Her effort didn't hide the giggles coming from behind her palm. She gave up and whooped until tears ran down her cheeks.

I looked at Little Bear, but he seemed as perplexed at Gina's source of mirth as I was.

She finally calmed down a bit, though an occasional chuckle escaped her lips. She swiped at her eyes with the hem of her cloak.

"What is so funny about the Reverend Father's public name?" I demanded.

"It's not a public name, Lady Justice," Gina admitted. "It's a word in Diné, but a phrase in ours. It means 'your father'. Essentially, he said, "I am your father."

"No," I drawled. "You're making that up."

Gina sighed, all humor leaving her. "I'm not playing games with you, Lady Justice." She looked away for a moment before eyeing me once again. "Nor do I wish to upset you. Gerd has been an active topic amongst the sisters of Love. Was the Reverend Father forty-seven or forty-eight winters?"

I frowned. "How did you know?"

"His eyes are so dark you can't tell where his pupils end and the irises begin," Donella volunteered. "He has wide shoulders and a trim figure for a man his age."

Everyone at the table stared at her.

Her face turned bright red. "Everyone saw him when the fleets restocked supplies."

"Everyone at Conflict has a trim figure," I snapped.

"I didn't see him. Did he have a scar on his chin?" Gina slashed her forefinger in a horizontal motion beneath her lower lip.

Donella nodded enthusiastically. "And he was left-handed."

Gina shrugged and faced me again. "That's the same description the sisters at Love gave for your father, Lady Justice."

"No." I shook my head. "No. I was a product of the Spring Rituals. Gerd would have lain with numerous men and women the week I was conceived."

"Except she didn't," Gina said softly. "In fact, she petitioned the High Sister of Love to leave when the Diné party went home before Gerd even knew she was with child. The petition was denied."

My hand flailed behind me, trying to find a chair. Little Bear jumped up and guided me to a seat. For once, I forgot to chide him for treating me as he would any other justice.

"H-how would he have known I was his daughter?" I looked up at Gina. "How would he have kept track of me unless . . ."

Thalia. It had to have been her. I couldn't hear Kam doing simply so ridiculously idiotic as informing the father of a Spring Rituals child.

There was only one person here at Balance who would have covered for my grandmother's second major indiscretion.

I pushed to my feet and stalked toward the door of the receiving room. "Anthea!"

I whirled at Little Bear's voice.

"Be gentle with him," my chief warden said more quietly. "He kept her secrets for all these years. It takes an extraordinary person to command such loyalty."

I nodded at his admonishment before I left the room. My throat was so tight I didn't trust my voice.

When I entered the stable, Hogarth was brushing down Nessa while Nathan and Ming Wei fed the other horses.

"Chief Justice!" Nathan immediately stopped when he spotted me and bowed. Ming Wei followed with a quick curtsey.

"M'lady." Hogarth nodded. When I didn't answer, he turned to the children. "You two go clean up 'fore the evening meal. I'll finish out here."

"Yes, sir," the squires answered in unison before they dashed out of the stable.

Hogarth leaned against Nessa's flank. "I'd just soon take the lashes, Chief Justice."

"Why do you think I'm going to have you lashed?"

"Lying to my Temple seat."

Nassa nudged my pockets for a treat. I stroked her nose. In my anger, I'd forgotten to bring something out for her. I always brought her something when I came to the stables. I visited her so rarely anymore.

"You were her chief warden, the only one Thalia would have trusted to get any message to my father," I said.

The old man sighed. "He told you, huh?"

"He tried." I shrugged. "I don't know the Diné language so he didn't say anything more. It explains why he knew so much about me." My weak laugh was self-deprecating. "For a time, I feared he was a renegade and had spies in Orrin."

"After—after what Gerd did, Thalia planned to have me take you to him once you were born." Hogarth rubbed his chin. "But then you came out of the womb blind . . ."

I laughed. I couldn't help it.

He cocked his head, a puzzled look on his face.

"Do you know how many children of the Spring Rituals fantasize about rich, powerful fathers coming to take us to some marvelous life?" I waved my left hand. Nassa nudged it to get me to resume petting her.

"All of us."

That was a new piece of information about my stablemaster.

"When was the last time you contacted him?"

"I wrote him a few days after Thalia died." Hogarth sighed. "You'd already been sent to Standora, but I couldn't ask about you after she was gone. Not without raising suspicions." He shrugged again. "After you were sworn to Balance, I'm sure he learned about you from our sister justices in Diné."

I stared at the stable floor for a moment, getting up the nerve to ask my question. "Do you think, sometime, we could, well, talk about my grandmother?" I peered up through my lashes at him.

"I'd be pleased to, m'lady."

I entered the receiving room. My staff still sat in their chairs, waiting. I cleared my throat. "My apologies to all of you. My conduct was not to the standard you have all set for this Temple. I will try to do better in the future."

I cleared my throat again. "Before we resume our meeting . . ." I turned to Gina. "Warden, would you please teach me the Diné language when you have the time? I don't want there to be any more misunderstandings on my side."

Gina smiled. "Of course, m'lady."

Maybe, just maybe, some good will come out of this stupid demon war after all.

If you are enjoying the adventures of Anthea
and the people of the Justice universe, drop me
a line through my website, Twitter or Facebook.
Recommending the Justice series to your friends
or writing a review would be even better.

**Turn the page for a sneak preview of the next
Justice story!**

A Touch of Mother

The soft knock on my door couldn't be my head of household and personal assistant Sivan with my second pot of tea. She would have simply barged into my office. The jingle of bells as the door opened immediately set my teeth on edge. I wish I could blame my reaction on my visitor. However, my past wasn't her fault.

"Good morningtide." I set aside the latest dispatches from the Issuran home Temple of Balance. Whatever else my own Reverend Mother prattled about could wait. "Ready for our next round of examinations?"

High Sister Dragonfly's veil fluttered with her sigh. "I hope you've had your first cup of tea." Her hands clutching the mound of scrolls and parchment were bright orange. Whatever bothered her would be worse than the audit of Orrin's Temple of Love. The poor priestess had inherited a royal mess when her predecessor, my birth mother, had been caught in a number of criminal acts, not the least of which were embezzling from her own order, demon dealing and high treason.

"Yes, but Sivan should be here any moment with a fresh pot." I cleared my desk of research grimoires from Light and Knowledge. "What has happened?"

Dragonfly flipped back her veil. Her cheeks were as bright orange as her hands.

The silk covered her face as required by all the priestesses of the Temple of Love when in public. Here in my office, neither of us stood on ceremony. The times we met privately at her office, she would switch between male and female civilian clothing. I could never decide if she made a more handsome woman or a prettier man, but such was the lot of a *berda* in the service of Love.

Neither of which mattered with the feeling of dread in the pit of my stomach.

She shook her head, and the bells lining her robes jingled. "You are not going to be pleased with this news."

I turned to the open doorway where my squire Nathan stood. Beyond in the hallway, Balance Warden Jonata and one of the new Love wardens stood guard, a leftover from the demon attack inside Orrin right before the Spring Rituals. No warden would let their priest or priestess go anywhere unescorted.

It had become damn annoying when I had to attend a privy other than the one in my personal quarters.

"Nathan, would you please tell Sivan my morning visitor has arrived early?"

"Yes, m'lady." He bobbed his head and took off in the direction of the kitchen.

Dragonfly closed the door Nathan had forgotten and dropped heavily into the chair on the other side of my desk. "Gerd has escaped. The Reverend Mother of Love believes she may be headed south."

"What?" My right hand automatically reached for my sword, but my scabbard and harness hung from their peg behind me. I forced myself to relax and lower my hand. "How? What happened?"

"No one seems to be sure on the details, according to my Reverend Mother." Dragonfly handed me the top parchment before she leaned forward and rested her elbows on the scarred oak of my desk.

I ran my fingers over the parchment. There were none of the raised marks used by my Temple for records. Though I wasn't blind like the rest of my order, even my odd sight couldn't quite discern between the ink and the skin. Which meant I couldn't read the demon-blasted original.

I rerolled the message. "May I have Donella make a copy of this?"

"That's the reason I brought it," Dragonfly answered sourly. "I rather suspected you didn't know about Gerd's escape yet."

There had been nothing of that sort in the dispatches from the home Temple of Balance in Standora. Why hadn't an alert gone out?

Unless the Reverend Mother's pride had gotten in the way. Losing a traitor of this magnitude would have the entire order questioning her competence.

I sucked in a deep breath and released it. "Tell me."

"The warden who delivered her evening meal was found in her cell beneath her blankets. Dead. He wasn't discovered until the next morning."

"What about the second warden? No one opens a cell door without a reinforcement." I couldn't see any warden breaking protocol, especially with a treason case.

"They haven't found him."

"Balance help us." I wiped my hands down my face. "This is not good." I pushed to my feet. I needed to move.

My birth mother on the loose meant the Reverend Mother of Balance was right. There was another traitor within her own Temple in the capital. Goddess, no wonder she wanted to keep this quiet. The dread in my stomach shifted to fury.

"Why does your Reverend Mother believe Gerd is fleeing south?" I asked as I paced in the small confines of my office.

"According to the Reverend Father of Child, Gerd's overriding desire is to kill you and torture me."

I stopped abruptly. My robes swirled around my ankles. "You say that very calmly."

Dragonfly shrugged. "It's not the first time Gerd has threatened me."

Which was true. Even though Dragonfly had been Gerd's second, she had never trusted the *berda* and often threatened her with castration if she didn't obey Gerd's every whim and command.

I shook my head as I rolled possibilities and probabilities through my mind. "Would any of the other Love priestesses here in Orrin help her?"

Dragonfly cocked her head and simply stared at me.

"That was an idiotic notion." I bowed. "My apologies to your sisters for even allowing the thought to enter my head." Gerd and her renegade allies had done worse things in order to keep the other priestesses and Dragonfly under control.

Dragonfly inclined her head in return.

I resumed pacing and tapped my index finger against my chin. "So who else would possibly help her?"

Dragonfly laughed. "Why do you make light of such serious matters?"

"Would you prefer I soil myself?" I grinned at her. "I'm assuming you have some proof of Gerd's additional misdeeds in those ledgers you carried here."

"That's what you and I have been verifying." She patted the topmost binding.

Sivan chose that moment to burst into my office with tea and cups.

"Find Chief Warden Little Bear for me," I ordered as she set down the tray on my desk.

Sivan frowned at my rudeness.

"Please," I amended. "It's a matter of Temple security."

Alarm filled her expression. "What happened?"

"The Reverend Mother managed to lose the Mad Whore."

Glossary

Words and Phrases Specific to the Justice Series

Apprentice – lowest rank of a trade or craft guild

Britannia – Toscan name for a series of islands off the western coast of the Old Continent. The two largest are Eire and Albion. Four hundred years before Anthea's time, the queens of Eire and Albion were losing their battle against the demons. They ordered the islands evacuated and the Temples of Death to launch their last resort spells. The islands are now barren, and no one who steps on them lives for long.

Briton Diaspora – refers to the survivors and their descendants of the evacuation of Britannia who are now scattered around the world

Brother – title for any fully ordained priest of any Temple that accepts men, except for the Temple of Father

Cant – Issura's neighboring nation-state to the south

Chengzhou – the capital of Jing, a nation-state in the western shore of the Old Continent

Chief Justice – title of the highest ranked priestess at a Temple of Balance

Chief [name of trade] – the highest ranking master guild member of a trade in a city or region

The Cradle – according to legend, the continent where Child created the first members of the human race

Duke/Duchess – highest ranking noble of a region

Distance-view glasses – a telescope

Father – title for any fully ordained priest of the Temple of Father

Gray Mountains – a mountain range that runs the entire length of the western side of the Long Continents

The Grand Canal – a human-built canal that passes through the isthmus connecting the Long Continents

Guild – a civil organization for a trade or craft

Guild Master – an expert tradesman's rank based on analysis of his/her peers

Healer – a person with the magical ability to heal illness and repair wounds

High Brother – title of the chief priest of a city Temple, except the Temple of Father

High Father – title of the chief priest of a city's Temple of Father

High Mother – title of the chief priestess of a city's Temple of Mother

High Sister – title of the chief priestess of a city Temple, except the Temples of Balance or Mother

Iberia – nation-state on the southwestern corner of the Old Continent

Issura – queendom on the western coast of Northern Long Continent; the Peaceful Sea forms its western border with the nation of Pagonia to the north, the nation of Cant to the south, the nations of the Cliffdwellers and Diné to the southeast and the Gray Mountains to the east

Jing – nation-state on the eastern side of the Old Continent

Journeyman/Journeywoman – middle rank of a trade or craft guild

Justice – title for any fully ordained priestess of the Temple of Balance; alternate term of address is Lady Justice

Kemet – nation-state on the northeast corner of the Cradle

The Long Continents – the two continents separating the Peaceful Sea from the Panthalassa Sea, they are connected by a narrow isthmus

The Lost Continent – southern continent between the Peaceful Sea and the Storm Sea. By Anthea's time, the original inhabitants were believed to be slaughtered by demons 500 years before. Sailors from the Sea Peoples and Maurya who landed there after the inhabitants' disappearance reported screams but found no one. Those with magic talents went mad. Not even the priests and priestesses from Child could save them. Those who tried went mad themselves.

Magistrate – elected official of a city or town in Issura who is responsible for civil and criminal law enforcement and the city or town's defense/care in an emergency

Master – senior member of a trade or craft guild; the clergyperson who is primarily responsible for the training of a novice class

Maurya – the southern-most nation of the Old Continent

Middle Sea – shallow sea that separate The Cradle from the Old Continent

Mother – title for any fully ordained priestess of the Temple of Father

National Road – main, paved road through the nation of Issura. It roughly parallels the western coastline.

New Thenos – an island city/state on the eastern coast of the Northern Long Continent

Novice – a person in training to become a priest/priestess of the Twelve

Orrin – third largest city in the queendom of Issura with the second largest port

Pagonia – Issura's neighboring nation to the north

Panthalassa Sea – ocean that separates the Long Continents from the western part of the Old Continent and the Cradle

Peaceful Sea – ocean that separates the Long Continents from the eastern part of the Old Continent, the islands and archipelagos of the Sea Peoples, and the Lost Continent

Peacekeepers – men and women who act as a city's police force. They report to the city's magistrate. They also act as an auxiliary defense force if their city or nation is attacked.

Rambla – a city in northern Cant, its people were used to hatch demon eggs off-screen during the events of *A Modicum of Truth*

Reverend Father – senior-most priest of a Temple order, the leader of that sect in the nation in which he resides

Reverend Mother – senior-most priestess of a Temple order, the leader of that sect in the nation in which she resides

Seat – person holding the highest ranking position of a Temple

Shakya – nation-state in the western portion of the Old Continent, southwest of Jing and northeast of Maurya

Sister – title for any fully ordained priestess of any Temple that accepts women, except for the Temples of Mother and Balance

Standora – capital and largest city of Issura

Storm Sea – ocean bordered by the eastern part of the Cradle, the southern part of the Old Continent, and the western part of the Lost Continent

Tandor – Issuran city that guards the border with Cant and Diné

Temple – a collection of people dedicated to the service of one of the twelve gods; a building that houses such people; the primary place of worship for one of the twelve gods

Tiwan – the capital of Cant

Toscana – nation-state on the southwest section of the Old Continent; location of the first battle against the demons

The Twelve – the collective name for the twelve deities of the Justice universe

Valencia – duchy in the nation-state of Iberia; know for their innovative shipbuilding designs

Warden – security guard of a Temple, they act as supplementary military personnel in the event of a demon invasion

The Twelve Temples

Mother

    Cloak Color – Light blue

    Motto – "To give without thought; to forgive with love."

The Temple of Mother is responsible for the teaching of household arts, such as spinning, weaving, food storage and preparation. The order is also responsible for caring for those who have lost their families.

Father

Cloak Color – Dark blue

Motto – "All tools are weapons, and weapons tools."
The Temple of Father is responsible for the constructive arts, such as carpentry and smithing.

Balance

Cloak Color – Black

Motto – "Balance in all things."
The Temple of Balance runs the judicial system. A justice is the judge in criminal and civil cases.

Light

Cloak Color – Medium brown

Motto – "Light brings truth, for without truth, there can be no justice."
The Temple of Light is responsible for codifying contracts and mediating contract disputes. A Light priest also acts as the bailiff for a justice, and is often the one to truthspell a witness or the accused. The Temple of Light also provides military support to a nation's civilian army.

Knowledge

Cloak Color – Gold

Motto – "With patience, knowledge comes."
The Temple of Knowledge is responsible for education and for recording historical events. They essentially act as the library system for the Justice universe.

Thief

Cloak Color – Grey

Motto – "Hiding in plain sight."
The Temple of Thief acts as the intelligence-gathering arm of both the Temples and the civilian leaders. They finance their efforts through gambling dens.

Conflict

Cloak Color – Dark Red

Motto – "Destruction is the necessary evil, for it clears the way for new growth."

The Temple of Conflict focuses on strategy and all martial arts. They are the primary support and teachers of a nation's army.

Love

Cloak Color – Medium Red

Motto – "Pleasure is life."

The Temple of Love are the holy prostitutes. They also deal with sex education and lead the Spring Rituals, the annual fertility rites which were first used to breed as many humans with magical talent as possible. Don't underestimate them. They fight just as hard and as nasty as their fellow clergy in Conflict.

Child

Cloak Color – Light green

Motto – "All things are new once."

The Temple of Child is responsible for the emotional health of citizens. They also develop and teach agriculture and animal husbandry techniques.

Wilding

Cloak Color – Dark green

Motto – "All creatures return to us."

The Temple of the Wildling God deals with management of wild animal populations, forestry, and the protection of ecosystems.

Vintner

Cloak Color – Purple

Motto – "The line between wisdom and madness is one sip."

The Temple of Vintner not only deals with the cultivation of grapes and the production of wine, but they also promote the gathering, cultivation and processing of all medicinal herbs.

Death

Cloak Color – Black

Motto – "For every life, there is a death."

The Temple of Death takes care of the gathering of the dead, the last rites, and disposal of the corpses. They also act as a repository for the last wills and testaments of all citizens.

Characters and Places

Queendom of Isurra

Orrin

Temple of Balance

Chief Justice Anthea – a circuit justice for ten winters until her appointment as Chief Justice at the age of thirty winters ("Justice")

Chief Justice Penelope – deceased, predecessor to Anthea as Chief Justice

Chief Justice Thalia – deceased, predecessor to Penelope as Chief Justice, maternal grandmother to Anthea

Justice Yanaba – junior justice after the events of *A Question of Balance*

Sivan – personal assistant to Chief Justice Anthea and head of the household staff

Donella – senior clerk

Lailani – junior clerk

Chief Warden Little Bear – head of the wardens

Warden Tyra – junior warden, killed in the Battle of Tandor

Warden Gina – junior warden

Warden Aglaia – junior warden, died in the battle to retake the Temple of Love (*A Question of Balance*)

Warden Daniel – junior warden

Warden Noko – junior warden

Warden Jonata – junior warden, Aglaia's replacement from the Standora Wardens' Academy

Warden Dezba – junior warden

Hogarth – former chief warden under Justices Thalia and Penelope, now stablemaster, husband of Deborah

Deborah – Head cook, wife of Hogarth

Nathan – squire to Chief Justice Anthea after he was sentenced to pay reparations for stealing bread, an orphan, age ten winters at the time of his sentencing in *A Question of Balance*

Ming Wei – squire to Justice Yanaba, nine winters old at the end of *A Question of Balance*. Originally from Jing, she was sold by her parents to a Jing noble as a sex slave and brought to Issura. When the noble's crimes were discovered, he immolated himself and his slaves. Ming Wei was the only survivor and has severe scar tissue on her face, back and arms.

Temple of Light

High Brother Luc – a circuit priest for twelve winters until his appointment as chief priest at the age of thirty-two winters between the events of "Justice" and "Diplomacy in the Dark"

High Brother Kam – semi-retired, predecessor to Luc as chief priest, poisoned and died during the events of *A Question of Balance*

Brother Mat – Second to Luc. His birth name is Micah. He murdered the real Mat on his way to Orrin from Standora. Died under Anthea's truthspell questioning in *A Question of Balance.*

Brother Jeremy – youngest junior priest

Istaqa – personal assistant to High Brother Luc and head of the household staff

Edberth – former personal assistant to High Brother Kam, he now acts as evening assistant to High Brother Luc

Henry – stablemaster

Chief Warden Nicholas – head of the wardens

Warden Gibb – junior warden, died shortly after the renegades' kidnapping of High Brother Luc in *A Question of Balance*

Warden Mateqai – junior warden, becomes Sister Shi Hua's personal bodyguard during the events of *A Modicum of Truth*

Warden Yar – junior warden

Warden Tadhg – junior warden

Warden Gad – junior warden

Temple of Love

High Sister Gerd – chief priestess, biological daughter of Thalia and Kam, biological mother of Anthea. She was removed from office on charges of fraud, bribery of a public official, unlawful magic, and conspiracy to commit murder. Later, the charges of dealing treason demon artifacts and treason were added.

Sister Dragonfly – Gerd's second, *berda* (genderfluid), is acting High Sister after the events in *A Question of Balance*, becomes High Sister after the events in *A Modicum of Truth*

Sister Gretchen – priestess, deceased. The discovery of her body in one of Duke Marco's wine barrels precipitates the events in *A Question of Balance*

Warden Jocasta – junior warden, one of the replacement after the events of *A Question of Balance*

Temple of Conflict

High Brother Han – chief priest

Temple of Death

High Sister Bertrice – chief priestess

High Brother Kai – deceased, predecessor of Bertrice, retired in Bertrice's favor as the temple seat and became a teaching brother in Standora until his death

Brother Xander – Bertrice's second

Chief Warden Axton – head of the wardens

Warden Hitari – junior warden

Temple of Vintner

High Brother Ben – chief priest

Temple of Mother

High Mother Bianca – chief priestess

Temple of Father

High Father Jerrod – chief priest

Temple of Child

High Sister Mya – chief priestess

Brother Turtle – junior priest, helps to save Justice Yanaba by pulling her soul back into her body during the events of *A Modicum of Truth*

Temple of Wildling

High Brother Jax – chief priest, second form is a wolf

Sister Farrah – Jax's second, second form is a fox

Temple of Thief

High Brother Talbert – chief priest

Temple of Knowledge

High Sister Mariana – chief priestess

Nobility

Duke Benedetto DiMara – father of Marco, Alessa, and Isabella, husband of Cora, convicted of conspiracy and conspiracy for illegal magic to mind wipe his son Marco during the events of "Justice"; imprisoned at Standora for life.

Lady Cora DiMara – mother of Marco, Alessa, and Isabella, convicted of treason and demon dealing, executed by the Reverend Mother Alara of Balance during the events of "Justice".

Duke Marco DiMara – duke of Orrin, inherited his post at the age of eighteen winters after his parents were found guilty of numerous offenses and stripped of their titles and property

Lady Katarina DiMara (nee' DiLove) – common-born wife of Marco, animal healer. Her mother was a priestess of the Temple of Love and died of the wasting sickness shortly before Katarina's eighteenth winter.

Lady Alessa DiMara – sister of Marco, a latent talent, lover of Sister Gretchen of Love

Lady Isabella DiMara – sister of Marco, attends the University of Standora

Bartholomew – retainer of Duke Marco's until it was learned he'd assaulted Lady Alessa and Sister Gretchen, Lady Alessa subsequently asked Chief Justice Anthea for clemency and hired him to manage the estates Sister Gretchen

William – retainer of Duke Marco's

Julian – retainer of Duke Marco's

Arturo – former captain of Duke Marco's flagship, his murder is the precipitating event of "Diplomacy in the Dark"

Titus – captain of Duke Marco's flagship, the *Mars Tranquilus*

Citizens

Malven DiCook – duly elected magistrate of Orrin

Dante – one of DiCook's peacekeepers, dies at the beginning of *A Modicum of Truth*

Barbora – wife of Dante, dies at the beginning of *A Modicum of Truth*

Jaime – one of DiCook's peacekeepers

Guilds

Chief Healer Aaron – head of the Healers' Guild

Master Healer Devin – second to Aaron in the Orrin Healer's Guild, originally from New Thenos

Journeywoman Bly – a junior healer, often assists Master Devin at autopsies

Tandor

High Brother Dav – chief priest of the Temple of Light

Chief Justice Elizabeth – chief justice of the Temple of Balance

Minerva – the new clerk with the Temple of Balance, a renegade, killed during the fight within the Temple of Balance (*A Modicum of Truth*)

High Brother Aduba – chief priest of the Temple of Conflict

Brother Tighan – second of the Temple of Conflict, a renegade, killed by Aduba during the fall of Tandor

High Brother Nantan – chief priest of the Temple of Death

Sister Reby – second of the Temple of the Wildling God, first introduced as a shapeshifting thief in "The Perfect Partner", second form is a polecat

Brother Sisquoc – surviving priest of the Temple of the Wildling God, second form is a panther

Brother Trajan – priest of the Temple of the Wilding God, second form is a wolf

Sister Jumping Mouse – priestess of the Temple of the Wildling God, second form is a kangaroo rat

Duke Enzo DiToscana – Duke of Tandor, murdered by a skinwalker possessing his wife

Duchess Nadine DiToscana – the widow of Duke Enzo of Tandor

Ural DiSand – merchant from Tandor, implicated in the Assassin Guild plots in Orrin, killed while possessed by a skinwalker (*A Modicum of Truth*)

Amarantha DiRoma – Tandorian merchant, rival of Ural DiSand, murdered by renegades shortly before they poisoned most of the personnel of the Tandorian Temples

The Wave Dancer – Duchess Nadine of Tandor's flagship, one of two remaining ships in Tandor prior to the Battle of Tandor

STANDORA – CAPITAL CITY OF ISSURA

Reverend Mother Alara – head of Issura's Temple of Balance

Justice Rose – novice training priestess of the main Temple of Balance in Standora when Anthea was a novice

Reverend Father Farrell – head of Issura's Temple of Light

Brother Elroy – a Light priest, aide to Reverend Father Farrell, and a distance speaker who accompanies the Isurran and Sea Peoples fleets to Tandor in *A Matter of Death*

Brother Long Wind – a Light priest and aide to Reverend Father Farrell; he accompanies the queen's army to Tandor in *A Matter of Death*

Brother Garbhan – a Light priest and aide to Reverend Father Farrell; he remains in Orrin during the events of *A Matter of Death*

Brother Jon – novice training priest at the main Temple of Light in Standora, murdered by the skinwalker at Samael DiRoy's abandoned manse prior to *A Question of Balance*

High Sister Imala – a Love priestess, considered to be the lead contender for position of Reverend Mother of Love; she accompanies the queen's army in A Matter of Death

Chief Warden Catherine – Imala's chief warden; she was a classmate of Mateqai's at the Warden Academy

Warden Hototo – a junior Love warden

Brother White Wolf – a senior priest of Thief; he's a personal friend of High Sister Imala

Queen Teodora – reigning monarch of Issura

Crown Princess Chiara – eldest child and heir of Queen Teodora of Issura; lady general of the queen's army

Duke White Eagle – former Conflict brother, left the order to marry Crown Princess Chiara; honorary title duke of Standora as the future queen's consort; lord general of the queen's army

Pana Valley

Lord Aleister DeGrove – noble noted for his vineyards

JING EMPIRE

Chengzhou

Empress Bao De – ruler of Jing a century before Bao Yu, she sacrificed herself to stop a demon army

Empress Bao Yu – ruler of Jing until her death from natural causes during "Courting Trouble"

Emperor Bao Chengwu – current ruler of Jing, succeeded his mother Bao Yu during "Courting Trouble"

Ambassador Quan Po – half-brother of the current Jing emperor Bao Chengwu; was heir to the throne until his nephew was born

Reverend Father Jin – head of Jing's Temple of Light

Sister Shi Hua – a priestess of Light, who was tapped as Po's bodyguard. She received additional training from Conflict, Thief, and Love. Originally from the town of Yintze in the southern province of Chu.

Brother Lin – novice master of Light

Brother Jian – a priest of Light, classmate of Shi Hua during their novice years

Brother Fa – a Wildling priest, his second form is a tiger, a friend of Shi Hua and Jian during their novice years

Justice Mei Wen – a priestess of Balance, Shi Hua's closest friend other than Jian during their novice years

Sister Yin Li – a priestess of Love, Shi Hua's maternal aunt

Reverend Father Chen – head of Jing's Temple of Conflict

Brother Shang – a priest of Conflict, Shi Hua's instructor when she was a novice

Reverend Father Biming – head of Jing's Temple of Thief

The Unbridled – spy ship used by the Temple of Thief, a four-masted carrack built in the Iberian duchy of Valencia, captained by Reverend Father Biming during *A Modicum of Truth*

Brother Hadar – a priest of Thief from the Kingdom of Hejaz, serving on board *The Unbridled*

ISLANDS OF THE SEA PEOPLES

KINGDOM OF O'AHU

Prince Alika – youngest son of the king of the Sea Peoples, one of Sister Gretchen's worshippers, the father of her unborn child

Captain Iakepa – senior captain of the O'ahu trading fleet

DINÉ NATION

Reverend Father Nizhé'é' – head of the Diné Temple of Conflict

Justice Spotted Fawn – the western circuit justice for the Diné Nation, killed in the Battle of Tandor

Bidzii – Spotted Fawn's clerk, he's fluent in Issuran so the justice speaks through him; killed in the Battle of Tandor

Brother Bumblebee – junior priest of Light with the Diné army

Sister Lizard – junior priestess of Knowledge with the Diné army

CLIFFDWELLERS

Healer Kotori – a physician with the Diné army

PLAINS NATIONS – COMANCHE

High Brother Pecos – a senior Conflict priest

ACKNOWLEDGMENTS

The plot of this book was outlined a couple of years ago. It feels ironic that my own father passed away a month and a half before I completed it. His passing made the last few chapters difficult to write. But as High Sister Bertrice would have said, for every life, there is a death. And the wheel keeps turning as my own son heads out into the world.

As always, I owe a great deal to Jaye Manus and Elaina Lee for making my books look enticing enough to pick up, both inside and out.

The love of my life and I would have celebrated our twenty-fourth anniversary as I was finishing this book. He understood I was under a time crunch and graciously suggested we celebrate after I was done. This kind of unselfishness is what true love is about.

And to Becky, Roshonda, and Shelley, thank you for getting me through the last year of hell. Your positive attitudes made a difference you can never imagine.

Suzan Harden is a recovering attorney who writes fiction to regain her sanity. She currently lives in the Great Lakes region with a husband who believes writing is a practical career option and a kid who thinks she's too enamored with superheroes.

www.ingramcontent.com/pod-product-compliance
Lightning Source LLC
Chambersburg PA
CBHW070631170726
48291CB00003B/972